INCORRIGIBLE

INCORRIGIBLE

LONNY LEE

Cover design by Lauren DeFoto

ISBN-13: 9780692673744
ISBN-10: 0692673741

AUTHORS NOTE:

All the characters in this story are fictional, with the exception of some political figures—Hugo Chávez and Fidel Castro and his wife—with whom I have taken many fictional liberties (personality, sexual behavior, and basically everything but their name and country of origin) so that in no way, shape, or form are they true accounts of anything that, to my knowledge, has ever occurred in real life. Any coincidence would be just too funny and strange, but heck, anything is possible! Reality is only a figment of our imagination.

This novel contains explicit sexual content not intended for minors.

This novel is a fictional satire with fantasy, mystery, adventure, and romantic elements, intended only as entertainment.

All illustrations in this book are from the author's private collection and were made specifically for this book.

"Change is always a possibility as long as there is life and you are willing to take the risk."

TABLE OF CONTENTS

Chapter 1

ESCAPE FROM CUBANTRAZ

If you had the opportunity to be your own God, would you? To have the power to manipulate your fate and make it your own will is grand indeed.

I am writing this today not just because I think it will be a best seller one day, but also because I want to share with you how I got away with murder, so to speak, and how to learn from my mistakes to become a better con. I've been holding on to too many secrets, and some are just too good to keep to oneself! (I am reminiscing with a shameless grin as I write these words.)

I have a really black heart and a hand with a watermark. The trick to owning a really black heart is not to let others know its true color so that they think you are as nice as any other person—so you blend in. We all like to pretend; we all like to think we are actors in our own movie, the one we call life. I just take it one step further and actually make good use of my acting skills. I dare to be what others sometimes find themselves too inhibited to be. Fear is such a shameful inhibitor!

I hide under a façade, a regular facade, just like most people. It's only that my facade is just more intricate and better thought out than most. I think of myself as having purpose, and this purpose gives me all the edge I need to dare to be who others won't.

My name is Maria. This is not my real name, but it serves a purpose. Every time I give somebody a name, they get a personality that goes along with it. In this case, Maria is such a common name that it can be you, the girl next door, or anybody for that matter. Beware of girls named Maria!

This story starts in Alcatraz—well, not quite Alcatraz but just as bad. I used to be Hugo Chávez's mistress, you see, and on one of his trips to Cuba, where he visited his friend Fidel, he took me with him. This was when Fidel became sweet on me—not a hard thing to do—and decided to keep me for himself. Hugo added me to his list of gifts to Fidel, giving more richness to their already lively friendship.

"*Como puede un hombre quitarle a otro a quien llama su amigo?* (How does a man take from a man he calls his friend?)," said Hugo, bantering.

Fidel walked over to Hugo and placed his hand on Hugo's shoulder and said, "It is not taking, my friend. Friends are generous with one another. Why don't you just give her to me as a gift? Sleep on it, dear friend,"

Fidel said in a tone that was as gentle as a summer breeze. If you know anything about Fidel, however, his friendship can be more than you bargained for, and asking no matter how nicely was really a command; after all, he didn't get to rule Cuba by being a kind and gentle leader. That just was not how it was done.

Hugo paced most of the night over this. I could tell part of him wondered whether "gifting" me would in some way demean his manhood. You know Spanish men—they are all about their male bravado. Needless to say, I felt I was being treated like a piece of cattle by two farmers.

I was really not happy to be stuck in that position, away from my country, about to lose all that I had known up until that point in my tiny life, probably never again to see my family or friends—about to be traded to a man who probably would keep me under his power until he grew tired of me, and then what? If I were lucky, he would let me go so that I could live the rest of my days in poverty somewhere in the slums that had been long forgotten by God.

Hugo looked over at me as if it would be the last time he would ever look at me with desire.

"*Mujer, seras mia una vez mas!* (Woman, you shall be mine one last time!)" His tone was decisive. He was a no-questions-asked type of man. This meant that if you, as his mistress, asked too many questions, he would not hesitate; you would just be saying hello to the back and front of his hand.

"*Papi ven,* (Daddy come here)," I said to him in my sexy voice, making one last attempt to seduce him and be in his graces, but I feared it was already too late, for his mind was made up, and clearly his relationship with Fidel was more important to him than any woman who was not loved by him. His bravado was not as important to him in this situation.

I debated whether or not to use my powers of influence on him once more, but in a way, the unexpected future was tempting to me. Perhaps it was time to change the breeze and inhale new airs. And I also thought that a fight between Hugo and Fidel over me would not benefit me in any way, even though I would have enjoyed the spectacle with some popcorn.

Hugo's penis grew possessive of me; he stabbed my vagina with it as a weapon of war. He showed off his prowess to an invisible audience, making my insides sore. As he was about to come, he pulled out his penis and hosed me down with his sperm, marking his territory as a woman who was once his. "Remember me, woman," his actions said to me as dawn grew closer into another day, and I rested, waiting for my fate.

He slept quite peacefully after that; his breath was deep and breezy with no recourse and no remorse.

The next day I was moved into a different room in one of Fidel's properties. The room was a shade of light blue and had a colonial feel with a European antique decor. There was a white vanity and an ocean view. The floor had an intricate mosaic pattern, and on the walls were several portraits from the eighteen hundreds of men and women who had once been important.

I was locked in that room for a couple of days before I saw Fidel. I guess a mistress must wait to be visited, as do all items of convenience. I was scared, but I didn't really have a choice but to go on or die resisting. These are not great choices to have.

He came to my room and asked me to get dressed in lingerie; it was in such a polite manner that it surprised me—not what I was expecting from a political or military tyrant. He waited on the bed and watched me for a few minutes and then asked me to come over toward him. He touched me softly with hands that felt like feathers on my skin. He undid my red lace bra and exposed my breasts. He smothered his face all over them in delight. I almost felt as if I was getting ready to nurture him like a mother would a child. I followed my instinct and, without words, did just that. I figured if he liked me enough, he might be good to me, and my time in Cuba wouldn't be so bad.

I grabbed his head in my hands and ran my red fingernails through his hair and coarse frizzy beard. He grabbed one of my hands and caressed his face tenderly with it; while doing so, he noticed the raised marks on the palm of my hand. I told him they were my watermark, and he looked at me, knowing I had been branded.

Fidel smelled like cigars smoked by a tranquil sea. When I kissed him, he tasted like a very strong aged rum. I sat on his lap like a child getting ready for a story. He liked this; I could tell. He smelled me like a bloodhound whenever his nose was close to my skin.

"You smell like magnolias," he said to me sweetly. Part of me felt this was how he manipulated people and won them over, but I was not sure how transparent he was with me yet. I decided not to think too much about his ploy with me; after all, he didn't have anything to gain from me at that point. I already was his. I, on the other hand, was forced to win him over and keep him happy for my own sake.

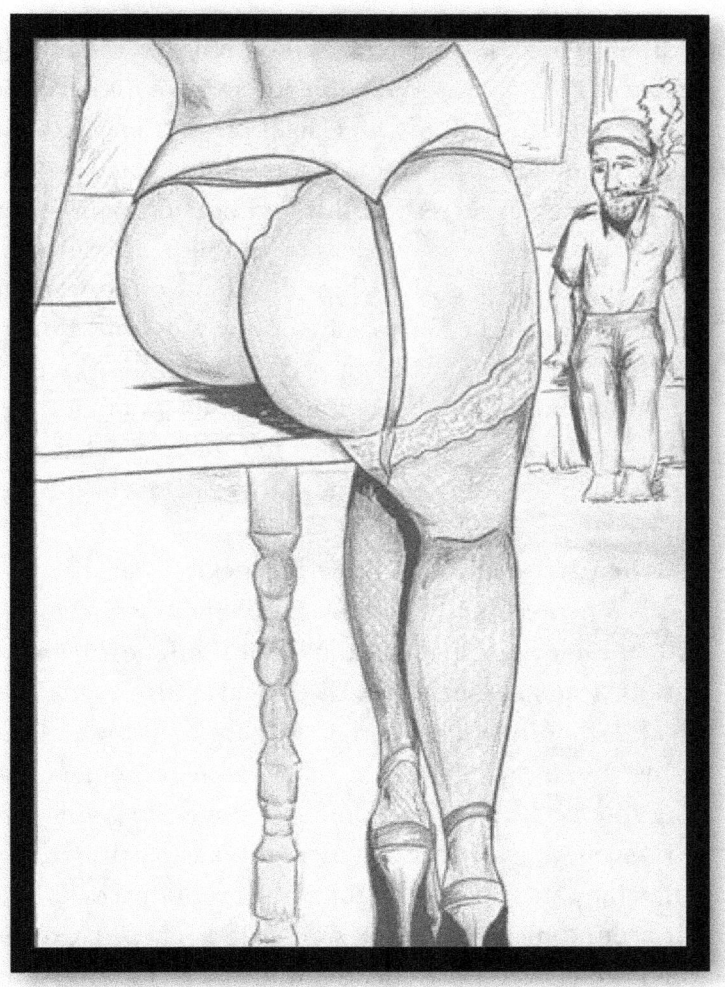

He laid me on the bed and started to caress my legs softly, and although I did not find him attractive, my body was reacting to the feeling of pleasure and erotic sensuality. This soothed me and left me vulnerable for an attack. He kissed my heels and even licked them with pleasure. This surprised me, for it was from a man with such power. He took my high heel off and played with my toes; he sniffed my feet, looking intoxicated by the aroma. I cringed secretly at this and hoped that my feet smelled good. He seemed pleased, so I didn't disturb his odd behavior; in fact, I let him do whatever he wanted with my feet. He began to suck on my toes, and I quivered from this new sensation; it was wet and squishy, and I was pretty sure I didn't like it. He then began to use his teeth, and I had to stop myself from flinching. He licked my toes as if he was eating meat that falls right off the bone.

When he was finally done, he tickled me with his beard as he went up my thighs and lapped over my intimate lips like a serpent sticking out his tongue, in a hissing way. I moaned at this with pleasure; his tongue felt soft and smooth in just the right way. It was like wet velvet against my clitoris. I began to quiver with excitement the more intense he got. He teased me, not quite giving me an orgasm, and when I was almost ready to climax, he pulled his pants down, revealing his throbbing cock. The hair around his cock looked similar to his beard, except it had a big hard nose sticking out. It was so abundant that his testicles disappeared under the lush shrubbery. The tip of his penis slipped around my wet lips before entering me—something I noticed he enjoyed. I climaxed from the excitement as soon as he entered my body, and it was a good thing I did because he nearly came before me.

We continued an affair for nearly four months. Life wasn't nearly as terrible as I had originally anticipated. The food was good; I ate generous portions of a beefy stew called *ropa vieja*, fried cassava plantains (both sweet and savory), beans, and all sorts of Latin delicacies that fill the hips with generous proportions. I had my own room, tons of beach time to enjoy by the ocean, and for the most part, when Fidel didn't need my services, I was on my own. I did notice, however, that I was often being watched. Fidel was always very careful not to speak too openly to me about his operations—or anything too serious, for that matter.

The presence of the armed forces was everywhere, even when I couldn't see them. It reminded me often of the reality of life there. The people looked resentful and scared despite their strong sense of pretense. Many distracted themselves in admirable ways, such as academic studies and the arts, as a way to focus on more pleasant and productive things. One thing that brought cheer to the community was salsa dancing and the contests held for it. I must say, I felt inspired to become the best dancer and secretly took it upon myself to find a partner to compete with. This did not take long.

When my feet touched the ground, I felt I had swift wings at my ankles and swiveled like a flame through the wind. My partner was a slim dark man with a very athletic figure. I often found myself admiring the perfection of his taut muscles. His skin had a natural glow to it. It was intriguing, in a way, how his skin glowed without the help of baby oil, but I guess we are all entitled to our secrets.

His name was Marco. His words when we practiced— and thank God that we practiced, because all that food I was eating would have stayed on my hips otherwise— were as follows: "*Muevete, mujer! Asi, así, mueve esas caderas. Seduceme, mujer!* (Move, woman! This way, that way, move those hips. Seduce me, woman!)" His voice was aggressive and commanding, suggesting the power of his passion.

He was intoxicating. There was something in his persona that was palpably strong and magnetically alluring in the way he carried himself. It was this indefinable sense of self that carried over into his dance like an electrical current. I wished I could have been his lover, but I was *intocable*, which means "untouchable." If any man was to be found with a woman who was Fidel's, at the very least they would have been thrown in jail, but a good beating was most likely the punishment, if not death.

Fidel's wife, Dalia, was a very jealous woman, something I guess I should have known, but somehow it had escaped me. I was as ignorant as always. It does happen to the best of us from time to time. We go walking down that red carpet, thinking we own the world in the palm of our hands, and suddenly the rug gets pulled, we lose our balance, and down we go, sideswiped by life's events. Then again, I lived a life where she didn't really matter. I only knew who she was because of who she was married to, not because she was something to be feared or venerated—but of course, I don't worship people who are not myself, anyways; that sort of thing is beneath me and only worthy of a true god.

When I walked through the streets during the day, mothers would often take their children and cover their eyes, some women would snarl at me, and others would hold on to their boyfriends or husbands and force them to look away. I was becoming aware of the public hatred that people were starting to have for me; even though nobody said anything to me, I could still feel it.

The invisible wall of isolation that others give you when they fear and hate you was always amusing to me. It was powerful; it was liberating not to live by the public's approval of self but rather your own. But it was also lonely to stand alone in the crowd and feel this way. I wondered why I was hated more. Was it because I was Fidel's lover, because I slept with a married man, or because I was viewed as some type of prostitute? Probably all the above. The thought made me smirk. Hate is a stronger emotion than love, and I wielded its power.

At first I avoided these looks by walking the streets at night instead of the daytime, but I refused to be a prisoner to society, so I walked the streets during the day anyway, flaunting myself lewdly in their faces just to make their day—or should I say mine? If I really wanted to be bold, I'd wink or flirt with their men just to see them grow insecure toward their loved ones, thinking they would stray to the warmth of my arms and then some. They weren't going to keep me from watching the sea roar against the cliffs by sunset or even enjoy my life. Who did they think they were? They were not more powerful than me!

It was coming close to my salsa dance competition. I opted to play it safe and let Fidel know what I was going to do, because Cuba is a small country; if I didn't tell him something he probably already knew, someone else would be more slanderous in telling him so.

He told me he hoped I would win. I told him if he asked the judges to favor me, they would. He smiled at me and looked down slightly, pretending to be abashed, that we both acknowledged the full force of his level of power.

The night of the competition came, and Marco and I walked down to the hall where people waited with cheer.

The first couple on the dance floor shook their hips to the rhythm of the trumpets and drums. The judges scored them based on style, inventiveness, tempo, and flavor. They were scored a seven, two eights, and a nine out of ten. The next couple was probably not as good as the first. The woman missed a step here and there, and together their movements seemed as jerky and clumsy as a duck on a slide. They had a crew of friends and relatives cheering for them, making it seem as though they were the kings of the dance floor with this intimidating crowd behind them. *Cocksuckers*, I thought as I smiled placidly on the outside.

Marco looked at me and smiled almost as if he could read my thoughts. "*No te apures linda, nosotros les ganaremos* (Don't sweat it, cutie; we'll beat them)," he said as my eyes widened fierily, taking up the dare.

The judges scored nines for the second couple, pissing me off even more as I tried my hardest to force a smile and applaud.

"The contest is fixed," I said to Marco with a snarl. "*Hijueputas desgraciados!* (Bastards, sons of bitches!)," I went on in a rant. Twenty more couples went on to compete, all averaging a score of eight. Most of them were decent salsa dancers, but I knew we were better; I just wanted to prove it!

When Marco and I got on the dance floor, we started slow with a dramatic entrance as the light shone on us. I slipped into his hand like a dove on a cloud. He brought me near, spun me, and teased me, and I teased him back with the flirty sway of my hips and a smile of happiness as if I had just been bedded by the god of sex. Our moves were so precise and coordinated that we were a pleasure to watch, if I do say so myself. Back and forth and back again, spin, twist, and over. By the time we were done, we were both sweating and panting as if we had just had the most vigorous of sexual sessions, and I was almost just as satisfied—that was, until I heard our scores. We scored three nines and an eight, getting only second place to that lousy couple who went second. They actually won, and I was stirring in a pot of flames, wanting to do something evil about it. There was a brief award ceremony where we took our places to be honored. When Marco and I were announced, I heard only a mild applause. This angered me. I had no idea this was supposed to be a popularity contest. When the crowd cheered for the winning couple, I could feel the blood burning in my face as I pretended to smile happy for them, once more swallowing my frustration.

Marco tried to console me, letting me know there would be other times for us to win, but the truth was, there was no better time for me than now! I nodded silently, making Marco feel as if he had done his job.

"*Vamonos. Te llevo a casa* (Let's go. I will take you home)," Marco said to me like a true gentleman.

"No, *esta bien quiero estar sola, papi. Déjame si?* (No, that's OK, I want to be alone, babe. Is that OK?)" He looked at me reluctantly, but having discovered my strong will, he decided to go off with Raul, his friend, and get a drink instead.

I waited outside, hoping for the woman who won the contest to come out alone. I wanted to attack her. I wasn't sure exactly how I would do this. I just wanted to tell her off or slap her in the face, but both would give enormous satisfaction. It simply would be enough just to upset her on the verge of her undeserved celebration.

The truth is, when you're this angry, you just want to do something you never really think things through. You get all this anticipation from the rage building up, and the next thing you know, something you can't take back happens, but that's OK; at least the anger is gone. You did something about it, so you can go home and have a peaceful night's sleep.

Before I could do anything at all, a car pulled up in front of me. A man came out from the backseat. He covered my head with a sack, bound my hands, shoved me into the vehicle quickly, and then we drove off somewhere into the night. However, none of these tasks were done obsequiously on my part.

The bag seemed to be made of some type of burlap. It was dusty and that made me cough as if I had just swallowed a gust of grainy sand. I was very nervous too. I could feel the adrenaline rushing back and forth, this time for a very different reason altogether than a few moments before. I kept wondering who or why this was being done.

My thoughts raced back and forth like a pendulum. I felt it was best not to talk or ask any questions at that moment. They might not have even answered me anyways.

I sensed there were three people in the car, at least that I could smell anyways. There was a man driving, a man next to me, and what felt like a woman. I felt it was a woman because of the strange distant aura she emanated and the musky sweet scent of her body. In my lifetime—and believe me, that is a while—I had never met a man who smelled as good as a woman.

They were all very silent at first, but the closer we got to our destination, the men started to talk.

"*Señora si nos agarran nos van a matar. No estamos siguiendo ordenes* (Ma'am, if they catch us, they will kill us. We are not following orders.)," a coarse voice said nervously.

"*Yo tengo familia, Señora. Sin mi no sobreviven* (I have family, ma'am. Without me, they won't survive)," said the other with temerity.

"*Callen, cobardes! Por algo quiero que desaparezca. Los muertos no hablan.* (Shut up, cowards! There is a reason I want her to disappear. The dead don't speak.)" The woman had a very dry way of saying this. Perhaps it was the chill up my spine as she spoke that made it seem that way. Or maybe it was the thought of a death being so near that worried me. I can't really remember the last time I dealt with my own death or why I felt this long-forgotten feeling again. Oh yes, it was because I was actually alive again!

The ride seemed endless. In a way that was good, I suppose. It potentially gave me the time to think about my situation and how to get out of it. I thought I could try and run as soon as the car stopped and they opened the door. Then I sighed; what a terrible idea! What if I got shot? I wouldn't be able to see, and I was also bound. Did I have any other options? Should I beg for my life? No, absolutely not! That was beneath me. Was there anything that I could say to change her mind about killing me? Hmm…

The car stopped, and I swallowed hard, thinking of the fate that awaited me. Life was pounding out of my chest and running away like a coward. There was no real value in cowardice even for somebody like me, so I went and got my fear and shoved it back where the sun don't shine! Then again, staying calm increases your chances for survival by 30 percent, and then there is another 10 percent that is merely associated with luck. But who really needs luck in a situation like this?

The driver got out and slammed the door; he came around and opened the other door for the woman who was riding next to me. Both the man and the woman in the backseat came out, and then the door opened, and I was jerked out of the car, falling abruptly on to the ground. I felt the dirt and the rocks all around my hands and knees as I hit the earth. There was this gritty feeling on my hands, and I had to try and dust the dirt off—a task that seemed quite hard when your hands were tied, but even so, I wasn't sure why clean hands mattered so much at a time like this. It wasn't like my tombstone would say, "And the woman died with clean hands." *How silly*, I thought, but I suppose the anxiety you get at a moment like this does spurt out unusual thoughts in the brain. Then, again, that just might be me.

They took me for a walk. I could feel the cobblestones underneath my feet, so I knew we weren't on a regular road anymore. I felt like my toes wanted to clench the edges of those cobblestones rather than move forward, but the dust made my foot slip off, so that wouldn't have worked anyway.

"Take the bag off!" growled the woman. I adjusted quickly to the low nighttime light. The color of the full moon was glistening with as much orange as reddish hues. It looked like a ominous bloody moon. Perhaps my imagination was becoming too vivid…

I was thankful for the light from the moon though, and the nighttime lighting from the bottom outside edges of the castle. It was quite romantic, in a way that meant I could at least witness my demise and not go from one dark place to another without being able to see how it happened.

I recognized where we were. We were at the edge of a cliff at the Castle El Morro, by the water, far from the main road, houses, and people.

The woman stood in front of me in an A position, her hipbones protruding forward, almost as if exaggerating her dominance in this situation. *That's OK*, I thought. I'd stay on my knees for now and wait to see what happens. She wore a white flowing cotton dress and a red belt fastened tightly on her small waist. She had shoulder-length curly black hair, and from my perspective, she seemed to have very thick legs for the rest of her body proportions, but just to show I am not a hater, I'll throw in that this actually worked for her, and it made her somewhat attractive.

"Do you know why you are here, you whore?" She was not just angry but also full of spite when she said this, almost as if she had been waiting to get something off her chest for a long time. As she spoke, my anger started to swell up painfully inside me. She had some nerve calling me a whore! The worst part was that I was not even in a position to be able to do anything about it.

"I guess you hate me because I'm prettier than you!" I showed her a piece of me with a big bold smile, mocking her. The blind side of her anger was making her pupils dilate and redden even more. The upper hand she so smugly had was washed off her face, and not knowing how to answer me, she gave me a villainous laugh instead, the type you normally see in children's cartoons. Then I began to think how humiliating it would be to be annihilated by someone with the emotional and intellectual maturity of a child.

"You make me laugh! I am Fidel's wife, Dalia. You thought you could screw around with my husband and not pay for it?" she said, recuperating her stance and gathering momentum for more. "I see you have a very vulgar type of so-called beauty, but that doesn't give you enough brains to stay out of my way," she said, waving her gloved hand as if she was swatting an imaginary fly.

Somewhere a long time ago, I had read that if someone was going to kill you, they would do it within the first thirty seconds; otherwise, they were too chicken to go ahead with it. Looking at the fact that this woman was dressed in white—how ironic—I somehow doubted she would actually want to get her hands dirty with my blood, but who knew? Maybe she might surprise me.

"Well, clearly I am important to you! Despite my so-called vulgarity, you actually know who I am—but me, up until this moment, I had no idea who you were. Clearly you're the one who needs to get off her high horse. I didn't get in your way. You put me in it!"

The two men around us looked as if the acid in the pit of their stomachs had made a nuclear explosion in their pants. They all stared at me as if I was crazy, because most people would be pleading for their lives, and I guess this is what Dalia wanted, but I refused to give her the satisfaction of seeing me beg. She even had my hands tied in the form of one who says a prayer. She clearly was overconfident about how things would turn out that night. I just didn't want to make it too easy for this ugly princess.

"You got in my way the moment you snaked yourself into Fidel's bed!" Clearly Dalia was more insane than me, but even more than that, she was stupid enough to fight for her two-faced man.

"Listen, you think I want Fidel? That's insane! You can keep the man and his bushy dick for all I care! You just have to try and keep him in your bed—that is, if you can!" I gave her my signature smirk of evil bravado—the one where I nearly wink with my cheekbone, it is so high up on my face.

"Gimme the gun. *Ya no quiero oir a esta puta!* (I don't want to hear this bitch anymore.)" The man closest to her hands her a small gun, something I later knew to be a .347 magnum. I could see why she would like to hold something so small and apparently easy to handle (that was not a sexual pun); however, it wasn't until she stood there aiming at me for what seemed to be an eternity that I realized she had never killed anybody or shot anybody before. She'd never used a gun. *Maybe she had practiced before and she was just nervous*, I thought, giving her the benefit of the doubt. This gave me hope that she might miss and give up, a thought that curled my lips upward for an instant. After a few more moments of hesitation, she lowered her gun and handed it back to the other man.

"Take care of her. I'll wait in the car." She walked away, looking undignified almost as if killing someone was below her stature, and in some way, this demeaned her position.

The driver followed her back into the car, where they both waited for the other man to shoot me. I sighed in mocking resignation, but with all the time that passed, I actually had an idea. I was willing to try anything to live; after all, death seemed certain. I had nothing to lose.

"You know, you should shoot me over the edge of the cliff. That way I'll just fall right into the water. No cleanup." The man looked at me quizzically, but some-how this made sense to him.

"Are you not afraid of death, senorita?"

"Well, when a woman like me dies, she doesn't go to heaven and tell God all the great deeds she has done. She goes to hell to get high fives by the devil. So what do you think? Aren't you afraid I will come back from the dead for you?" I said this like a true devil worshiper staring boldly in his eyes, and seeing the fear of God in the man's face, I could tell he hesitated just as much as Dalia did when she tried to shoot me.

He laughed nervously, trying to brush the thought off.

I continued, saying, "You know, when they find my body washed up ashore tied, Fidel is going to know my death was no accident, and he is not a very forgiving man." I could tell my words were making plenty of sense to him, and he began to worry even more.

"What else can I do then? I have to shoot you." Clearly Dalia had some power over this man as well.

"Listen, I got an idea. Why don't you shoot to my side? I'll pretend that you hit me and jump in the water. That way I won't come and haunt you and your family at night. You know how annoying *las limpias son*, and they don't always work anyway. Even better, you can hand me a knife so that I can untie myself on the way down, and it will look like I committed suicide instead of being murdered," I said, bobbing my head in agreement lightly and hypnotically.

Las Limpias is a practice commonly done around these places to rid oneself of evil spirits and bad *yu-yu*.

Most natives have not only a strong fear of God but also a stronger fear of the unknown malevolence of the spirit world. So no matter how illogical something may be, fear is a strong motivator—or shall I say inhibitor?

"What if you survive?" he asked, sensing that there might be a hole in the plan.

"Have you seen the rocks and the rough current here? Survival—don't make me laugh!" I tried my most convincing voice ever, even though this was not hard. Surviving a dive here was not easy even for someone who is an expert diver. Unfortunately, that wasn't me. Even if I managed to convince this man to pull a hoax here, I still had to face what looked like certain death with rough cliffs at open sea. After a moment of deep thought, he bobbed his head in agreement with me. My magical persuasion never fails.

He grabbed his chin between his index finger and thumb, when Dalia screamed from the car to hurry up.

"OK, OK!" he said both to me and her, I assumed. "Climb onto the ledge," he said to me, handing me a knife and putting it in between my hands covertly. I stood facing the ocean, and I started cutting the rope discreetly with the blade. The man counted to three in a very low tone so that I could prepare to dive without screaming on my way down and also to jump on cue.

One...*thump, thump.* My heart pounded. Two...louder and quicker *thump, thump, thump.* Three! *Bang!*

I inclined three quarters of the way on the ledge, with my feet still touching it, so that I looked as if I just fell from the shot and not leaped into a dive. I managed to untie my hands, and as I continued to incline from the fall in slow motion, I pushed with the strength of my toes off the ledge with as much might as I could to avoid the rocks from the bottom of the castle. I tried my best to position my body, as vertical as possible for an amateur diver, in order to avoid injury to my body by falling flat. I calculated the distance from the water in order to time accurately when to take as deep a breath as I could to sustain life under water and adjust my need for oxygen while I cut the rope tied to my feet and tried to swim my way out. It was the adrenaline surging through my body that kept me focused on the best possibilities for survival; however, it was my keen optimism that led me to believe this stunt might actually work.

"I am made of fire and water. I rise from the steam. From the core of the earth, I bear life," I recalled my mantra in prayer to give me the strength to reawaken who I carry within.

At the time, this seemed to be insanity, but then, again, insanity had become like an old friend you acquired an odd taste for. You see, you start doing crazy things long enough, you'll begin to wonder how you ever went about life without doing so before. Crazy becomes an exciting addiction and there is no life worth living without excitement.

I felt like I was falling in slow motion. I suspended time, and then my hands touched the water; I took a gulp of air and went under. One thousand and one... one thousand and two...one thousand and three...The seconds go by, and my heart exploded at ninety miles per hour.

Chapter 2

ESCAPE INTO THE LAST BREATH

At another place and time the gods came together…

And so she blew air so hot that the sea boiled, and from the depths, another God held the fire in his hands and forged circles of rocks.

From their souls combined a purity of light and power—a source so bright it made the sun jealous, and he cried long and hard until vegetation started to grow, covering the orb with softness.

Sometime later, while they looked down on earth they found a soul on the verge of perdition. They observed her and pondered upon humanity.

"I am angry, yet I weep in silence. I am hungry, yet I starve. My sorrow feeds me but does not sustain me." Her soul, her thoughts were the song of solemnness.

She wept from the side where the sand touched the soft wetness of the foamy water. She wanted to go into the sea; she wanted to forget. So many tears had come down from her eyes that the sea itself could be a puddle of lament.

It was almost dusk, and her white dress fluttered away in the wind, another weightless item that needed to come off and vanish into the air like nothingness, carried invisibly by Helios. Her hair swept in the air a graceful dance of good-bye as she walked into a cold, wet end.

It was a slow march, and in every step, a lightness would continue to evaporate her soul to another place. It was a somber peace at last, as her alabaster skin would start to shine in glimpses of mother or pearl and crystal sand. She shone like a falling star about to go out. It is those stars that leave behind the vast fearsome darkness of the unknown, the same type that once could have been the brightest. She was suddenly more fabled in agony than precious in life.

"Oh my life!" she lamented. Suddenly, "alive" and "living" were two different things; one was once an aspiration and the other just a heartbeat about to take its last pump of blood. It was the air that changed from peaceful to violent and in it the last breath that choked in water. She tried to hold her breath at first, but with that inevitable reflex of survival that had kicked in, it only made surrender to breathe in the wetness of a puddle of tears that much more pleasurable. It was a painful resistance at first, but soon she understood that all change is painful when you resist, and change is almost always better.

"What could be worse than being alive?" she would ask herself, but arrogance lay in her ignorance.

"Could anything be worse than this life?"

This was the last thought, a thought that was cut short of her last breath and into another unknown state.

Chapter 3

A SWIM WITH THE FISHIES

*"I resolved to telling stories, because when
I actually tell people the truth, they don't
believe me. This is the Cassandra principle."*

— *M.*

I woke up resting ashore like a bum in an alley with a hangover. My heels washed up ashore beside me. Oh! My aching body was falling off limb by limb. These were the perils of having a mortal body! I smelled like the sewer of the sea, and my hair looked like seaweed. I squinted my eyes and thought, "Evil lives to see another day!" I smiled as I gripped my new pocketknife and stuffed it into my bra or rather what was left of it.

I wanted to lay there on that beach, but if I did, I would be found, and I was not going to wait and find out what my fate would be like if I did. I couldn't go to Fidel and tell him his wife tried to kill me. He might just have had me incarcerated for saying so, and there would have gone my life of bliss in Cuba. What if the men said I tried to escape to cover up my attempted murder? Then death or jail too awaited me. Perhaps it seems ludicrous that I say this, but the word of a woman like me around here… well, let's just say it held no value.

I needed help; I needed somewhere to hide, but who could I trust? It was not as if I was the most beloved woman on earth, either. I had no choice. I had to take a risk, and looking in my pocket for the last chance of hope was the only card in the deck left.

I walked across the beach and into a slummy bar. The turquoise paint was peeling off the sides on the outside. I guess I fit right in, with my ripped clothes and the overall look as if I had been back from hell. I made a beeline to the bathroom and fixed myself as much as possible, by pulling my hair back, watering the blood off my scratched skin, and wringing my clothes. Boy, did those scratches sting from the salt water! *Augh!*

I walked the streets as covertly as possible, making my way to Marco's place—the only person I thought could help. When I got there, I wondered whether I should just knock on the door, but I didn't want to wake anybody else in his house, so I moved over to the window of his room. It was covered by a flowery, yellow, and dingy curtain with a few small holes. I looked inside from the holes and could see him sleeping. I sighed and knocked on the window.

"Marco, Marco!" I saw him roll over in his bed. Great! I knocked harder, calling out his name. He squinted an eye and saw my shadow. He walked toward the window a little groggy and pulled his curtain.

"*Ay Dios mio!*" he vociferated, putting his hands to his mouth in amazement.

"Shh! Shh! Let me in, Marco. Please."

"What happened to you?"

"I'll tell you if you let me in." He looked at me half curious and half scared since I was an untouchable woman.

He debated for a moment and then nodded. I went to the door and waited. He opened the door, and it creaked as it opened. I walked in and saw Raul camping out on the couch. He looked like a potato that was squashed, with his saliva oozing out from the sides. I followed Marco back to his room as quietly as I could, trying not to wake the rest of his family. When he closed the door, he seemed eager to know what happened.

"Can I get a towel?"

"Yes, yes, of course." He rushed to get me a towel. As I undressed, in front of him, from my wet clothes, I began to relate what happened the night before after we left the competition. I saw him trying not to look at me out of some level of respect, but he was still having a hard time following my story as a result of the distraction.

"Marco, it's OK to look. I'm supposed to be dead, remember?" I gave him a devilish smile and asked to get showered as I covered myself with the towel.

"I have to heat the water," he said as he went and placed a pot of water on the stove. I was not used to the antiquated way people heated their baths, since the bathroom in my room had hot water already, a small privilege I was giving up to be part of the living. I pouted my lips when thinking of this.

"Well, what are you going to do now?" he asked me as if telling me I couldn't hide there forever.

"Let's shower and discuss, shall we?" He seemed taken aback by my forward behavior but didn't mind it one bit.

I undressed Marco, revealing the rest of the muscles I had imagined about until then, and when I was close enough to him, I encouraged a kiss. He fell right into me, kissing me with hunger, and my towel fell to the floor carelessly in an "oops" motion. He was fully erect, perhaps a morning thing; nonetheless, I played with his big hard cock in my hands as I talked business.

"I need a way off the island, Marco. Staying here would be like suicide." I stroked him, making it hard for him to resist anything I said. I looked into his eyes and enamored him with my magical persuasion that never fails me. He groaned eagerly. I pushed my body next to his in the shower stall as he closed his eyes, enjoying my hands. I grabbed the soap and made soapsuds appear as I smoothed them over, cleaning my chest, neck, and stomach and making my way down between my legs as he watched with excitement.

"I know of some people who are trying to get off the island. Maybe I can talk them into taking you with them. But it is risky, Maria. Even if they take you, you may not make it to the other end."

"Riskier than staying here?" I asked.

He gave me a look as if to say, "You have a point." Then he squinted his eyes as I squeezed the shaft of his cock out of my soapy hand.

"If I stay, I am as good as dead or worse. If I leave, I at least have a fighting chance, and even if I die, it would be on my own terms."

"I see, Maria, it's just that the chances of survival are not that great."

I stroked his cock hard, twisting with both my hands as if to stop him from talking to me with such a doomsday attitude. Men are easily subdued with pleasure, but you must not pin them against the wall and make it obvious to them; they buck up like mules against you if you do, and all the seduction, no matter how good, is null and void from that point—they become too aware of what is going on to fall for the antic.

I kept squeezing his shaft, loving the fleshy hardness he had acquired as I played with it like a child at a fair with a corn dog. *Let me eat the sweetness*, I thought, but then I remembered this wasn't about me getting off; it was about me getting off this island. As I finished that thought, my hands were coated with his thick hot-man juice. I massaged my hands and his cock together with his juice for a few moments and then I was done.

He gave me some clothes just to be able to walk around covertly; it wasn't much but a regular T-shirt and some shorts. I kicked the high heels for some flip-flops—not that my heels made it very far anyway. I tied my hair up in a ponytail and just fixed my lips with some red lipstick that lay around from his sister's stash. I wanted to make sure I looked good but in a low-key sort of way.

I followed Marco to a local hangout. It was what they called a "Soda," a casual place to eat or get takeout, usually with some tables and in this case a dance floor upstairs for nighttime entertainment or even an afternoon romp. This one particular hangout seemed pretty rundown on the outside, but on the inside, it was extremely clean and well-kept, which made you forget the cracks on the walls and overall signs of aging the building had. The floor was red and highly waxed. Over at these places, they polished the floor with half a dried coconut facedown on the floor and a stick pushing it down with sheer manual force; the fact that it was this shiny involved a lot of time and/or force.

"Is Pedro around?" asked Marco.

"Pedro is very busy today. Can't you see the sky is clear and it is still early in the morning?" the clerk said to Marco slightly annoyed, almost as if Marco should have known better. Marco put two and two together, and we left abruptly toward the beach.

The armed forces were making their usual rounds; they liked to think they were working alongside the people and rounding up resources from the local businesses. This kept them healthy. In some cases, business owners had no choice but to barter what little success they owned, giving up the possibility of any real riches. The armed forces made sure nobody got to be too powerful or had much more than they actually needed to carry on. Smart, I suppose; they wouldn't want anybody to conspire enough manpower and resources to overthrow the government in a political coup now, would they?

Anytime they were coming close to us, I embraced Marco against the wall, like two lovers who can't keep their hands off each other. Marco, of course, was not complaining. It was like saying good-bye a little bit at a time. I thought about how romantic that sounded in my head, and was glad I didn't say it out loud.

"Maria, when we get to Pedro, you will have to be at his mercy—that is, if he decides to take you with him, you know."

"Marco, how do you know about this?"

"They asked me to help and to go with them," he said with a slight tone of sorrow.

"And you don't want to leave?" In a way it surprised me he wanted to stay.

"I can't leave my family and venture out into the unknown to start over somewhere where I would be considered a nobody."

I wanted to ask whether he thought he was somebody there because he was a salsa instructor and known as a community celebrity for livening up a crowd, but no matter how I would have said that, it would just have sounded like an insult.

He looked at the floor rather pensive as he walked. He had other plans for staying, I thought, or so it seemed almost as if he didn't want to leave the land that gave him birth; maybe he was planning a revolt. Here goes my dramatic imagination again, getting into trouble. I felt it best to quit while I was ahead and not say anything more for fear Marco might change his mind and my ticket off the island would evaporate and disappear like the sunset after a long, hot day.

"I'm not like you," he said after a long pause. "I have a land and a place in life. I can't run away hoping for a better life. I want my life to be better here." His eyes had a glare of passion and conviction in them that I had only seen when he danced, except this look was ten times more intense.

"I am running away, Marco, but unlike you, I don't belong here, and I also have to try and survive. I am not yet at the point where I can say I am looking for a better life yet. I need to have a life to live before I can make it better."

He looked at me and smiled. I felt as if we were opposite sides of a coin paying off the same thing.

When we got to the beach, four men were working quickly to finish putting the last touches of what looked like a raft together. It was strung together by palm tree parts, pieces of wood from furniture and similar scraps of wood from God knows where. Necessity and desperation bring forth a humbling form of creativity to survival.

"Pedro!" Marco yelled.

"Shhh!" one of the men, whom I later found out to be named Julio, said.

"Sorry." Marco cringed at being careless. "Listen, Pedro, Maria needs to go with you guys."

"And why should I take her?" Pedro looked up at me, and his eyes widened for a moment, taking in my image. I could tell he liked what he saw, but I suppose convincing him to take me was my next challenge.

"Because she'll be taking my place."

Pedro scratched his head. I gave him a suggestive look full of my magic to help his thinking process. He glanced over at some garbage next to him. There were a few frying pans and some wood planks. After a moment, my eyes were more focused on what he was looking at, and then I realized those were our paddles.

"I can paddle long and hard," I said with conviction. These were the words Pedro was looking for to make up his mind.

"OK!" Pedro said, and I sighed with relief. The three other men were done and getting ready to throw the makeshift raft on the water, as we all said our good-byes to Marco, who disappeared into the streets quickly after that.

The three men and I pushed the raft onto the ocean with what seemed some provisions and what I thought was once garbage. We all climbed onto the raft and then started to paddle like crazy with the frying pans and wood planks. It took us a few moments to get our coordination and momentum going. In unison, we all paddled on the count of three so we could fade as quickly into the horizon as possible and not be seen.

The water in the Caribbean was choppy; in a way, this gave it a certain charm. At times it felt we paddled forward and the ocean threw us back the same distance, pushing us back onto the shore. It was a futile feeling, but we all were clinging to the same fight of not going back. It seemed like a fierce fight of will, the elements, and fate.

The sun beamed mercilessly on us. I was beginning to feel a fever on my skin. Pedro's curly black hair seemed to want to catch fire. We began to tire from all the emphatic paddling and so we decided to take a break once we were out in open water. The men decided it was time for a snack, and I concurred with them. I didn't want to ask for food even though I was hungry since I wasn't sure what these men would ask me to barter in return. However, I will not lie and say I was not up for suggestions.

"Pedro," I said, "how long do you think it will take us to reach land?" I looked at him as grateful and as sweet as possible. He didn't respond right away; instead, he broke his loaf of bread and handed me a piece. He also offered me water from his cantina. It was only after I had accepted his food and drink that he spoke.

"Four days if we are lucky to make it alive. Perhaps a day or two more depending on the currents and the weather," he said, squinting his eye to the sun. The other two men whom I was introduced to as Julio and Ronaldo looked hopeful at Pedro. It was as if this was a test of the sea: man beats the sea for survival or sea swallows men and washes them ashore. I pursed my lips at this thought.

"Oh!" I said, half expecting to be in a different land by the afternoon. Sensing my naïve nature, Pedro chuckled a little.

"Did you think we would just arrive first class in a couple of hours, princess?" asked Ronaldo facetiously as all men laughed now at my expense. I shook my head, unable to respond.

When night fell on to the sea and the evening breeze made slumber a little too brisk for my taste, we huddled together for sleep. It was hard to keep the body warm when the heart is always so cold. I looked at Pedro with desire and asked him if it was OK to cuddle up next to him for warmth. He did not resist. I snuggled so close that my breasts seemed to hug him. He secretly felt me up several times during the night, concealing his motives with discreet movement shifts in the tight quarters of the raft.

I felt exhausted at that moment, and restless as well. Resting somehow made my limbs heavy as lead and throbbing sore. I thought the others felt somewhat similar. Julio had decided to become chatty at night, lulling us all to sleep with hypothetical stories of how great his life was going to be in America. The typical dreamer.

Ronaldo looked at him, skeptical about it, and taunted him, until all we could hear from him were his loud snores. Soon Julio fell asleep; at first I thought he had somehow become a zombie because his pupils became white, but Pedro assured me he was just sleeping.

"Maria, I was wondering," said Pedro in a low and in what seemed his best attempt of a romantic voice, "if we make it to land, will you be my woman?"

I snuggled up to him, in a way looking for the security of the moment.

"You mean as in your wife?" I asked skeptically.

"If you are good, then maybe, but I mean as in being a couple," he said nervously.

"Sure, why not, Pedro. We've been through so much." I sighed on the inside, thinking, *Spanish men, they never miss an opportunity to score with a woman!*

"You are very pretty, and you have an incredible energy about you." Pedro sounded almost sincere about his words, but I, on the other hand, was not raised to believe in the lies of men. Besides, he was also under my charm, so nothing he really said was real, even if he so thought he could feel it. I went along with him, thinking of the food he would share with me over the next few days and the potential need for him, so it was best to keep him in my back pocket for now. I gave him a little peck on the lips. He kissed me back romantically, tongue and all, and cuddling together, we drifted into slumber soothed by the movement of the waves under our raft.

The next day Pedro shared some of his breakfast with me, enough to keep my body away from being famished but not enough to be completely satisfied. We all rationed our portions to make them last the duration of our trip.

"What happened to your legs and arms?" Pedro pointed quizzically at my scrapes, and if Julio and Ronaldo hadn't noticed before, they did at that point. I looked at them and imagined we all had the same look of being scorched by the sun with thoughts of survival, hope, anxiety, and boredom; so instead of telling them the truth, I decided to tell them a story to keep their minds off our troubles at sea.

"I'm not sure you want to hear this story—all of you seem too good a people to listen to my story," I said, goading them to beg me for the story. I used a slight exaggerated tone to cue them into asking, as if I were lying and they needed to call my bluff. Luckily these men were of enough intelligence to catch on to their cue, even though I had my doubts.

"Oh, c'mon!" said Julio. "We're alone at sea. We don't know if we are going to make it to the other side, so why don't you just tell us your damn story to at least kill time."

"Oh, I don't know. It's really not that good anyway," I said, making an obvious attempt to appear to make myself interesting. All the men on the raft looked at me bug-eyed, expectant, no longer wanting to plead with me for a story they already knew I was going to tell them anyway. So I sniggered as I started my tale.

"It all started two nights ago. I was lying in bed unable to sleep. I took my sheets off, thinking it was just too warm. I tossed and turned for a bit, and I even masturbated to see if it was my heat that prevented me from going to sleep." My supposed admission of self-love caught the men's interest by surprise, who, at this point, were paddling without me. I decided to speak a slower pace in order to prevent myself from needing to paddle alongside the men, an unspoken privilege I had just acquired for entertaining them.

"What do women masturbate about?" asked Julio with great curiosity; he seemed to voice the feelings of the others who continued to look expectant of my words.

"Do you want me to tell you the story or tell you what women masturbate to?" I asked, pretending to be annoyed.

"Both," said Pedro. "Just add it in to the story and continue. It's not like we don't have all day. Besides, I rarely get to hear this sort of story." The men nodded in agreement with Pedro, and suddenly I became a novelty.

"You have a point," I said, and putting my quasi-modesty to the side, I lowered my voice to a seductive tone, as I continued to relate the story. "I imagined myself bringing food to a rugged soldier held captive at the Castle Morro. I had fixed him plantains, refried beans, yellow rice, a skirt steak fried in onions, and some corn tortillas to feed him with my hands." The men now looked hungry and nostalgic of home food.

"Everything should be eaten with a corn tortilla!" Ronaldo cheered with a loud hoot like he would on Independence Day. I laughed at his comment as the others nodded in agreement.

"I wore a yellow spandex tank top with low cleavage, which pushed my breasts up, displaying them for his view. I was half expecting to nurture my soldier not just with food but also with the motivation and warmth that only a woman can provide." As I said this, I grabbed my breasts and bounced them up, mocking the behavior of myself in the story. The men seemed to salivate at this despite still being scorched and delirious by the heat of the sun and the salt from the sea that was felt in the air.

"My black skirt was barely covering my butt. I entered the room wearing my high heels and complaining about the heat as I swept a tendril of my hair off my face. The man was sitting on the floor with a bushy beard from so many days of being in the cell without shaving. I love the way a rugged man looks. I was forced to kneel down in front of him with my plate of food, since he seemed too weak to get up. I fed him with my hands as he looked attentively at my cleavage with desire, but then, suddenly, he also noticed my skirt was too tight and short to cover my privates from view. He stared in between my legs as he ate silently, letting out an occasional manly grunt and breathing heavy as he inhaled his food. When he was done, I snuck out a small flask from in between my breasts. It was still mildly cold. I had told the man I placed it there to help me cool off a bit and apologized if the drink was warm. He looked me in the eyes and said it didn't really matter as long as I showed him my breasts, that he hadn't seen breasts in a long time. In some way, his hunger made me want to feed him even more."

I mocked the movement with my hands as if to show my breasts to the men just to tease them and add drama to my story.

"I lowered my spandex top, and out bounced my chest toward his face, and in a pleasant synchrony, my nipples stared right at him as he licked his lips, ready for his next meal. 'Are you wet, woman?' he asked. I responded by telling him to check for himself and, if not, to make me wet, with a daring tone."

All three of the men were dazed so far at my story, and I wondered whether my eroticism was going to prove useful in some way, but I guess I was to find out.

"He grabbed me and explored every inch of my private parts with his fingers until he had made me slick enough to taste me. I filled the entire jail cell with my womanly aroma, and that was when he said, 'A woman who wears no panties is begging to get cock.' He looked down at his pants to show me he was fully erect and ready to give me what I was pretending I hadn't gone down there for. 'I didn't think you would notice I wasn't wearing anything,' I said to him, feigning innocence, but of course, the soldier didn't buy it, although he did seem amused by my play. 'It's hard not to. I could see your pussy from this point on the floor from the moment you clunked your heels together and walked in,' he said. I kept quiet as he petted me with his finger, and I closed my eyes in pleasure, waiting for him to continue. He buried his face in my chest, caressing my plump clouds with his whiskers. I shivered and grew more aroused. I was curious to see his cock, so I unzipped his pants and took it out to play with it in my hands. He was as hard as a steel pipe and hot as a wood stove, and both these things made me grow more impatient to feel him inside me, rubbing up against the walls of my snug and tight vagina."

I tried my best not to look at the men's crotches, but curiosity got the best of me, and I couldn't resist. It could be my creative imagination in conjunction with the excitement of the moment, but I could have sworn all three men were hard as rocks.

"The man noticed my angst," I continued, "and he smiled, kissing me heavy on the lips. He grabbed my hips with his hands and motioned me to sit on top of his cock. He groaned with pleasure as inch by inch he went in, engorging every space inside me with his girth. He held my hips with his hands and rocked me on his cock up and down and to the sides in small calculated but hard movements, caressing the insides of my G-spot mercilessly while he sucked hungrily on my nipples. After a while, I unfolded like a flower showered by the sun, opening up more and more to the soldier as he made me orgasm and submit to him in the best way, by sheer pleasure. He grabbed my breasts and squeezed them tightly as I straddled along, feeling his cock pulsing and becoming harder; he was getting ready to come. His thighs tightened, and my breasts were squeezed even tighter as he groaned loudly from orgasm. I could feel his juice hot and thick like lava erupting and coating my insides. He lay on my chest exhausted but happy, and that is how a woman masturbates to a fantasy."

"That's a great story," said Pedro, and the others nodded in agreement. I simply smiled and continued but was interrupted with a question.

"Well, when you masturbate, do you come?" asked Ronaldo. Suddenly I had a psychic moment; it was telling me Ronaldo was not the brightest.

"Of course, you have the need and the desire, and the only thing that would keep me from climax would be

an interruption." He looked at me abashed as I enunciated the word "interruption." I looked away into the sea,
so as not to make it more painful and uncomfortable for
him, and continued my story.

"When I was done with myself, I still couldn't sleep,
and I began to hear a voice calling me. I thought I was
delirious from lack of sleep, and so I ignored it. The more
I heard the voice, the more I grew restless in my bed, and
I still couldn't sleep. It became even stranger that the
voice sounded like the soldier from my fantasy. I knew
then nothing was really calling me. However, the voice
wouldn't go away. I remembered Dona Armenia, my landlady, telling me that sometimes the tenants hear things at
night. When I asked her, she told me not to worry, that it
was nothing but the wind or the voices of other tenants
talking, because the walls were too thin. But then I wondered if she meant this to be something else.

"All night that night I couldn't sleep. The next day I
went about my day as best I could, almost forgetting the
soldier's voice in the middle of the night. When I got back
home from my daily routine the next night, I was tired,
and I completely undressed myself and went under my
covers to try to sleep again. My body was weary, but my
mind did not quiet down to plummet to an unconscious
realm as I normally do every night. Then I felt myself
light, and my body overcame my mind. I was almost
asleep, when I heard the soldier's voice once more. I
felt a little chill in my bed," I said, adding a horror tone

to my voice, building up the suspense for the men, as they gripped the frying pans hard in terror when they paddled.

"I dug deeply into the mattress, unwilling to show my back to the wall or the window or anything for that matter. Out of instinct, I suppose, I turned my lamp on and gripped onto the corners of my sheets. I was quite unaware why I was so frightened that night and not the one before, but I guess that, in part, it had to do with the consistency of hearing the voices. One night could have been some sort of fluke, and if it goes away, you forget, but when it comes back, you begin to wonder if it is more than just your mind playing games with you. The voice seemed to call my name out into the open. It beckoned me. I had scattered thoughts in my brain about whether or not this was some type of urban legend coming to life there in my bed, and as I did, my heart started to pound heavy in my chest. It pounded partly from fear but also expectant for something to happen. It was then that I remembered the story of the broken soldier who takes his lusty victims, who are never to be seen again. You know, the stories moms tell their young girls in order to preserve their purity for marriage?" I looked at the men to see if they knew that story, but they all nodded their head from side to side in disagreement with me.

"C'mon, you seriously have never heard of the legend of the broken soldier?" I sniggered on the inside because there was no such legend of the broken soldier, and that was great, because I could make it up and string them along.

"Well…when I was young, my mother told me of a maiden who fell in love with a soldier who had been tortured for months. She first took care of his wounds and later fed him every day until the soldier felt healthy enough to seduce the young maiden. When he succeeded, unbeknownst to him, the maiden was unable to marry another man due to her impure status and was shamed in her town for being a slut. Such was the humiliation; the woman had no other choice but to plot with the soldier to run away together. The soldier, of course, agreed to the escape plan, and on the day the plan was to take place, the woman drugged the sentinel guarding the post and stole his key. She smuggled the man out, and they ran into the nearby woods. Seconds after she had fulfilled the escape, the authorities sent the bloodhounds and the guards out to catch them. Obviously, the woman had such a powerful scent that all the dogs could clearly smell her, and motivated by not just the duty of their species but also by the lusty desire the woman inflicted in them, the dogs and the soldiers who followed caught up with her very quickly. One of the guards managed to catch the soldier with a bullet, killing him on the spot, while the men grabbed the woman and took her back to the jail cell. She was used for the guards' personal pleasure and at times also given to the dogs from that point on until the end of her days. The soldier's soul remained vagrant in the woods, luring young maidens in 'heat' to run away with him, hoping to accomplish in the afterlife what he fell short of doing in his previous life."

I sensed the men pensive at this for a moment, almost as if they would have heard a similar story somewhere in the vault of myths.

"I had no idea moms said these types of stories to scare young women," said Julio, bewildered. Then I secretly prided myself in the ability to be able to summon feelings of fear in men with belief. The truth is, no matter what a man says he believes in, always in the back of his mind there is a fear of the unknown lurking to occupy his thoughts, even if that fear in itself contradicts his beliefs. They just can't resist it despite it being illogical.

"So I thought of this myth for a moment," I continued, "all the while hearing the haunting voice of the soldier in my mind, but then the feeling got worse, the chill got colder, and I began to feel something grabbing on to my sheets and pulling them down. I tried to hold on to my ends, but the sheets just slipped through my fingers as if I was grabbing on to a metal bar with buttered hands. I began to tremble with fear as tears rolled down my face. Then I felt a cold hand climb up my leg to try to touch me privately. It was then that I screamed in terror and jumped out of my bed, waking up the other tenants and my landlady. They all came running into my room, and I had to quickly grab a long T-shirt to cover my body."

I made my best impression of a horrified face without over-exaggerating, but somehow that was difficult for me. When you recount an event in your mind or by speaking to someone, your face makes these unconscious gestures under normal circumstances, as if reliving the moment, so when you tell a story that is supposed to be factual and not a fabrication, you should do the same; that's good lying 101, a.k.a. acting.

"Dona Armenia asked me what had happened, and I was near hysteria when I answered her. 'There was a man in the room, pulling my sheets and touching my legs.' Immediately one of the other female tenants began to stir uncomfortably as if she'd had a similar experience. I got on my knees, and one of the other tenants went down to hug me as I sobbed out of control. In between my sobs, I managed to say in a low trembling voice, 'The broken soldier.' It was then that the other female tenants 'oooed' with terror, putting their hands to their mouths. I knew then that even if they hadn't experienced something similar, they, at the very least, knew what I was talking about, and they too were frightened by the myth.

"Dona Armenia said it was nonsense to believe in such myths and that it was probably just the wind through my window. I turned around in the midst of my sobs and said to her that there was a truth to every myth. I gave a dramatic pause and then continued to mention that the window was closed. 'Then it must have been something else,' she said. One of the other tenants simply said, 'Well, it must have been something for sure. A woman doesn't reach this state over nothing, Dona Armenia.' After we all settled down, it was decided that I would sleep with one of the other female tenants for the night so that I wouldn't be alone. It seemed like a good idea, except that as soon as I felt comfortable enough to sleep, I heard the broken soldier call out my name again, who, by coincidence, happened to be the other tenant's name as well. The other Maria and I both looked at each other, not wanting to acknowledge out loud what was going on, but with our eyes we said enough. She too was being haunted by this voice—I could tell by her frightened stare.

"I was in a way too embarrassed to ask her if she had the same fantasy with the soldier, but my assumption was that she did. The calls continued through the night intermittently. Once they had seemingly stopped, and we were about to fall asleep, they would start again, more haunting than before. The last time this happened, I was about to drift off to sleep, when the lights from the lamps went out, and the door burst open. Then the impressive form of an imposing authoritative figure stood there for a quick second, hovering over us. He reached in and grabbed the other Maria and walked out as we both screamed vociferously, alarming everybody in the building.

"I tried to help the other Maria and chased after the figure, who seemed to move rather slow. However, no matter how quickly I tried to move, I could not catch up to him. It was like those dreams where you are going in slow motion, almost paralyzed, and you start to feel the importance and dire need to move quickly to fend off an attacker, but somehow you just can't.

"The other tenants and Dona Armenia all ran up again to see what the ruckus was about. Some seemed annoyed, others scared, but the general consensus was that the other Maria who was missing and I both had the same strange story. Some of the tenants offered to go out and look for the other Maria, thinking she must've been sleepwalking.

"I was looking with Raul, another tenant, in the nearby woods, because I was convinced that's where the specter of the soldier took her. Raul was not only nice enough to accompany me but also salacious enough to stare rudely at my nipples more than looking through the woods to find the other Maria, revealing to me the real reason a man goes out into the woods with a half-clothed woman in the middle of the night.

"Sometime before dawn, I heard the creak of the branches nearby. Apparently, Raul was too distracted to pay any attention to his surroundings. When I looked back, I was shocked to see where the noise came from, it was from an abrupt oncoming club in the head, that knocked Raul to the ground unconscious. It was so dark that it was the only thing to be seen. I was quite unwilling to find out if he was dead. As if by instinct, I ran as fast as I could, getting caught in several branches, and that is how I got these scratches." I attempted to finish my story here, knowing how abruptly and poorly I was giving it an ending just to see their reaction.

"Well, then what happened?" they all seemed to ask in unison.

"Well, you guys wanted to know how I got these scratches—that's how." They all looked at me as if I had stolen from their mother and bitch-slapped her in the process.

"My mouth is a little dry, and I am a little hungry. Is it OK if we take a break and eat something?" The men realized for the first time in the day that they had paddled like machines and had failed to feel hungry or tired and that it was now deep into dusk, almost nighttime.

"Yeah, sure," said Pedro as if a rock suddenly fell into his brain, knocking for clarity.

This time both Julio and Ronaldo shared portions of their food with me. Pedro offered me some of his, but I felt it prudent to ration his generosity and wait for another day. He would have normally been offended if I hadn't accepted his food if this had been a different situation, I know, but he understood.

"Maria, do you have any more stories like that to tell us tomorrow?" asked Ronaldo. The others seemed just as eager.

"I think I speak for all of us—when I say we really liked your story and feel happy, we have your company to make us forget our troubles," said Pedro.

"I'm sure I can come up with something. You all know those stories about El Cadejos and La Llorona, right?" I asked as they all nodded in agreement. For those of you who don't know, the Cadejos takes drunks with him to hell or protects them safely home, depending on which side of the road you walk on. La Llorona lures lonely drivers to take her in as their passenger (she poses as a damsel in distress on the side of the road) to help her find her children who drowned in the water, only for the drivers never to be seen again.

"Tomorrow I can tell you about La Sirena, (the siren)," I said.

"Oh, and who is that?" asked Ronaldo.

"A mythical woman who lures men at sea to their doom," I said this with my dramatically grave tone of voice and my theatrical hands.

"Oh really? How?"

"She looks like a goddess and uses her voice to hypnotize the men into a trance, but I will say no more until tomorrow," I said as I gave them all a devilishly evil smile that made them wonder about me.

The sea that night was unusually calm, and this was good because it helped us all sleep better that night. That night I positioned myself between Pedro and Ronaldo to gain more warmth. I get cold at night, no matter the temperature. Coldness has always been a part of me.

The next day was to be the third day at sea; we started off in our usual fashion. I suggested to the men to speak about their dreams, if they had any, before I went into my story. Pedro volunteered to go first. He had mentioned he dreamed all the time.

"I must have been influenced by what you said yesterday about the siren because I dreamt you took my hand, and we leapt off this raft, taking a swim below the water. The weirdest thing was that I was not scared of drowning. I felt happy as a pig in shit." He grinned at me when he said this, almost as if he had won a prize.

"I had a similar dream to that," said Julio. "I dreamt I was swimming in water that was as clear as a window, and I never dream at all. I felt a big sense of freedom, like peace maybe, almost like when you die."

When Julio said his last word, it was as if he did not think before speaking, but when he said it, he realized something: it sounded like an omen; suddenly the dreamy look of peace was wiped off and replaced with one of gloom.

Ronaldo, who either didn't catch on that quickly or just plainly was not smart enough to catch on at all, still conserved the dreamy look on his face as if nothing bad had happened.

"Well, it's impressive what an overactive imagination does to the mind, isn't it?" I said. "I read somewhere a long time ago about the powers of suggestion. It is said that if you laced fact and fable together, as in a myth, the symbolism behind it stayed in the mind longer than mere fact alone."

"Really," said Pedro, shifting uncomfortably with Julio as Ronaldo stared out into the sea, still in a dreamy state.

"Yea, haven't you ever noticed when you study history, for example, and try to memorize dates, how you keep it memorized for, maybe, less than five minutes and then forget, but if I tell you that when Christopher Columbus came to America, the natives thought he was cursed with the hand of death, you may think it superstitiously funny, until I mention the fact that the natives contracted diseases they had no immunity for and died. Christopher Columbus went down in history for fact, but the natives have him down for being a servant of death. So my question is, are you more likely to remember the story or the year in which he discovered America?"

"The story of course, but then, again, I was never good at history, or dates, so ha!" said Ronaldo, while Pedro and Julio remained pensive. I nodded at them as if agreeing with them.

"How old are you?" asked Julio, intrigued.

"Ha-ha!" I roared as loudly and shamelessly as a street-corner hooker. "How many women do you know would actually tell you the truth about their age?" All three men laughed at this, knowing the significance of vanity to a woman.

"It is just that I've never heard a woman talk like you, let alone one who looked as young as you," said Julio.

"Well, all I can say is that I am ancient." I gave him a smirk, and with a few more jokes, the tense ambience lifted. Pedro and Julio had resolved their queries and lightened up for the next story I was about to tell them.

I started my story by describing the siren to the men, taking particular care to mention the softness of her voice and how the siren's voice was her most powerful tool of seduction because her music hypnotized the men.

"Her voice had the power to revoke the most powerful logic from any man, injecting her prey with such a powerful cocktail of chemicals and overriding their own need for survival. She infiltrated their entire being and made men zombies of love, willing to do anything the siren pleased."

The waves continued to become rougher, and the men swayed to the movement of the sea. They were all too hypnotized by my story to notice it as they moved back and forth like a pendulum. The rope that was holding the raft closely together was beginning to become undone. The men continued not to notice or perhaps they simply were too focused on my words to care.

The clouds approached the sea in shades of coal and lead; they moved in with such stealth that when you glanced back at the sky, they were just there right on top of you, even though you wouldn't have noticed them just a moment before. The air thickened, making us all heave, compressing the lungs in a dank prelude to a tempest. In a swift sudden movement, like the roll of dice on a table, the ropes that held our raft became undone, and the wood pieces and scraps began to float away. The downpour came as the air twirled violently all around us.

"She coaxed the men to drown…" I said in my story, and those were the last words they heard as the men sank to the bottom of the sea like rocks. I grabbed on tightly to the bag of provisions and a plank of wood, propelling myself as further north as I could.

Not everybody can swim as well as me in open sea, I thought. You would either have to be a fish or have good luck to survive. And a big smirk came to my face as I swam away.

Chapter 4

A DAMNED SOUL

And then there was water, painted in small universes; the sweet sound of its soothing melody was very vast and incalculable. It was a circle within a circle of a wall of water, simply held by the power of sound. Like the force of gravity attracting the stars and planets to one another in a constant waltz was this water held by a sound; maybe it was a symphony, so carefully designed that it could not be a simple matter of mind in a man but of God. Men were made to God's liking, but is it too pretentious to think that one is to the likes of God?

"Can I think of you?" It was a very soothing voice, but it was not really asking for permission. Unknown voices and sounds sought her ear, and she chose to remain silent in thoughtful fear of the unknown. "Can you be my worldly ally, you little beauty?" it asked.

"Can I be beautiful even after death? Have I not yet suffered enough with this wicked gift that has filled me with such pain?" she cried, blinded by the light of the figure.

"Beauty that pretends modesty, being modestly beautiful in its transparency, can be quite charming," it spoke and then paused for a moment, changed its tone, and continued. "You took your mother's beauty when you were born and laid her to rest with your life. Surely you understood there was a price to pay for that? A debt that hasn't been paid. All debts must always be paid. If we do not willingly give up to our debts, life has a way to always take from us," it said gravely.

"How could I know there was such a price to be paid and that all my life was a debt to a gift I could never enjoy?" she retorted.

"A gift you didn't know how to use. Any gift that you are born with is always a culmination of your soul's earnings, in your case you did not earn the beauty you were born with, you stole it. So it was not a gift and you had to pay for those things you took from your mother even her life. You cut her short of fulfillment as a mother, as a wife and as a woman, her soul now wanders in purgatory as she did not get a chance to redeem her soul," it vociferated with contempt.

"Who are you?" asked Acaricia in an innocence that wanted to refuse judgment and justification.

"I am not here by choice, little insolent one. I was asked to show you mercy. I am simply trying to determine whether to grant you another gift that you do not deserve or send you on your way to be purged from sin," it continued with the same tone, now inspiring fear.

Her body glimmered against the reflection of the water, and her skin was so smooth and so light it was shining like a moonlike sun, pale yet bright. Her long, silky, midnight-black hair, which was so sweetly naked and so dark, was in contrast to her skin. She was a true beauty, lying in such pleasing delight to the pupils that she made all ache with lust, fascinating even the prude at heart.

"All I wanted was an end to my misery..." Acaricia cried.

"It's the Devil that does not want you. You are not bad enough to deserve hell, and it is I who can't let you in, for you are not good enough to be here either. You don't deserve purgatory. We all pity you, for you don't belong anywhere! And then here you are defiantly lamenting your poor life—the one you cowardly chose not to carry out. You are a damned soul. You paid loveless violent passion in layers of forced, unwanted love..." it said.

"It was years and days and hours until it all became blurred that there was no start, so there would never be an end to such incessant calamity. Can you pity the fact that I was not pardoned by my father? Can you believe that not even my brother or the thirteen siblings across the street or the baker bringing the bread or the mason on a break—none spared me? Can't *you* have mercy on me?" Acaricia cried, and from afar, more souls cried with her to the tune of their own laments.

"It was your penance, but you chose not to carry it. You chose not to relieve your soul. Rather, you chose to escape from your burden. None dared hit you, for your beauty protected you. Although forceful, they all showed you a love you could not give yourself. They forced love to show you what you needed. You had to learn to love yourself, but you couldn't, and here you are now, a negation of life I so generously gave you, but you took it away in insolence. How dare you try to escape? How dare you avoid your penance? Who made you equal to me to take your own life?" The disdain in his voice slobbered in wrath and hit like thunder. She no longer had the will to argue and accepted her fate in silence. She cowered in death just as much as she did in life.

"I had no more will to go on and nothing to hold me…" Acaricia trailed off in a whimper.

"Silence! I will not stand for weakness. Your actions prove to me that you are too selfish to love me the way I deserve. You are now a damned soul, Acaricia…You will be trapped in perpetual agony without love, until you can redeem yourself. You will have choices, but until you make the right ones, your soul will never be saved. You will wander aimlessly and without rest forever, but if and when you redeem yourself, you will know the purest form of true love, and I will have you sit beside me as my favorite. This is my promise to you. This shall be your gift."

Her ivory skin never looked so soft and vulnerable beside him. He was a pure white light that blinded, revealing only a silhouette of a tall, well-built man. His head seemed to be larger than expected to the proportions of his ten-foot stature.

With one big bolt of lightning, Acaricia was sent back to earth from the planet where she was in order to try again what in life she had once already failed.

Chapter 5

THE OLD MAN BY THE SEA

I could have felt despondent; I could have felt helpless, but that just wasn't me. The storm had washed me away, and I had lost track of where I was, not that I really ever knew anyway.

The sea and I had a strange understanding, one where I was allowed to navigate as long as I paid tribute. We had an intuitive way of understanding one another. I swam the rest of the way alone.

My skin looked like a dark roasted peanut by the end of the sixth day at sea. My skin had some minor sores from the sun burning down on me. I began to feel disoriented. All around me was the sight of the sky meeting the sun. When there is no sun in the sky, you can't tell whether you are going north or back south. I wouldn't be surprised if with my heat stroke I swam a couple of miles back south.

I drifted in the sea for a while, losing track of time, or maybe time was just suspended; I couldn't tell the difference. I wondered whether or not evil would endure once more. You may wonder why I say I am evil, but by now you must have figured out I am not a saintly individual. I shall tell you then. When I was a child, the mother whom I knew always said that men loved evil women more than they ever could love a good girl, and they were more willing to go to hell for a bad woman than they would ever sacrifice for a good girl. She would also say that evil never dies. When I asked her why that was, she said it was because good people are called to heaven, while the bad ones stay on earth, purging their sins forevermore. I've wondered whether Mother was right about men, but as far as "evil never dies," I made sure to be bad just to find out.

I had started small at first; being bad was like testing the limits. You try something when nobody is looking, and then you progress to bigger, bolder, more cunning things. You start to feel grandiose in a way because you are guided by no moral compass, no fear of God, so you become wicked for just the joy of being what others are too afraid or "good" to be. I don't care to be judged; I simply abide by my own acceptance of self. It is a strong and defiant stance, and only a few have it in them to try.

When I was six (by most humans' measurement of age), I went to my best friend's birthday party. My family was too poor at the time for me to afford a gift to give her, so instead of suffering the humiliation of showing up to a party without a gift and being branded the poor kid, I stole from my friends piggy bank during a play-date and bought her a gift with her own money. I got her something we both wanted, and in a future playdate, I stole the toy back so I could keep it for myself. Whenever I looked at the toy, I smiled and thought, *Stolen goods taste better than purchased goods.*

Often, during all my grade-school years, I would steal from the kindergarteners' lunch boxes (I went to a private school that had a section on grounds for the babies) or other grade schoolers. I would take their good stuff to eat, like pop tarts, candy bars and such, but leave them my lunch instead. It consisted of a squished smelly banana and a liverwurst sandwich on cheap white bread that had been mangled by the butter knife. One day I noticed, as one of my raided lunch boxes was being opened, that the little kid looked inside with disgust as he picked up the wet, dripping banana. I was laughing on the inside for days after that.

I often thought of my evil ways, and somehow they always seemed to bring a smile to my face, even when my cracked lips hurt as they moved upward. Evil is always present, and it grows just like a flower; it takes over even the purest of hearts.

I looked at the sky, searching for a sign, or anything for that matter. I saw birds in the sky, and even though I am no ornithologist, I would guess what I saw were a common breed of pelican. I decided to follow the path of the birds, since they are always close to land, in hopes that I would get there soon, too.

Sure enough, I soon saw land. I felt a jolt of excitement at this, and the closer I got, the more energy I seemed to get to swim. I let go of my plank of wood, since my provisions had run out over a day ago, and that was all I had on me. I didn't want to look like salvage from a wreck. I wanted to look as if I belonged somewhere. If there were any authorities or lifeguards, I certainly didn't want to raise their radar. It is always best to attack in silence when the enemy least expects it.

When I arrived ashore, I noticed I was on a section of the beach where all the other sunbathers were stark naked. Not the greatest sight, I might add! I walked out of the sea feeling numb and off balance from being in the water for so many days. My skin was pruney, and my scratches were still there since they couldn't quite heal from the excess of moisture. I took off my ragged T-shirt and shorts and decided it was best to blend in with the sunbathers. I must admit I was slightly embarrassed at first, as I had an overgrown bush of pubic hear going on, but heck! I became one with the sea over the last few days, so cut me a little slack! I walked around a bit, observing, taking everything in, and thinking of a strategy as to what to do next.

The beach itself was about a mile and a half long, and on the other side of a fence were regular sunbathers in bathing suits. I looked at both beaches, trying to decide what would be best and where my chances would increase for success. I stayed there by the fence most of the day, waiting and observing. Whenever anybody looked at me, I smiled in a friendly fashion. I noticed that many of the men on the nude beach were between their forties and sixties and alone.

One particular guy, sensing my inviting demeanor, came over and offered me a beer. "Hey, I noticed you've been out here all day alone, and I wondered if you were thirsty," he said.

I smiled at him, and brushing my hair behind my ear in a flirtatious manner, I responded, "You must have read my mind." I cranked open the can of beer and took several jolly gulps down my throat.

"Would you like some shade? You look as if you have spent a lot of time in the sun," he said in a very polite and pleasant demeanor.

"So do you," I retorted, because his skin was so tan he looked like an apache soldier, only that his skin was thin from age and leathery from sun abuse. Luckily, he had a sense of humor, and we both roared with laughter together.

"So do you want to come to my tent?" he insisted; then I really felt I was in native land, being introduced to the chief.

"Well, since you ask so nicely, why not?" I looked over at him as if he had won me over with a smile.

We walked across the beach a few feet in front of some sunbathers and reached his tent. Something I observed as I went along was how many people he was friendly with and saying hello to. I guess this guy was popular on this beach. I wasn't sure that was a good thing, yet…

He was sunbathing in high style, I might add; he had a cooler full of drinks, snacks; he also had plenty of beach chairs, towels, and sunblock and suntan lotion in several presentations. I was in awe.

He looked as if he wanted to ask me a lot of questions but somehow couldn't without being rude. He had blue eyes that looked tired from age but cheerful from a good disposition. His hair was as white as salt, and it also smelled like the seasoning too. He had an average-looking penis, but I am not sure I know a man who looks large or impressive when flaccid, so I guess it was OK. He was overall slim, with a slight sag and a slight belly. For his age, I would say he had good muscle tone. I was trying to decide what to do with him and sizing everything up around him.

"Do you want sunblock?" he asked in his usual polite demeanor, and I nodded in agreement. He handed me over a yellow bottle of SPF seventy, and I smoothed it over on my body as seductively as possible. It's a trick of the trade.

"Can you get my back?" I asked, and his eyes twinkled with delight as he said yes.

"You are in great shape, you know. How old are you?"

I gave him my signature street-corner-hooker laugh and said, "Young enough to have plenty of fun!"

He laughed with me, as if that was the best answer I could have given him. "Are you from around here?"

"Well, don't you hear my Spanish accent!" I said and chuckled.

"Oh yea, in a way we're all Cuban around here. My grandfather was Cuban," he admitted.

"Oh boy, I sense trouble. Should I run now or hold off until it's too late and you got my heart hostage?"

He giggled at this, and his face turned redder than it had been from the sun. "You're funny. When I saw you on the beach, you seemed different," he said, as if impressed and pleased by the change. His right cheek had a deep impish dimple that over time had became more like a wrinkle. He also had these lush expressive eyebrows; they were so thick you could do a comb-over. His gestures were so rich and dramatic that it was hard not to be engaged with him in an animated way.

"Do you have a name?" I asked, chugging some more beer.

"My name is Eric. Would you like something to eat? I got cheese, crackers, and some grapes."

"Sure, I am hungry," I said, trying not to appear too eager to eat after the exhausting swim. "Do you always pick up strange women from the beach?" I asked, rather skeptical.

"I'm a friendly SO, and I normally make friends at the beach. I am considered a regular here. Always on the lookout for Sha-boo-a. But it isn't every day I see a woman on this beach that looks like you," he said slyly.

"I sense the Cuban in you talking!" I cheered with a giggle. He smiled back, raising his hands slightly as if to say I can't help it. "But what does SO mean, and Sha-boo-a? Is that nude-beach lingo?" I asked innocently, not realizing how loaded that question really was. He took out the snacks, and I chomped them down like a squirrel with a nut as I listened.

"S.O in these areas stands for Sex Object." He used his signature grin with a little too much dimple. He was as open as his ass was to the air, and his sincerity and lack of pretense were refreshing. He did, however, change the subject before giving me any more nude-beach culture.

"I'm gonna get a smoothie at the concession stand. Do you want anything?"

"Sure, bring me one too!" I said as another cracker with cheese made love to my mouth. I was suddenly loving America. As Eric left our tent, and I looked out toward the sea, the sun actually came out for the first time in days. I watched Eric as he walked away; he was rather tall and looked like a light post walking.

If I had to guess, I would say Eric was in his late sixties; however, it is hard to tell sometimes. Once you pass

LONNY LEE

a certain threshold in age, old is old. Another thing I've noticed is that the older you get, the old-age threshold also goes up in number, so you conveniently never reach it. I guess old age always creeps up on you, no matter how you try to lie to yourself.

Eric was a great host by feeding me and giving me drinks while entertaining me. I became slightly leery that I was going to become Gretel and he, the witch, laying out the crumbs to the gingerbread house.

What happens often to people like me is that we often meet people who are our same kind, people who are not necessarily out for our best interest, but, on the other hand, you can also meet the complete opposite and prey upon them until you suck them dry. I wondered which Eric would be.

When Eric came back with our smoothies, we continued to eat and be merry. All the while, Eric was trying to close in on an answer he was seeking to find about me and ridding the conversation lightly and politely around the subject.

"Is that all the clothes you brought?" he asked, sensing how bare I was.

"Well, the truth is, I have this long-drawn-out story, but the short answer is, this is all I have on me now."

This immediately spiked his curiosity. I failed at making it sound like a dull story; I should have tried to save it for another day.

He looked pensive for a moment, almost as if hesitating. I guess he thought he would be rude for asking, but at the same time, he was interested in knowing. Maybe he just didn't want to get too personal with a friendly stranger. I assure you that is never good.

"Well, I am a great listener if you want to tell me about it," he said.

"Since you insist," I sighed and paused but then continued. "Six months ago, I decided to move in with my boyfriend." I looked over at him as I spoke, but rather than look me in the eye, like he had been doing up until that point, he looked straight ahead, almost as if rationalizing my story. This worried me a little, and I wondered how effective my story would be.

"He was supporting me because I lost my job," I said.

"What kind of job did you have?"

"I worked as an assistant manager in a retail store."

"What store?" he asked, almost as if trying to trip me up. I scavenged quickly in my memory bank and cable TV for the name of a store.

"Do you know the designer name brand Fendiwittz? They make a lot of high-end luggage and purses."

"Ah! Yes, I do. I've also seen the prices. Who knew baggage could be so expensive!" he said, seeming more convinced but curiously avoiding eye contact.

"Literally and figuratively!" We smirked at each other as he awed at our sudden joint wit.

"Yea, I was going to open a new store around here."

"You mean the shops up the block?"

"Yea." I reacted instinctively, unaware if I had messed up or not, but hesitation would be a dead giveaway that

I was lying. I began to think that if I was to tell this man stories, they needed to be better than the one I was laying out for him.

I sighed on the inside; I knew that six days out at sea, escaping death the night before that and a salsa competition crammed together in a week's time, had me running on fumes, but I still needed to survive. I was taking a stab at the dark at survival, also because I had no idea Eric was the golden ticket I was looking for. In either case, he was a regular here, and if I failed with him, I would have to move to another beach and try something different elsewhere. I ran the risk of getting burned at the nude beach. Ha! I love my dual-purpose sentences.

I then continued my story. "Anyway, my boyfriend was the very jealous type. When he called and I didn't pick up, he would get annoyed, thinking I was out with somebody else. When he texted and I didn't get back to him right away, he would think the same."

"So when you stayed home all that time, what did you do?" His line of questioning was beginning to make me uneasy. I began to feel he was going to be harder to win over than I thought.

"Everything," I said, sounding affronted and making no pretense to hide it. I also paused with an uncomfortable silence, cuing him to apologize or, at the very least, to ease up on his questioning. That was, of course, if he was to take me home with him, something I was beginning to doubt he wanted.

"I'm sorry," he said. "I didn't mean to offend you. It's force of habit to ask questions like this."

"You mean, ask questions where you demean the sanctity of a woman's natural place in life—the home?" I take on a defensive tone.

"No," he smirks, "asking questions to get to the bottom of things."

I nod for a moment, taking in his last comment and digesting it.

"Well, it's just that staying home and doing everything around the house and feeling helpless for not being able to do more to feel independent doesn't make my self-esteem feel any better. I guess you could say I feel kind of sensitive about it."

Eric looked at me for the first time since he started this interrogation, and in his eye I could see he felt my words. I wondered if he ever was unemployed at any point or if he simply sided with a more independent nature. Too soon to tell.

"Well, go on. Tell me what happened," he said, this time sounding more sympathetic.

"I can't say I was surprised." I looked down at the floor solemnly and shook my head from side to side. "He came home one day to find the neighbor in our home having coffee in the living room. Tony—my boyfriend—grabbed my neighbor and kicked him out. We got into a huge argument, where he kicked me out of the house. I thought he would calm down, and we could talk it out later, so I went for a walk," I said, waving my hands emphatically in a distressed manner, and this is when he noticed my watermark, the three raised wavy lines on the palm of my hand.

"Did he hit you?" asked Eric, concerned. I demurely looked over at my scrapes and soothed them with my hand as if hugging and nurturing myself from a painful memory. He must have thought my watermark was a sign of domestic abuse; then, again, I also had all these scrapes.

"No," I said softly and forced my eyes to welt up a bit by thinking the sad thought of my first breakup.

"It's OK," he said softly. I extended my arms, pretending to need the comfort of a hug.

"He said he loved me, Eric. I just don't understand why," I said, sobbing and wailing in mocked pain. Eric hugged me, like you would a child who was abandoned at a park. He rubbed my back and did something else in the process. He was consoling me in his own way, but you have to understand we were both naked, and as he was consoling me, he compressed my round, voluptuous breasts onto his chest with a sense of lusty desire. It was creepy in a way, but I, of course, went with it. Creepy was my thing, and I loved it!

"What do you want to do? Do you want to get your things back from his place? Do you have a place to stay?" His line of questioning changed to something more pleasing to my ears.

"I can't," I sobbed. "He took all my things, which weren't much, and burned them in the yard, all this while yelling out to the neighbors what a whore I was," I cried out, adding more pain to my tune.

"I left with the clothes on my back. I have absolutely nothing, Eric. I have no job, no place to stay, no clothes. Up until you showed up, I hadn't even remembered to eat in a day."

"You slept on the beach then?" he asked, astounded that I was pretty much homeless.

LONNY LEE

"Not exactly. I have been vagabonding since last night. I haven't slept at all. I prayed to God for a solution because I really have nowhere to go. I don't have family here and really no friends. Tony really consumed all my life, and for him, friends were a threat," I said, secretly priding myself on how convincing I sounded.

"And you allowed that?" Eric sounded upset that a person could be so controlling of another's life, as if he couldn't picture that something like that could and does happen every day to some people.

"Well, how do you say no to somebody who has helped me since I got into this country? He has helped me with everything, and now, I feel devastated I lost him. I wish I could go back in time. I wish he could forgive me. I just feel so lost," I cried in Eric's arms.

"Listen, why don't you come to my house, wash up a bit, rest, and I will help you figure something out, OK? I want to help you."

I sobbed in his arms and hugged him. I savored my first success by smothering my breasts against his chest. I felt proud but also grateful.

"C'mon, we can do some shopping to cheer you up on the way home. I want to take you to dinner tonight." The cheer and excitement in his voice was quite uplifting.

I put my T-shirt and shorts back on and helped Eric pack up his things. I carried the umbrella tent. When folded, it was actually easy to carry. Eric had this down to a science, I thought. When he got dressed, he simply put on a red speedo bottom and strutted along the beach as if he was the Adonis of the geriatric community. I raised an eyebrow at this and chuckled on the inside. The only thing he could possibly be missing was a peacock's tail, but that, however, would not be flashier than the lewd bulges he carried in his dangerously tight bottoms.

He looked over at me as we walked away. I kind of hoped I didn't look as bad as I thought I did.

"I look different dressed, don't I?" I asked, and we both laughed.

"Yes, but there is always something that can be done about that," he said with innuendo. I chuckled; he was quite the character.

When we got to the parking lot, I noticed he parked in the handicap spot, but even more than that, he had a high-end sports car. It was a red-and-silver Hybrid Miser-ratti 910 Spyder. This was a magical car that wasn't even out on the market for consumers to buy. It had two electric motors (for those of you who are ecosavvy) to produce zero emissions. Of course, don't let me fool you into thinking I knew that kind of stuff back then.

"This is my baby," he said with pride.

"I can see that," I said, chuckling. "I noticed you are not the least bit bashful at showing off."

"Well, that is because I have reached a point in my life where I gave myself license to show off!" he said refreshingly.

"I bet it can be a lot of fun."

"Indeed it is!" he said, winking at me.

I began to wonder what it was that he did for a living because I couldn't assume he lived so lavishly on a pension and social security. We sat in his car, and he began to drive off to the stores. He then sped off in his car, and as he hit the gas, I felt I was going to suffer from whiplash; my head went back so far from the impact.

"This car has V8 and goes zero to sixty in two point five seconds," he bragged.

"No kidding! I thought you said this was an electric vehicle?" I asked innocently, playing along with his need to show off his toy to me.

"Well, I had this car imported from Japan just because you can toggle back and forth from using gas or electric, and when you plug it in, it charges quick!" he said emphatically.

"Wow! I had no idea they even made vehicles like this." Part of me said this impressed, but there was a secret part of me that really didn't care about cars like this, that was until I got to drive it. At that point I had totally overlooked that this was the perfect getaway car, but the important thing was I had the thought eventually and that was what counted. We stopped by at the pharmacy first, where Eric was kind enough to get me my toiletries.

At the pharmacy, I asked Eric if it was OK to buy makeup, since I didn't like to go for the natural look.

"Please do!" he said it in a jerk-like tone of voice. I shot him a sharp glare, and he quickly continued with, "I love a woman who takes care of herself."

"So do I," I said, holding my ground.

As we approached the register, this young woman in a hot yellow string bikini bounced in front of us in line. She had a slender physique with well-proportioned curves. Eric flashed her a big saber-toothed tiger grin.

"That woman is in great shape," he said to me, ogling over her round hips as they bounced to the rhythm of her impatient tapping foot.

"You are a true admirer of the female form," I said, not quite sure if I should feel offended yet.

He approached the register with my stuff, where the heavyset mature female clerk said with a very pleasant tone, "Did you find everything you needed?"

"No, but that's because, unfortunately, you don't sell what I need," he said suggestively and grinned at her, exposing his dimple with his rosy Christmas cheeks. The clerk's mouth and mine dropped in awe, not quite knowing how to respond.

I began to giggle nervously.

"He's harmless, I promise." The woman looked at me with a forced smile.

As we walked out of the store, I felt like putting Eric on a leash.

"I had no idea you were in heat," I said to him, joking.

"You have no idea how happy women make me."

I shook my head at him, gritting my teeth as he said this. "Well, I am beginning to notice."

He smiled at me with a twinkle in his eye as we walked back into his car. We drove toward some clothing stores.

"Is it OK if I take you to this store I like?"

This question automatically raised a red flag with me, as I began to wonder where he was going to take me. I smiled suggestively. "Is it a sex-toy store?" I looked at him, insisting for honesty in his answer.

"No," he said, giggling. "But if you want, it can be on the menu."

I cracked up, a little winded from his boldness. "For a moment I thought I had encountered an adorable old man!"

"I thought I *was* being an adorable old man," he said slyly.

I bit my lips and nodded in agreement, thinking, *Ah, Caramba, estoy jodida!* (Uff! I'm screwed.) He looked at me as if he took pleasure in giving me a run for his money and wondered how else to make me work hard.

"Well, I know this store downtown that sells all these high heels and nice form-fitting dresses that I think you would look great in. It is called Skin!" He sounded cautious for once, so I began to realize that maybe his salacious nature was perhaps just a front.

"OK," I coughed out. *I am in over my head with this man,* I thought. He clearly thought of himself as the type of man to whom the rules of decorum no longer applied when it came to courtship. Old age definitely gave him license to be an incorrigible flirt, or rather he gave himself that right.

"Do you live alone?"

"Yes, unfortunately. My wife died a long time ago," he said, nostalgic.

"I am sorry to hear that."

"Thank you. It's OK now. For the first five years, I mourned her. I thought life was over. Then I decided to make up for lost time, but age and stuff are not the same," he said, lamenting.

"So you regressed back to being a teenager!" I said, making light the situation, and we both chuckled as we walked in to Skin.

Skin was the type of store that sold a lot of club wear—things like tight latex dresses, anything leather, and plenty of high heels. There was everything from the standard to platforms with rhinestones and then more. I looked around and decided that maybe it was time for a makeover. Eric gave me some very approving looks at some of the clothes that I picked out and even made some suggestions himself. Clearly this was a gift that he was giving himself.

After we were done shopping, he took me to his home. It was a two-story home in an Art Deco style decor painted in a light turquoise. The roof was made with Spanish tiles, and this gave it a familiar homey look to me. The driveway was paved by a skilled mason, who had created a very intricate design on rock that looked like a centaur.

There was also a very interesting sculpture in the front lawn that doubled as a water fountain. It was a bare-breasted mermaid reaching out of the water to caress a centaur in the face. It was an interesting composition, since I was quite unaware of any story where a mermaid fell in love with a centaur. His landscaping was very clean and well groomed with some simple shrubbery, a few palm trees, and some flowerbeds.

We went in, and then he showed me to a guest room on the first floor. It had its own bathroom. Every wall in my room had a different color: one was bright yellow, another jade green, the next flamenco pink, and the other a shade of sky blue. The bed had a seashell design on a white bedspread. There were two lamps with sand and seashells, settled on nightstands.

There was a white shaggy area rug on the floor. The floor seemed like some type of Carrara marble tile. Whatever it was, it was definitely cold. Eric let me know he would like to go to dinner at eight and asked me what I wanted to eat, but before leaving, he also asked, "What is your name?"

"You can call me M," I said, leaving Eric intrigued as I closed the door to the room behind me to get ready for events later.

You see how I just did that? I gave myself a new name, and now I had to own up to this new persona. You break in half and subdivide, leaving a piece of the old life behind and start brick by brick, building a new one. You reinvent yourself to become something or someone else, something stronger. You can start by pretending, but at some point you have to own up to this life you're making up as you go along. When you plot for the future, you must also allot for variables. I could sit around and wait for life to happen, but that was just not M's style.

Chapter 6

THE HOLY DOME

Almost suspended in a timeless warp, Acaricia landed in a place not known to her. The air smelled like fresh dew after a morning rain. The sun beamed high, and she was in a public outdoor market, where plenty of people were dressed in solid robes of linen and cotton.

Everybody seemed very tall, and most of them were very young. Their heads also appeared to have an uncommon largeness about them and were paired with big almond eyes. *This must be a different race of people*, Acaricia thought.

She walked around but seemed and felt lost in a sea of people. The marketplace was filled with foods she had never seen before.

There were round fruits that looked like oranges with spiky red-and-orange hair coming from them, long orange-avocado-like vegetables, and food with various kelp or seaweed dressings, which were all to her left. To the right of the market were live animals and cured meats, but on either side she looked, there were plenty of knickknacks and food to eat.

The sun was so high in the sky it must have been noon; the rays were burning her cheeks. Acaricia realized quickly why all these strangers had a protective headdress to shield them from the sun. The general ambience was one of peaceful activity.

In bewilderment, she started walking around disoriented and wondering what she was to do there. Since she was not told her mission, she simply needed to figure that out for herself; she ran the risk of becoming a wanderer. *I am alive again*, she thought, but in a way, she felt different than in her past life. Under her yellow loosely fitted gauze dress, there was a light warm breeze, making her feel quite naked as she walked.

She listened to the townspeople speak; they appeared to be speaking in a language that was very foreign to Acaricia, but despite that, she seemed to understand what they were saying. It was as though language didn't matter, for she knew the meaning in her heart.

"I will drop off five loaves of bread to your home later for these fire fruit," said a young lady with a child who appeared to be six years old. Both had the lightest blond hair and largest dark eyes Acacia had ever seen before.

"Sure enough. Have a happy fire day. See you later," said the clerk, who was a young man with eyes as dark as a black hole. He seemed to stare at Acaricia as she walked by. It was a familiar type of stare to her—the same she had many times in her past life.

As Acaricia continued to stroll down the market, each step seemed to bring her closer to being discovered. She paused for a moment, looking at her now-silky blond hair. It navigated in waves similar to the people around her. *Where am I?* she thought.

Not so far on the horizon, she could see the luscious green mountains; they looked so warm, friendly, and inviting. The animals she saw were so exotic to her, but then, again, what could an uneducated girl from the farmlands possibly know about the world, let alone other countries, that is, of course, if that was where she was?

An old lady came walking in her direction; it was the first old lady she had seen since she had been there. She seemed to have her eyes closed, but despite that, she somehow managed to walk on by as if she could see where she was going. A small colorful bird with a long tail flew around her, moving equidistant toward her with every step. It flashed around pompously its iridescent plumage in such a fashion it was hard not to see them coming. The closer the lady came, the more aware Acaricia felt she was moving toward her, until she stood right in front of her, preventing any movement forward. Without hesitation, the old lady grabbed her hand and said, "My dear, you wander as if you are lost, but you are exactly where you are supposed to be. You bear the mark of water on your hand."

Having the lady this close to her, she saw that her eyes were sewn together. The stitches were so minute and elegant you could barely tell they were there. This was clearly something that was handled by an expert hand. The lady continued to caress her hand in a sensual way. Her fingertips rubbed against her palm, and this was when she saw the three wavy lines on her right hand. This was her watermark. Intrigued and bewildered, Acaricia tried to ask something of the old woman, but before she could say anything, the elder walked away, with her bird swarming around gracefully as if dancing to her own mental tune.

Acaricia continued to walk, now in a sense of more wonder than before with every new discovery she made. Some of the merchants hung far from their posts into the walkways unencumbered by the traffic of people or the need to guard their goods. Poverty or need seemed to be a distant nonevent that happened in other places but not there.

The women all had a variety of bright berry-stained lips and flushed glows, and although all of them seemed to be at healthy varied weights, none of them was, by any means, overweight. Even the men all seemed to possess a natural attractiveness about them. Truly another anomaly Acacia had never seen in her prior life.

Acaricia began to wonder where they left the ugly and old people, although another bigger oddity was how large their heads and eyes were. They all had an extremely statuesque height. Acaricia had never seen a race of people like this, but what she wondered more was if she stood out for having distinctly different features. It was not until she looked at herself in the reflection of the marble on one of the adjacent buildings that she saw her features had changed from those that she had once had known before. Her hair was a large wavy-blond spectacle that swept the air romantically, and her eyes were oval and large by proportion to her face just like the others, but what she noticed was that her head appeared to be a lot larger than ever before. *Could it be my hair?* she thought. Even then, without her noticing, she walked with more balance and grace than ever before just like the others. For once she felt she didn't stand out for her features; she simply fit right in.

She walked some more and meandered for a while. Her feet started to become sore and blistered in her leather thongs. She sat on a perch near a dome to give herself some respite from her mundane ailments, and they seemed to be many. Being alive again was not what she had wanted when she took her last breath. How contrary to life is death, where the only pain is in the indelible spirit as opposed to being mortal and taxed with such heavy burdens on top of the physical ones. Her feet continued to throb like a heartbeat the more she rested. Her swollen toes were bound by the leather of her footwear. Her normally little feet seemed too large for her body. Maybe she too had grown to the height of these giants and just not yet noticed. Walking on the soles of your heart is torture, and the bigger you are, the more weight you bear.

She noticed the people congregating inside the dome. *Attracted, perhaps, to some form of entertainment,* she thought at first. Most of these people did not look well. Their eyes were a solid black, but unlike the eyes of the others she saw before at the market, the color turned to a very high degree of opaqueness, unlike the vibrant dazzling onyx tone.

Curiosity seems to be the great driver to do mischief in any of its many forms. At times this may come as an inopportune questionable action and at others downright adventure, and for Acaricia, the lure of both was just too much to resist, and so she walked in.

Considering her ailing feet, it was not hard to pretend affliction, and limping as she did, she found a seat, complaining in silence so as not to draw any attention toward her.

The inside of the structure was circular, and the seating was arranged in such a way that all faced toward the center where the most curious object was to be observed. At the center of the dome was this golden globe suspended in midair, rotating slowly on its axis. It seemed to be made of very light and pliable metal, almost like mercury. Acaricia was bewildered and amazed, as in her prior life, she had never seen such a thing. Even though she was curious to know what was going on, she kept it to herself. Doing or asking anything might give away her position, and until you know the lay of the land, it is best to simply observe.

Everybody sat quietly and orderly. The very first line of the seats by the metal globe were made of some type of solid-looking sand. From seemingly nowhere, five old women and a man appeared by the globe. The old women all wore lilac robes and had their eyes sewn shut. Each one of these women had an animal with them. Acaricia immediately recognized the lady from earlier in the day. She stood there as her bird continued to fly in circles around her, humming with the hovering flutter of its wings.

"The sages are here," said one of the onlookers in the crowd in their native tongue.

Most of the audience was looking down at the sages, but one attendant was pointing at the sky, and this prompted Acaricia to look up at the dome. The dome had a smaller dome with no enclosure, allowing the sun to shine from above and onto the orb. The structure was purposely designed to receive the midday sunlight. The intensity of the sun on the metal became a blinding spectacle of splendor. Everyone's eyes could see clearly despite the brightness in part because the inky darkness in them would not reflect the light that bounced off their pupils.

Acaricia was stunned by the sight. It was like being able to see the sun straight on with your naked eyes. The heat started to enclose the dome like a sauna of sorts, an event that lasted an entire twelve minutes. The orb in the middle moved amorphously during this time, creating these hypnotic shapes for everyone to see.

After this, Acaricia couldn't feel the pain in her feet; it was as though it never existed. There were some small blisters on her feet, but even they were fading from sight.

The man on the bottom seemed very young by comparison to the women. His hair was so blond, it looked like golden crimson; his eyes resembled emerald marbles even in their darkness, and beside him was a golden dog that looked as if his tail, feet, and ears had been dipped in dark tar. His look was somewhat of disdain, perhaps the sense of entitlement that he bore. *He must be somebody*, thought Acaricia.

The sages looked at one another or rather moved their heads toward one another in a sense of union, before commencing what still seemed unknown at this point. Acaricia felt it was almost a circus show, with lights, animals, and odd people, but she soon realized this was a naïve thought.

"Our God has spoken to us through the stars. Our Holy Ephemeris has given us a daily reading and has let us know that there is one among us today who has the power to raise us to higher existence. There is a strong power within her, and it is important to recognize this person and aid her in every single aspect of our way of life. She is part of our prophecy," the man with the dog said, staring at the crowd, while the crowd stared back at him nervously as if the prophecy was something to be feared.

The next sage was one of the women; this one had a large purple gemlike snake that resembled an amethyst. Her snake slithered around her body in circles, almost in a rhythmic pattern. She seemed to be seeing images in her mind.

"This year we will celebrate the Festival of Fire in the Garden of Pharos. We will publicly announce our designations for future sages and honor the games. I see there will be a very gifted alumni this year. The planets are in retrograde, so sorting students will be particularly difficult this year. We must remember this is a year of rest and not activity, so we mustn't put forth any new ventures until the following year." While this sage spoke, the orb continued to shape-shift into what seemed to be animal forms.

"For many years now, we have concentrated on growing our resources, planning the future, and practicing our talents. I am proud to announce that next year we will expand our Hall of Knowledge. Our scribes and writers continue to produce great works that tell upon the paths we have followed as the favorites of God."

All the other sages looked or rather acknowledged each other. This apparently was a cue to the end of the civil congregation. The crowd started to chatter, and some started to leave, while others lined up to speak to the sages.

Acaricia got a little closer to hear better. She still tried to conceal her bewilderment, not realizing she stood out more by not participating.

Each sage had a different line of people. Most of them were seeking answers or guidance of some sort—advice for decisions they felt needed God's approval. A little boy from the crowd and his mother approached one of the sages, looking a bit groggy and swollen, and the sage looked at him and said:

"You have an ear infection because you do not want to listen, my boy. If you open your eyes to what is being said to you, your ear infections will go away. Learn to listen or not have ears at all," said the sage with the snake around her neck with her head tilted down as if looking at the boy or struggling for breath. She then touched the boy's hand. The little boy had an annoyed look on his face for what he was told, but it soon followed one of relief almost as if the pain in his ears had gone away.

A man with a cough approached a sage with a snowy white rat on her shoulder, and he extended his hand toward the sage.

"Your cough will go away when you have said the things that you have stuck in your throat. Speak them freely, and see your cough gone."

"I seek guidance to have a child, Sage Incandida," said this young woman, who apparently was barren, as she put out her hand and bowed at the sage.

Incandida was the sage with the rabbit, the rabbit clearly being an infallible symbol of fertility and new beginnings. When she touched the woman's hand, her face turned to the side as if she saw something bad in the girl's future; she paused for a moment, making the young girl clearly upset there, where she stood waiting for her to speak.

"Women who are barren have either creativity issues or female issues, and then there is God's will. You must reassess your femininity and channel it in creative pursuits. Children will come, but not as you expect." The young woman looked disappointed, almost as if she had expected the sage to give her a clearer, easier message, one with an ending she had prescribed for herself.

"Bear in mind the thirteenth law," said the sage, and the young woman bowed and left the dome.

Acaricia's eyes narrowed. The thirteenth law. What could that be?

The woman looked as if she thought she could forge her own fate, mocked acceptance, and bowed out into the crowd outside.

Chapter 7

I FIND A NEW IDENTITY

Oh! Finally a nice clean shave! It's amazing what a little soap and water does to a woman. I wore these cute peep-toe sling-back seven-inch heels and a skintight tiger-print dress. I felt like such a predator, and I bet I looked like it too being next to an old man with a few bucks and the jolly goodness of a Santa Claus.

I had been running on fumes this last week. I had been clapping together my last two pesos against an invisible can, asking for charity. Maybe it was Christmas, and Eric was my Santa Claus. Perhaps this was my new thing, Santa.

Eric held on tightly to me and decided to valet park the car at a very well-known reservation-only seafood restaurant, the type where the hostess acts all snotty until she sees your name on the roster and a twenty-dollar tip in her hand.

"I thought this would be better than the diner," he said, half joking.

"Maybe you can take me to the diner sometime," I said innocently, not yet quite knowing what a diner really was.

The hours seemed to weigh on me, the excitement pushed me further to go on, but I was exhausted; I couldn't wait for dinner to end so I could rest.

We got seated at a table by candlelight, and in a way the dim lights gave us a romantic ambience.

"You look absolutely lovely and sexy tonight," he said in his usual incorrigible tone.

"Thanks," I said and smiled. "I wanted to thank you for helping, Eric," I said. "I didn't think there were knights in shining armor anymore."

"Don't thank me quite yet. How do you know I don't have a secret agenda?"

"Don't we all?" I said suggestively.

"I'll tell you mine if you tell me yours," he taunted me like a little boy holding his hands behind his back but still showing me the mischief in his dimple.

"Then it wouldn't be so secret, would it?" I gave him a coy face as he gazed intently into my eyes. *If he stares enough into them, I can hook him with my magic*, I thought.

"I know who you are, M," he said, suddenly changing the tone.

"Do you?" I asked, bewildered and alarmed. "And what may that be?"

"If I tell you, you might think I am crazy," he said, almost as if declaring some forlorn type of love.

"You are in luck. I happen to love crazy," I said, inviting the challenge.

"OK, I just don't want to scare you," he said with trepidation.

"I am not the type who scares easily, but I am the type *you* should be scared of," I said, and we both giggled and then paused. My statement sounded like a threat, but it was really just a fact.

"I have been very lonely these past few years, M. I reached a point where everybody I loved and cared for has died or is dying. Every week that goes by, I go to somebody's funeral. When my wife died, I was upset at first because it wasn't me. Then I was upset she didn't outlive me like statistically she was supposed to. I lived an entire life thinking I would always have her and how I would retire and play golf, visit my friends, and live a life of blissful leisure until my dying day. All through my life I worked so hard looking forward to this life I had planned for myself, and then I get here, and I have nothing but an empty space. I have this huge house and all the money I worked tirelessly for but with no real meaning to my life. I can do whatever I want, but I have no one to keep me company, and ironically, even though I don't have to, I still work just to keep me busy—except that my work now is different. I used to be a defense attorney—I guess I still am. It's just that now I take only certain cases and work pro bono at my will."

"Is that why you ask so many questions in an interrogation style?" I interrupted.

"Guilty as charge," he said and laughed. This was a scary scene: a law-abiding citizen with a dubious woman in the middle of the night. I sighed discreetly at this thought. Him being the righteous type kind of put a kink in my plans.

"A couple of weeks ago, after being angry with God for sometime, I decided to reconcile my differences with him and prayed for him to show me a sign, to give me something or someone, hopefully someone, to keep me company and share with. I went to mass last Sunday and prayed for the same thing, not really expecting him to hear me, but when I saw you today at the beach, you seemed to be praying for something too. You looked lonely and—I hope this doesn't sound like an insult—but desperate too, and in some way I felt drawn to you," he said. He seemed so sincere he made me think twice about my elder-abuse heist.

"When you told me your story, I felt you were the answer to my prayers. I wanted to help you almost immediately, but I didn't want to overwhelm you with attention and scare you away into thinking I am just a dirty old man," he said with an honesty that was refreshing. However, his words did cause a reaction of pain in my heart—a stabbing feeling that I just had to ignore for my own well-being, because when you have a black heart, and it is struck by goodness, the result can only be pain.

"Eric, you are a dirty old man, and an incorrigible one at that! You can't scare me away. I have nowhere to go," I said, immediately regretting the bluntness in my words. This abruptness wouldn't help my cause, but somehow my normally slick behavior disappeared at sea after I became M.

"Ouch!" Eric laughed at my comment, thinking its honesty was rather cute. You can't get rid of a dirty old man that easily, I suppose.

"Does this mean that if I ask you to stay at my house in a romantic context you would?" He hesitated, waiting for the potential rejection.

"Hmmm…" I said, thinking what to do not to sour my cherry. "I would stay indefinitely at your place as long as you will have me, but aren't you concerned of what people are going to say? Aren't you concerned about the age difference and such?" I asked cautiously. Despite my ageless look, it was hard to tell how much older I really was, but of course, who would know?

"I am not at the point in my life where what others think of me matters as long as I am happy. And you think too much. Why don't we just try out this arrangement and see how it goes? I can help you accomplish whatever you want if you just let me. I'll support you, help you get back on your feet, and if after that point you wish to leave, you can go," he said with a hint of sadness.

"It's hard to say no to a good deal, but what if I end up being too expensive?" I asked, setting the bar of expectation high.

Eric laughed out loud, losing all composure, and said, "All women are the same!"

I shot him an affronted glare. "Stereotypes are over-rated!" I said.

"It isn't a stereotype. It's biology. Women are hard-wired that way from birth to seek security," he retorted.

The waitress came around and introduced herself. Eric flashed her his signature saber-tooth tiger grin; he threw in his mischievous dimple for an extra dramatic effect. I felt her take a step back. She looked at him as if concerned for her safety in the midst of his creepiness.

"You have a lovely name," he said. "Do you still go to school?"

I sighed, feeling very embarrassed about this. It was just at this very moment that I felt my creative imagination at play. We drifted in smoke to a playground, and when the smoke dissipated, I saw Eric sitting on a park bench, ogling at the little girls with lollipops in his pocket. He continued to have this distorted creepy grin as if dirty thoughts were invading his brain, and suddenly I got a revolting chill down my spine. This was like a limbo dance; how low (young) can you go?

Our waitress made polite conversation about the weather, trying to divert his attention into dinner matters, and then she took our order. Looking back at this, Eric didn't always say things that were necessarily bad; it was more the way he said things, with that suggestive look in his eye and overtly personal vibe that reached out and touched women inappropriately. When our waitress left, I looked at him aghast.

"You are absolutely incorrigible," I said, this was suddenly my new pet phrase.

"Guilty as charge," he said as he chuckled proudly.

"I am surprised you haven't gotten into trouble."

"That's because my wife used to keep me on a leash." We both giggled.

I suspected it was more than his wife taking one down for the team like a champ, but more so, the fact that not that many women within his desired age group would want to be with a man of his generation. I sighed, thinking back at his words earlier and how pleasant they sounded to me—almost ideal. We had a fated encounter and I was the answer to his prayers, but this last stunt somehow managed to take away that fairy-tale dream. Whether this was going to be tolerable for me was yet to be seen. I did, however, encounter a strange feeling of familiarity with Eric. I couldn't quite place it yet, but it was as though I already knew him.

After dinner on our way back home…

"So if our arrangement works out. Can I drive your car?" I asked, not really knowing how he would respond.

"Over my dead body!" he said with a chuckle as he stepped on the gas, showing off. *I might just have to*, I thought as I puckered my lips to these last words.

"What happened to the adorable man I met on the beach?"

"When the sun goes down, that man goes to bed, and the other one comes out to play."

"Hmm…" My eyes widened. Eric was more than I expected.

"You like to live dangerously, don't you?"

He again used his signature saber-tooth tiger grin and dimple to respond.

When we got home, he took me to my room so I could finally get some rest.

"Good night," he said, extending his arms for a hug. I fell into him as he squeezed me so hard that I felt my breasts were going to pop. He went to kiss me on the mouth, and I simply surrendered to him.

I had been with Fidel and Hugo and a long list of other unsavory characters; what was one more at this point? But maybe Eric was different.

I heard him grunting as he kissed me, causing an odd and unexpected effect in me. I had felt this way before, but it was so long ago that I had forgotten. I kept getting that sensation of things passed happening again. A déjà vu feeling, a repetitious moment, without the clear memory of the true event anywhere to be found.

He lightly advanced his hands, like soldiers, onto my butt, trying to ease in unnoticed or perhaps just so lightly I wouldn't counterattack. As soon as his hands felt comfortable in their new territory, his soldiers started marching like cat paws on plushy terrain.

I couldn't figure what it was, but the overt desire and excitement he showed for me made me feel aroused. This was another unexpected feeling between us. I felt uneasy about having these feelings and went to bed wondering whether or not I actually was starting to like Eric; maybe I wasn't going to do him dirty, and I could just stay there and live a sybaritic life with him like he wanted. In either case, I needed to get an identity before I would decide to settle down into any lifestyle whatsoever.

When I got up the next day, it was deep in the afternoon. I still felt tired and groggy. I made my way into the kitchen and found the sliding glass doors that led into the patio open, where the pool was. I heard voices and realized that Eric wasn't alone.

"Good morning, M." Eric gave me his signature grin. "Why don't you get your bikini on and join us at the pool?"

I nodded in agreement, and after a brief snack, I got my canary yellow string bikini on. It looked great in contrast to my olive-toned skin and highlighted my turquoise eyes. I let my brown hair fall in its usual casual ringlets, put on some lip gloss, and headed back out to the pool party.

"M, these are my neighbors, the Gruebers. This is Shelly, her husband Boyd, and their children, Marcus and Ann."

By all accounts they looked like a picture-perfect suburban family. Shelly was a middle-aged woman who looked like she went to Zumba classes daily, Boyd was a tall blond with a potbelly and a general "life is work" attitude, and their children seemed to be nine and eight years old, both mini versions of their parents with the carefree nature of no responsibilities because they were still children.

"Guys, this is my friend, M. She's staying with me for a while." Mr. and Mrs. Grueber both looked at me in amazement but out of decorum did nothing more than give me a sleazy smile.

"M, the Gruebers are here because we organize a block party for our neighbors every year. We do one in the summer with the kids and another around winter or fall for the holidays," he said.

I began to feel the social pressures of having to conform to this prissy little cookie-cutter lifestyle. How different was this from the life I was used to earlier. This must have been an American thing, a block party.

"Will there be dancing?" I asked rather naïvely, and they all looked at me as if I asked them to go clubbing in downtown Miami.

"It's not that type of party. These parties are the type where neighbors socialize over food and drink and chat about family, life, work, and current events—that sort of thing," said Eric, making me feel even more out of place.

"Oh, I see. To me that's not a party that's having coffee with a friend."

They all chuckled at me, and clearly I felt it was going to take a lot more than good looks to fit into this crowd.

After the Gruebers left, Eric told me he was going to his office to prep for one of his cases. It was close to nighttime, and I did wonder why he simply didn't just do this from his home office. He told me to make myself at home, but if I wanted to leave to go to his gym, or anything at all; I could use his other car. He took me to the garage and showed me a Grunge Rover in olive green; he said the gym, the bank, the mall, and the spa were all GPS programed for me so that I wouldn't have to think about where I was going.

"I left you a weekly allowance on the kitchen counter. Use it wisely," he said. If you're a good girl, I will give you more this time next week. He kissed me and squeezed my ass cheek as he left.

"Wear something nice when I come back home." He gave me his signature smile and a wink.

As soon as Eric left, I ran discreetly to the kitchen in case he was coming back suddenly and looked at the wad of cash he had left me. I smiled deeply with satisfaction. I had put it away for then and decided to go to work on my other issue.

I got dressed in my black workout pants, tank top, and my brand-new sneakers. I was all in black and felt like a cat sneaking around the neighborhood. I wanted to make sure that it was nice and dark as I left so that I wouldn't be seen that easily stalking prey. This was my modus operandi. I tied my hair in a bun and, by all accounts, looked like any suburban woman would jogging around the neighborhood. Clearly a master of hiding within plain sight.

All the houses in the neighborhood had a similar look even though they varied in color and size. They all had an Art Deco style with the rendered brick and the Spanish tiles; most of the houses were colored in shades of sunset, bone, burnt sienna, and cadmium orange, while others went into the aquas and the sky blues.

As I jogged around, I went looking to see who was home and which lights were turning on at dusk. Most of these houses had outdoor lighting that illuminated things dimly around the walls and the landscaping. I looked at the mailboxes for last names and the corners of the houses by the gutters for cameras. *If this is something I am going to do, I would need to conceal my face just in case,* I thought. Then there was the issue of an alarm system—if the house had one—but luckily, this was something easy to spot on the lawn by a little sign that read "This house is protected by ATP" or, in some other cases, another generic protection system. The issue wasn't the alarm system; that would be easy to bypass if I really wanted to, but what I really needed was a woman who looked enough like me and was young enough, whose identity I could duplicate with ease. This was something that I needed to do quickly before Eric started asking too many questions and handed me over to the law, something that I had no doubt with his background he would do.

It would be very tricky to take someone's identity from the neighborhood. That would be too close for comfort and way too risky if I did decide to make a life here. In either case, I still had to stake all the possibilities of my surrounding; you never know when an opportunity would come in handy, and I would need to take advantage of it as backup. I checked the clock real quick; not even an hour had gone by, and I still wasn't close to spotting what I needed. Perhaps it was time to branch out.

I went home and grabbed the Grunge Rover. It was a rather big car, definitely not what I normally was used to; then, again, girls like me can quickly get used to anything. I decided to go to the gym, since I already was dressed as if I was going there anyway.

At that time of day, most of the women who would go there were the working women's crowd, trying to get in shape after work and before going home.

The gym was maybe ten minutes away; it had a spacious parking lot, lit dimly with a couple of lights. The windows on the gym were sweating, and even before I went in, I could feel the heat inside and the atmosphere stickier than it was outside. When I entered the gym, I noticed that there were people of all physical designations, people who looked like they spent too much time working out, people who needed a lot of work and the in-betweens; those were people who looked decently in shape in clothes but naked. Well...let's just say you better close your eyes and turn off the lights.

The clerk at the reception area stopped me in my tracks and asked me for my membership card as another member scanned their keychain fog and walked right in. I looked at the keys of my Grunge Rover and saw a little tag. I scanned it for the guy.

"You aren't Eric Lieberman," he said, as if I was trying to get in for free.

"I know, and are you really Pike?" I retorted, staring impolitely at his nametag as if Pike couldn't have been a real name.

"Yea," he said, giving me a little attitude.

"Well, I'm staying with Eric, and he said I could come to his gym as a guest."

"Oh," he said, changing his tone and disposition quickly. He gave me some paperwork and a temporary pass. "Listen, I'm sorry. I wasn't trying to give you a hard time. We just don't like freeloaders, but please send our regards to Mr. Lieberman."

Pike used a tone of voice to say this that made me feel like Eric wasn't just a regular member; it sounded almost as if he had some level of royalty. My imagination at play probably, for all I know he was just notorious for flirting with the girls.

"Do you want a tour of the facility?"

'Sure," I said.

We walked around the machine area.

"This is our most venerated StairMaster. This is the best thing that could happen to an ass in thirty days. You get on this thing and 'Spartan' it out for an hour a day for a month and you will have prizewinning buns guaranteed," he said with a sense of honor for the rear that I had never known before.

"We have a 'before' and 'after' wall of fame for those who choose to take the challenge," he added proudly.

"Really?" I was shocked with disbelief. He signaled over to the wall on my left, and I saw a series of pictures that looked like the "before" and "after" pictures of a plastic surgeon's office.

"Yes, we have one member who even did the coin-toss challenge." Pike spoke of this as if it was religion.

"The coin-toss challenge?" I asked with curiosity.

"Yup, that's where our member gets such a taut rear that they get tossed a coin on the left gluteus maximus, and the member must bounce it to the right using only muscle movement to prove definition, strength and agility. Not many people can do that, and you bet it's an honor."

I wanted to laugh, as this seemed so ludicrous, but I abstained as we walked past the rooms where they gave the aerobics classes.

There was a room full of odd stationary bicycles with a screen that played an all-terrain danger of the outdoors sort of movie. Pike explained to me it was for the rider to feel as if they were outdoors and facing the elements of the road as they rode.

"So, for example, if I was going uphill, I would feel the bike and my thighs tightening up as I go upward in motion," I said, taking in the idea.

"Exactly. It's like going on an extreme bike adventure but never leaving the room."

I thought of that for a moment, and I guess it was one of those things that you needed to experience to really understand, because where I came from, there was nothing like it. It mimicked the real thing, so in a way it felt like an elaborate farce, except the rider was admittedly faking it. I thought it to be so inane I wanted to laugh, but I still left it alone and shook my head behind Pike's back just to feel true to my new self. He showed me a section for yoga and mentioned how the class was offered mostly in the mornings and very late nights.

"So this gym is twenty-four hours?" I asked, wondering who goes to the gym so late at night or who actually sacrifices sleep to do that sort of thing.

"Yes, we are closed only for natural disasters, state of emergency, five holidays out of the year, and alien attacks as stipulated by our employee manual." Pike continued to speak as if under oath and with the seriousness that led me to believe this was a culture to be reckoned with.

"Alien attacks?"

"Yes, our owner was an abductee, and he takes that sort of thing very seriously," he said courtly, as if it was something that had been mocked before.

"How often does that happen?" My curiosity seemed so insatiable I almost forgot why I really was there.

"Since the gym has been open never," he said.

I nodded demurely and continued to walk, this time making sure to take notice of the women around me for a potential doppelgänger.

"We have an Olympic-size swimming pool in the basement where they give swimming lessons, if you wish to take them."

"That won't be necessary. I am an accomplished diver now and an excellent swimmer," I said, perhaps with an exaggerated sense of hubris.

He looked back at me, intrigued by how I said that sentence, so I decided to work my magical voice. I looked at Pike dreamily into his eyes and, almost as if singing in the language of love, asked him to take me to the locker room.

"I can't go in there," he said, trying to resist me.

"I think you can," I said softly as I touched lightly his shoulder. He failed to realize I didn't want him in the locker room; I just wanted to know where it was. We walked past an indoor tennis court, a volleyball court, and a basketball court, until we finally got to the lockers. The locker room was equipped with a steam room, showers, and tanning beds.

There were three women talking as they got changed, one in particular I felt I could easily pass as. She had black hair and green eyes, and her skin tone was also slightly off, but for just a face on a small picture ID, it would work.

"Hey, I was thinking of becoming a member of this gym, and I was wondering if I could ask you guys some questions about it, if that is OK?" I asked.

They all nodded, not thinking there was anything strange to this.

"My name is M," I said, hoping to prompt them into giving me their names.

"My name is Emilia," said my target, and the other two were Fernanda and Amanda.

"Do you like the ambience here?" I asked.

"I was a little intimidated at first, but then I got over it," said Amanda.

"The facilities are great and always clean," said Fernanda.

"Yea, I think that's why I ask. I am getting the tour right now by Pike, and I saw some pretty hard-core stuff and wondered if this was for me."

"Don't sweat it. If you wanna be hard core, do it, but work out and do as much as your heart's content," said Emilia.

"What do you think of the twenty-four-hour convenience?"

"Well, I work as a teacher, so for me it doesn't really make a difference, but it's nice to know I can come at any hour," said Amanda.

"So if you can't sleep at night, would you really work out instead?" I asked, joking.

"Maybe, but it's never happened," she replied and chuckled softly.

"I'm a nurse, and with rotating schedules, it actually helps me come more frequently," said Emilia. I thought that was great because I needed someone with a clean record.

"I travel sometimes for extended periods. Have you guys had any issue with suspending membership?" I asked innocently, trying to dig for information.

"I haven't taken a vacation in a long time, so I wouldn't know," said Emilia, while the others nodded in agreement. That was great news because the possibility of having a passport was low. I thanked them and walked away. I tried to stick around for a bit, looking at Emilia's locker. It's not easy not to look creepy standing alone while staring at three women dress and undress, so I moved on for a better opportunity later.

Pike was still waiting for me like an obedient little dog outside. His eyes had a blank hypnotic stare. I told Pike I might need him again soon but thanked him for the tour. He took both my hands in his, lovingly, the same way one would when saying good-bye to a priest after having relieved you from your sins, and then he walked back to his post.

I saw Emilia walk out, and I discreetly walked behind her, waiting for the right moment. I saw her get her keys ready and walk toward her car. For a moment she appeared to feel a little chill. I could have just walked up to her and said the most celebrated predator phrase just to make her nervous—"I'm not going to hurt you"—with an added touch of creepiness in my tone. That always wigs them out just before I take them down, but the truth was this: I didn't have the time to toy around with my victim before lunging at them.

I walked several paces behind her, while she still failed to notice anything wrong. I was in the background like a regular bush on the side of the street that had always been, looking quite inoffensive.

I looked at both sides, getting ready to pounce on her and feeling the blood rush through me to move forward without fear. Cars were still driving by on their way toward their final destination, and I had to make sure to be quick, quiet, and discreet. The air was still sticky from the humidity that always befalls the swampland of Florida. Part of me wondered why the Spanish conquistadors fought so hard to protect this place.

I sped up quickly behind her, and before she could even turn around to see what hit her, I grabbed her by her hair and, with all my might, hit her head against the side of her car on the window, quickly and swiftly so she wouldn't have time to react. It was interesting to see that even though her head wasn't made of rubber, it kind of bounced off the window when I cracked it. The window didn't shatter but rather formed a circle that looked like a spider web where I hit her head. This probably was a safety feature for cars nowadays—being shatter resistant or shatterproof. I was kind of disappointed as to how this simple item made the moment less dramatic, but I had to remember this was an emergency and not my usual play.

Emilia lay on the asphalt. It was lights out. I sat her inside the car so she would look like she was sleeping, and it would take longer for people to figure out that there had been some type of malfeasance going on. Her body was ten times as heavy as it normally would be, and moving it would have been nearly impossible to do quickly had she not been so close to the seat.

"And you say you work out! You're heavy!" I said in a low voice to the dormant body of Emilia, cracking a half smile and compensating with a joke for all this hard work.

I looked inside her car quickly to see if there was anything else I could use. I didn't really see anything of real value to me, but there was this small pocket-sized tin with mints; I figured, *Why not stay fresh while I am at it?*, and so I grabbed it and took it along with her black purse. I wiped her car keys carefully, unaware if they fingerprinted those days for petty theft, but heck, why take any unnecessary risks.

I drove off, not quite ready to get home yet. I needed to come down from my high. The adrenaline pumped through my body in a very deliciously lively way, bringing back memories, as I took the air of freedom to my skin and owned the road with every speedy curve. I looked for a lonely area to park my car and go over my new things. Her wallet had exactly what I was looking for: her ID. I even lucked out, as it had her social security card behind it, which was just winking at me and telling me, "You did a good job." I always thought how convenient it was to be on the good side of evil. I found some jewelry in her purse, too. I suppose she took it off before working out. I looked at her phone and decided it was very important to lose it. I shut the phone off immediately, wiped it down, cracked it, and tossed it.

Cell phones are the biggest tracking devices—very risky to own one these days; people always know where you are, even when you want to go below the radar.

I went to my new home and found Eric waiting for me in the living room, tapping his foot. He seemed annoyed I was gone for so long, even though it really wasn't that long. I tried to walk past him real quick to get my new purse to my room.

"Where were you?" he asked, with a mixture of concerned parent and possessive love. It was quite annoying, especially because not even Fidel pulled this kind of stuff on me; then again, he did lock me up sometimes.

"I went to the gym and my neighbor's house. He said he had rescued my purse from the fire," I said coldly.

"Is this the neighbor your ex thought you were cheating on him with?"

"Yes," I said, giving a dramatic pause. "Are you jealous?"

"No," he said, changing his tone for a softer one. "I just haven't lived with someone in a while, and maybe this might seem premature, but I worry about your safety. I guess also part of me felt like you decided not to come back." He gave me this sad, lonely puppy look that oddly moved me a little, even though I was still not quite sure why. Feelings are terrible for someone with a black heart; it is always best not to have them.

"You thought you scared me away? I told you I don't scare easily. But why are you so afraid I would leave you? Did something happen to you?"

"Well, I told you my wife died. I guess I am just afraid of losing the people I care about in my life," he said, pausing for a moment. "I know. It's just been so long since I had a woman in my life, let alone one as beautiful as you. I just want to grab you and squeeze you all the time. But maybe I have been just very lonely," he said, making me feel sorry for him. Damn it! Another feeling!

I secretly became concerned for my safety. I had these emerging emotions, a secret agenda, and a man with possessive attitudes who wanted to squeeze me, maybe to death. To me this was becoming less objective, and I wasn't having that. But then I thought, *He is just an old man. What do I have to be afraid of?*

"I've noticed!" I said, and we both chuckled. I was glad he was a lighthearted individual. "I think we both are going through an adjustment period, and that takes time," I said, mediating the situation.

I walked over toward Eric with seductive stealth and sat on his lap like a slick cat.

"You know, you remind me of a skinny Santa," I said, and we both chuckled. "I might be looking to sit on your lap every day, asking for wishes," I said with innuendo.

"Well, only if you're good you get wishes," he said in a way suggesting as to how our relationship works.

"What happens if I am bad?" I whispered in his ear.

He gave me his signature saber-tooth smile and kissed me. "Then you get even more," he said with a breathy surrender.

Being this close to him made me, for the first time, acknowledge a very interesting scent he had. He smelled like a blend between an animal and the woods, perhaps some cedarwood in there. It was an odd scent but, at the same time, strangely familiar. It had a very comforting effect on me.

"I like the way you smell. What is it?" I asked wide-eyed, like a child with curiosity.

"It's called Eau de Lieberman," he said jokingly.

We kissed some more, and for the first time in a long time, I found myself enjoying a man, one extremely unsuspecting man. These were dangerous slopes for me. Women like me are never allowed to fall in love. It's because of the curse of the black heart—a curse that I knew too well.

"Do you want to sleep in my room tonight?" He hesitated as he said this.

"Hmmm..." I gave him a long pause. "OK," I said, looking into his eyes and sprinkling him with the magic I needed to subdue him even more.

I couldn't believe I was eager to jump into bed with an old man, but heck, I was! I had to be careful; Eric was making things too convenient for me, and if I wasn't sure of what I was doing, I might just stay and pretend to be a Stepford wife.

It was at moments like this with Eric that I began to wonder which one of us was the predator.

Chapter 8

THE THIRTEENTH LAW

Acaricia didn't want to be noticed, so she tried to duck out of the dome when the sage with the dog came after her.

"What is your name?" he asked before she could dodge him.

"Acaricia."

"You seem lost. Are you new here? I don't believe I've seen you before," he said, trying to be polite but knowing the truth already.

"You could say that. I don't remember a day before today," she lied.

"Come with me. Let me be your oracle."

Acaricia stopped him with her hand, trying to be prudent of knowing such things.

"You spoke of a prophecy today?" she asked, changing the subject.

"Yes, our land is blessed. It has been spoken that a woman is going to enter our civilization, and if we help her achieve enlightenment, our entire civilization would progress to the next level."

"What happens if you don't?" she asked.

"You mean if she doesn't achieve enlightenment? Then we are all doomed," he said, somewhat worried.

Bewildered, Acaricia remained pensive. "I've never heard people speak like you do."

"Well, since technically you were born today, I suppose I will tell you what you may or may not already know. We here live on different spheres. On every sphere that a soul lives, it must undergo certain tribulations in order to get to the path to enlightenment."

"The path to enlightenment?"

"That is where the soul reaches the highest level and, in essence, becomes godlike. Unfortunately, souls often commit sins, not just against others but also against their own soul. Every life a soul chooses to live in essence is an opportunity for redemption and enlightenment, but, unfortunately, only a few souls see it that way. Most often, a soul chooses to relive cycles and patterns, mostly destructive, regressing their soul back a sphere or keeping it in the same place with no evolution. When that happens, that soul needs to work twice as hard to break free and progress to the next sphere or level."

"How many spheres are there?"

"As many as a soul needs to reach enlightenment," he said, not quite giving Acaricia the answer she was looking for.

"That sounds like it could take a long time!"

"Sometimes it does, but time doesn't really matter. Time is a man-created thing," he said, intriguing Acaricia.

"So everybody on this island is on the same sphere?"

"Not quite," said the sage, being more intriguing with a smile.

"What is the thirteenth law?"

"The thirteenth law is about doing a selfless act. Every so often, a soul gets the opportunity to do a selfless act—an act that in no way would benefit the soul and, in fact, something where the soul would need to do some type of sacrifice to accomplish the thirteenth law. If the soul succeeds in accomplishing the selfless act, it will manage to reconstruct and heal his own soul in the process. But it must be completely selfless to work, and few ever succeed at it."

"Is the selfless act something that can be chosen? Like charity work, for example?"

"It can be, but it doesn't necessarily work that way. The selfless act is something that, during a particular life path, finds the soul of the individual, something the individual must do that warms his soul regardless of it being rewarding, which, at times, is not."

"In essence, I understand what you are saying—although rather vague, it seems like a religious dogma of sorts."

"I take it you are not religious?"

"I have a hard time believing in good deeds when none have come to pass in the life I remember. I feel there is no God to look upon, no saving grace, no enlightenment."

The sage looked at her and seemed deeply hurt at her comment, almost as if her lack of belief was a negation of life itself and all it stood for.

"God is not an entity that chooses your life's burdens. *You* do. You choose to overcome or to fail. God is only there to oversee you and to come when you call. He is not meant to be the provider of your ailments." The sage spoke peacefully, although in a self-righteous tone.

"I'm sorry I did not mean to hurt you. I just don't feel the same way."

It was here that the sage began to understand that Acaricia was his opportunity at the thirteenth law. Acaricia needed to find a source or motivation to come to the light of God. Her own enlightenment.

"Why is self-sacrifice or the selfless act called a law?"

"Because those who encounter it often do not want to carry out the selfless act. They'd rather ignore it, pretend they never saw it, and walk away. The law obliges them or at least it should. They are reminded of why it needs to be done. It's the thirteenth law," he simply said solemnly.

"Why are there no old people on this island aside from the sages?"

"People on this island choose not to age past thirty-four. The sages continue to age because we renounce that type of vanity. You are full of questions. However, it's been a lot of information today, and you need to rest."

Chapter 9

THE MERMAID AND THE ARCHER

Eric's room was a loud expression of boldness. He had all these gaudy animal prints and fake animal rugs. He said he liked nature a lot but couldn't bring himself down to kill an animal (or knowing someone else did) just for its skin. It was an odd juxtaposition that encased him, and I didn't know what to make of this tacky and extravagant taste or of his anti-animal-cruelty stance.

"Is M short for something else?"

"It's short for Emilia." I cringed a little as I said this.

"I take it you don't like your name."

Eric was a very keen observer of obvious cues. They do say hints don't work with men; however, I believe differently. They do matter to men when they truly want to pay attention. They prefer to play stupid when they just don't want to be bothered. It's like the light-switch syndrome: on and off.

"I could have been given a nicer name, but I can't go back to birth and fight with my mother over it now." We both chuckled.

"I'm going to change into something more comfortable, if that is OK," I said.

"I thought you wanted to go to dinner."

"Hmmm, I can't recall the last time I had to talk a man into dessert." I giggled a little as Eric's wrinkled dimple gave me a more perverse version of his signature grin—if that was possible! I felt a chill go down my spine due to the creepiness.

"Well, I was just trying to be good," he said.

"OK, let's be good then. I'll get dressed, and we can go to dinner."

Eric sulked for a second but quickly brightened up as I started to strip for him.

I sang to him with my siren's voice and slowly swayed my hips from side to side like a pendulum. My hand seductively invited him toward my chest, where my black heart lay.

> "Eres el amor del cual yo he sonado,
> un amor que desborda ríos;
> Un ídolo al cual yo he adorado,
> un hombre que me inunda de amoríos.

Ah Amor! como te he anorado,
Ah Amor! como me has calmado;
Sígueme amor coronado,
Sígueme amor colmado."

(You are the love I have dreamt of, a love that overflows rivers. An idol of whom I adored, a man who floods me with love affairs. Oh love! How I have longed for you, Oh love! How you've calmed me! Follow me, crowned lover. Follow me, copious love.)

A lot gets lost in translation. However, Eric looked too encumbered by love and lust to do anything but admire me openmouthed. I continued to sing to him, refueling my power with his desire for me. His desire increased the more he heard my melodious voice.

Eric came to me obsequiously and grabbed on to my hands as if an invisible pull beckoned him. It was the power of my magic. He seemed weaker with pleasure but not minding it at all. He submitted to me with ease. Better than I had ever expected.

I kissed him softly, having my body fall into him like a floating feather onto a surface. He was hungry and couldn't seem to stop consuming me voraciously, like an animal devouring fresh prey whose flesh was exposed. I felt intoxicated by desire and growing stronger with power, regenerating myself with every sip of lust. I wanted to drown him in the waters of my desire as he grunted like a horse eating hay.

He kissed my neck with just enough tongue and wet-ness to make my legs tremble and my blood gush toward my hips. I could feel his hard cock poking through his casual slacks. He begged to be free of all constriction. He took his hands and touched my skin smoothly, enticing more desire in me, teasing me gently with all the things he was going to do to me. He began to massage me. His fingers dug into my hips in a circular motion, following a rhythmic pattern similar to my song. He was moving his fingertips so lightly my skin got goose bumps from the delight. He massaged my breasts like dough with his hands, perking up my nipples like a master sculptor. He kneaded them in careful echelons of intensity, making me moan, and as the sound waves bounced off the walls, it drew his body closer and closer to me.

Suddenly he paused and went into the bathroom quickly to grab a bottle of baby oil. When he came back, he oiled my body that slipped as slickly as the cocoon of my vagina did. I enjoyed the friction of his fingers pene-trating my limbs with his movement. He swayed me back and forth between subtle erotica and blasted euphoria.

I felt so moist it was almost as good as being in the water. He took extra care to arouse me one more level up when massaging my legs, pulling and tugging my muscles toward him and then pushing upward with his thumbs up to my vaginal lips, separating them with soft circular touches. I could see his glee the more he raised my lust. I was so undone in pleasure and growing hotter in his hands as they made love to my body and explored all my nooks and crannies. He pulsed his fingers around my anus, massaging the same way his thumbs had just touched my intimate lips and vagina. He pushed through, easing me into him more intimate than just a moment before. He penetrated my vagina with another finger and moved in and out, giving more pleasure on both ends.

"Are you my little girl?" he asked.

"Yes, daddy, I've been bad. Why don't you punish me? Spank me hard, daddy," I said, playing along with him.

He looked as if his penis was about to explode in an outcry of excitement. His cock was hot like a roaring flame. He spanked me on my behind, as if taking claim of that piece of meat, and turned me over and fed from the challis between my legs. His talented tongue caressed softly around my clitoris. It tingled me lick by lick further into orgasmic ecstasy. I moaned and started contracting the insides of my pelvis as all the blood began to pool like hot lava, ready to erupt from a volcano. Eric continued feeding from me and building momentum to my body. The feeling of him savoring from the taste and aroma of my body and knowing how this hardened his bold erection was the thought that pushed me into climax, as all the tightening from my body released and let go into the zenith of my pleasure.

The sounds of Eric's tongue still echoed in my head. It was as if he craved fried chicken for weeks and then was finally able to indulge in the meal, showing no decorum by licking his fingers and making loud pleasurable noises as he ate. It was the type of guilty pleasure you can only enjoy shamelessly in private. This thought made me grin. A complicit secret between two people is a bonding elixir for better or worse. Eric smiled at me more placidly than usual, feeling the accomplishment of his prowess.

"More?"

"Do you want to make me a spoiled lover?" I said, panting.

"Why not?"

"Hmmm…" I purred, and Eric took that as a yes and got back to work. I began to think of Eric as my own personal sex toy, only that this toy came with a built-in ATM.

He lapped tirelessly between my legs as I rejoiced in the pleasure we both felt until my desires were fulfilled.

Eric kissed me; he tasted sweet. His face was sticky and musky-smelling, all things that seemed to make him really happy. His enthusiasm for sex was intoxicating. It was as though he was finally alive, fist pumping, blood gushing, heart thumping, adrenaline rushing, alive.

I went for the counterattack and gripped his cock in my hands, and he grew bigger and harder. This was pleasantly different from my first impression at the beach. I placed my lips gently over the tip of his penis, and with the tip of my tongue, I flicked the little opening, causing Eric's toes to curl. I motioned Eric to lie on his back and, for the first time, saw his naked body in full splendor. His chest was covered with salt-and-pepper hairs, just like his arms and his thighs; the lower of his legs by his calves were hair-free. From this angle (that was me on top), I could see the curls of nose hairs peeking through; they looked like little tornados. I was really hoping a storm wouldn't come along with them. His eyebrows seemed curiously bushy, like tufts of white snow with sprinkles of dirt. The dimness in the room made him seem dirtier and lustier than ever before (if that was at all possible). These thoughts were growing on me as much as his lust had made his cock grow from a little mushroom to nearly a foot long. *Quite impressive!* I thought. He was aiming to represent a hushed community of old men with needs.

As I lowered myself to insert his length in me, I felt the sides of my vaginal walls expanding to fit his thickness. I moaned and saw his eagerness through his light bright eyes. I felt myself collecting all the fuel I needed to preserve myself this young-looking while I sucked all the energy he was giving me through his lust.

I straddled and grinded on his dick rough and hard, a pace that made Eric excited with the unexpected. He began to shake and convulse, grabbing tightly on to my arms as he expelled from the pit of his stomach all the energy he put forth in his seed. He then collapsed onto the bed exhausted but satisfied with a smile on his face.

"Wow, I don't think I have ever had sex so intense before," he said, breathless. I giggled.

"We can still make it to dinner if you want," I said, teasing.

Eric laughed as if that somehow seemed like a very remote possibility.

"I need a moment before I can move," he said. "How do you feel?"

"I feel like I just got dipped in the fountain of youth." I grinned slyly and raised one palm up in the air as if to say "who knows." He laughed at my unexpected comment and appeared to coo softly with his eyes closed.

He grabbed my hand and caressed it tenderly, noticing the raised mark on my hand with his touch. He looked at it bewildered because it looked like it was a natural formation on the palm of my hand. It was not a burn mark, not a scar, but there were three wavy lines in a distinct pattern. He asked me nothing about it.

We snuggled together, and my hand began to have this strange fascination with his chest hair. It was fun to coil my fingers on his curly bushes. He resembled and smelled like I would imagine a big foot would.

"Do you like it?" he asked, touching my hand again but still saying nothing about the mark on it.

"How could I not? It is like having a fury pet." We both giggled together, something I noticed we did very often, and this made our association so easy.

"I get the feeling you and I will get along just fine," I said.

"I think so too. I'm just afraid you will get tired of me someday and move on."

"Do you always see the dark clouds instead of the sunshine?"

"Force of habit, I suppose. Just when I think I will be happy, doom and gloom happens, casting a shadow. It just seems inevitable." We both pause in silence, moving along with the sudden change of mood. He sighed deeply as if wanting to let something out that pressed on him, and so he spoke:

"During my career, I perhaps was a little too idealistic in believing I would be defending innocent people. Then I realized only sometimes they were innocent, until eventually I took their so-called truths with a grain of salt. But then I would find the truth by being humiliated in court when a client had lied to me. I learned not to be too optimistic because I always ended up disappointed."

"How many times have you found out the truth about a client in court?"

"More than I care to remember, augh!"

"That must stink."

I noticed how pensive Eric was; he appeared to be reliving a moment in the past that I dared not ask about.

I went to shower but when I entered the room again I smelled this intense animal and cedarwood scent in the room. It was interesting in the fact that this was uncommon for any man to give off this type of scent.

That night as we cuddled together naked in bed, Eric laid his head on my chest, caressing the softness of my breasts with his hands. The feeling was mutually soothing to both of us as we drifted to sleep. In my slumber I dreamt I was searching through the woods. It was bright and sunny when I found this handsome young man. He had an arrow and a bow, and he smiled at me. We appeared to be playing a nice game of tag, when he told me to run in a dialect I somehow could understand. When I looked back, I saw this huge animal. The animal was so enormous that he covered the setting sun with his body, and then nighttime fell upon us. The archer shot several arrows at the animal, but he still couldn't take it down. I could not see the animal very well, but his scent alone made me afraid. The closer he came, the colder I felt. The animal invaded every space in the woods. I tried to escape from it, and the more I ran, the closer I felt it was to catching me.

The archer was trying to protect me from this hellish animal, but nothing he did would make him go away.

The animal was on top of me, concealed by the darkness; all I could feel was its warm stagnant breath. It smelled like dead meat that was rotting, perhaps even something more putrid than that. I cried out, anticipating the pain, but the animal would not eat me—not yet at least. The air was cold, and I felt colder. I was embraced by its darkness and dragged through the woods and then into a body of water. The dirt and the rocks burned and scratched my skin painfully; the heat and the cold were ripping me apart into pieces of raw flesh. The coldness increased when I began to feel wet. It was the mixture of my cold aching limbs as the warm blood dripped out, staining the body of water a crimson brown. The heat was leaving my body as my pain decreased with it.

The animal turned into a dark specter-like cloud; it appeared to be a blanket of darkness at times, and it dragged me down into the water furiously. I knew in my dream I had resigned myself to my fate, no longer in fear. I was not afraid of the water. I was not afraid of what awaited me there; it was a place of comfort but not one of happiness. My feelings seemed to drain from me with the blood that seeped out. This was what the specter was waiting for—all the blood to leave me, for where I was going, I was not going to need it.

It was then that I saw the archer reaching out to me to save me, but I was beyond saving. It was too late.

I woke up feeling cold, covered in water (it was really sweat), panting and heaving dramatically and in panic.

"What's wrong?" said Eric, clearly alarmed.

"I think I ate too much for dinner," I said, trying to hide the truth once more.

"Hmm," mumbled Eric, sounding unconvinced. "Tell me the truth."

I told him my dream: no stories for once, no "mythomania" (compulsive lying); I was beginning to feel for once in a long time that I could just be honest, and the feeling was liberating. Was this me becoming Emilia?

Eric looked pensive for a moment, almost as if I touched something deep within his heart; then again, he was also tired and sleepy. Perhaps my imagination was playing with me once more. My imagination always tended to do that—prey on my vulnerabilities, since it was so much nicer to live in the thought of more beautiful things and believe they could actually exist than the crude reality of boredom many live.

"Do you think you can go back to sleep?" he asked.

"I can try, but I feel too awake right now even though I feel tired," I replied.

"I bet you do feel tired. I wore you out," he said with a proud nuance to his prowess. I laughed at his incorrigible comment.

"You don't miss an opportunity, do you?"

"No, but I want to tell you a story, if that is OK." I felt reluctant at this; normally it was me telling the stories, and now the chalupa switched sides, but heck, maybe a story would be nice, so I nodded in his arms, and he knew it was OK to proceed. If I had to guess, I suspected I would have gotten a fictional story anyway, since that is what age and time give the elders license to do. It was what I normally did.

"I had an ancestor, who is so many generations old that he be best described simply as Uncle Bernie. Uncle Bernie was an unusual character, and so many stories and myths came about during his existence that it was hard to distinguish truth from fable. He stirred such controversy that he ultimately ended up dividing the family between those who believed in his stories and those who didn't.

"It all started when he went on a walkabout in some nearby woods by his house, and it took him months to come back home. When he did eventually return, he was never quite the same as he had been before. He spent the rest of his years at home, writing his stories to which he believed were factual; although some were so fantastic, they were hard to believe. To those who were incredulous, he would always say, 'Impossible is not impossible. That is just a thought in a narrow and limited mind.' At other times, he would say his other celebrated phrase, 'Just because something hasn't been discovered, it don't mean it don't exist.'

"He had a story written in one of his volumes that reminds me of your dream. It was a story of a mermaid and a man who fell in love. He said the mermaid was cursed. She was not allowed to fall in love because she had to first learn to love herself. In life, the creature had been wronged by love, so she took her own life in a moment of desperation and despair. The gods made a cruel example of her, never to be able to experience the peace of the afterlife; instead, her soul was to reincarnate and/or be immortal until it learned its lesson. The creature was confined to the water in some way, even when it took human form. One day, it so happened that while the creature was in human form, she met an archer in the woods. The woman and the man fell deeply in love, and just after they had sealed such a love did the angel of darkness come for her to take her away to where she truly belonged. The woman was taken to sea, and as all her human form was leaving her body, she managed to hold on to the archer's hand that tried to pull her out of the sea. He tried to cure her with his love, not realizing that his imposition offended the gods deeply. He truly believed that his love could right all her evil, but by trying to save her, he became cursed as well.

"Eventually, the weight of the mermaid that was pushed down by the angel of darkness was too much to sustain, and it nearly broke his arm off in the attempt to save her. When they finally did let go of one another did another entity come before the archer to speak to him. It was a self-righteous voice that spoke to him. 'You love a damned soul. Are you willing to condemn yourself for her love?'

"'Yes,' replied the archer without hesitation.

"'You know not what you do. Because of your lust for the creature, you will be half-animal, going forward. The beast inside you will always prevail, no matter the intellect. You will forever shoot to the stars dreaming and always end in bitter disappointment. Because you love her, you will always sacrifice yourself for those you love with little or no satisfaction. You and all generations of your bloodline will be confined to this fate until her love manages to free her soul to be with you. Only then will you be free to be with her—free to love her and free from this curse. You are to be confined to the land and she to the sea, forcing both of you to never cross paths for more than a bittersweet moment.'

"The archer's body began to contort and twitch. He sprung out fur from the waist down. He was then down to his knees, when two legs with hooves sprung out from his lower abdomen, touching the ground as they too grew furry with hair. Those legs stood firm on the ground, as did the legs he already had. He then kicked up his front legs to the sky as a reflex, showing how they matched his other pair. Suddenly he was no longer a man; he was a centaur." Eric paused.

"Is there more to this story?"

"There might be, but I haven't read my uncle Bernie's manuscripts in a long time," he said in a way that I easily recognized as my own way of hiding some important detail.

I must admit that hearing this story made me feel like I had found an odd hole in a long-forgotten space and at an unusual time that made sense only to me. I just wasn't quite sure why at the time, but all this was very familiar to me; I just didn't quite remember why, but I knew it would eventually come to me.

"When you said this story, I kind of got the feeling that it was dear to you for some reason, almost as if you believed your uncle Bernie. You also have that sculpture on the front of your home," I said, looking for answers.

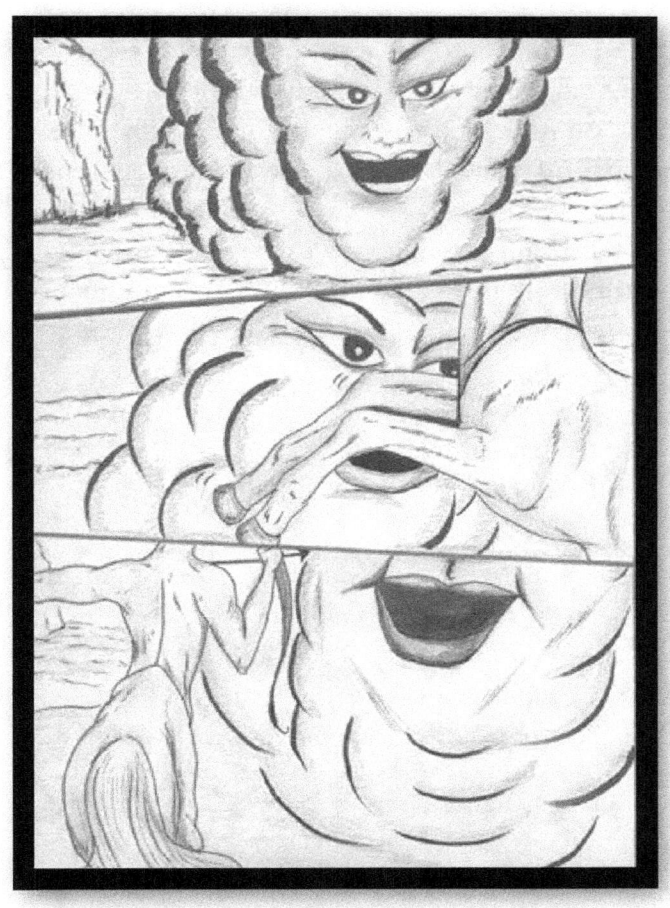

"I don't know if I believed his stories. I think it simply was nicer to believe that they could be true," he said with a certain sense of nostalgia. His words were my ideas spoken out loud. I have always felt that way. This sentence he said just bonded me more to him, making me feel a love for him I didn't want to admit to myself; I could have, but I was starting to feel a strong pain in my black heart again, and I knew this could not be good.

"I suppose a lie is much easier to believe than the painful truth," I blurted without even censoring myself.

I felt I said too much by expressing my thoughts; it was time to feign being tired and try and go back to sleep.

Chapter 10

THE FIRE IN THE HEART

Acaricia was tired and with nowhere to go. She thought she didn't appear tired; however knowing that the sages had special psychic powers, she did not attempt to question the sage with the dog and acquiescently followed him to a place of rest.

The sage lured her to a small cottage-like home. It was circular in shape like a dome. All the houses presented a similar shape and shade; however, when looking at the houses from a distance, they presented an appearance of a bright rainbow with all the spectrum of color. After further observation, Acacia noticed that the shades of the houses varied slightly in color from one to the next. It was imperceptible up close but majestic from afar—another very intriguing detail from this unknown land.

The sage did not set forth any more words of wisdom for a while; instead, he offered her food. All the food had been seared by the fire in some way. No matter how exotic, it all tasted sweet. The fruit was cut by nature like a star in bright shades of orange, red, and yellow; the meat was tender and glazed in red; and the entire assortment was colorful and provided the necessary sustenance as expected.

"This is the sustenance of life," said the sage in a church-priest tone. "There are those who feel empty inside and often seek things in life to fulfill them temporarily but feel disappointed when those things leave them more empty than before." The sage made a motion with his hands toward the food.

"I do not know what you mean," said Acaricia. She looked truly lost as if he was saying something very profound about the food or perhaps something very inane.

"All the food in our land comes from the fire of the heart. The land has heat, our souls have heat, and we both feed from one another. Some are born with a fire in their heart that burns brightly for generations and generations to come, while for others, the fire is so low that just a small breeze of disappointment puts it out, and then there are people like you, Acaricia, who have no fire at all and have given up completely long before they even started. You have been forced to look for this fire, but you have no will to search for it. This is why you are here now," said the sage.

Acaricia kept quiet for a moment, digesting the sage's words that not only made her feel more uncomfortable and vulnerable, but she also felt no more need for this type of reproachful conversation. She'd had enough contempt in her life; she simply wanted to take every day and every moment as it came until her last breath in hopes that it would be a more definitive last breath.

"You lost something in your heart so long ago that you wouldn't recognize it even if you saw it again," the sage continued.

"So you think I can find something that I am missing without the will to find it?" she asked.

"You can, but even if you do manage to find it, under these conditions, it would have no meaning to you whatsoever, so you wouldn't truly value it."

"I am sorry for what I am about to say, but I am tired, and this is not a conversation I wish to have right now," she replied, again closing herself off.

The sage looked solemnly at the floor and, in an "as you wish" gesture, bowed his head and closed his eyes. The sage was aware that if he failed in his mission with Acaricia, it would mean the doom of his people. He knew that their God was giving them one last chance before regressing them a sphere. He thought why all souls would regress one sphere if only some were responsible, only some were nonbelievers, and only some were offenders toward him. But all the same, those who were nonbelievers offended God deeply just as much as any offense. As their God, he expected a deep level of worship for all the powers he had given to those he believed to be his favorites and whom he had placed on that island so they could rejoice and honor him, but that was not always the case.

The sage was about to speak but he withdrew his words one more time and allowed Acaricia to go to bed once and for all.

The sage then left his home and went off to meet the other three sages in private at their Holy Dome.

"Are you sure she is the one?" asked the sage with the rat.

"Yes," said the sage with the dog.

All three sages had the look of worry etched in their wrinkly faces, and even without eyes to express their feelings, it was still quite clear to see their concern. The sage with the bird remembered the mark on Acaricia's hand and knew without a doubt she was the one.

"It is hard to foresee in these matters what the future will bring. We will have no choice but to do our best and await the outcome," said one sage.

"I am fearful, for this is a future that I cannot see with certainty, and failure will cost us," said another sage.

"The future is always being built by the actions of the present—we mustn't forget that," said yet the fourth sage.

"She is a damned soul, who is very lost. We must show her how to find herself to regain her soul. This will be no easy task," said the sage with the dog.

"What happened to the thirteenth law? Are we suddenly discouraged that easily, or are we only doing this for our own selfish needs?" asked the sage with the rat.

"We can't be selfish if this involves saving everybody. But if it is this easy for one of us to lose sight of our ways, then perhaps we are truly lost ourselves," said the sage with the rabbit.

The sage with the dog sighed heavily, filling his heart with gloom. "I need to pray then," he said.

The other sages glanced at him and joined him in prayer. They all needed the motivation of a true thirteenth law.

Chapter 11

THE NEIGHBORS

All through the night I felt Eric's soothingly tender touch on the length of my body, on my hips, and on my breasts…These erotic little touches reminded me of the waves from the sea when it sits peacefully serene. I woke up feeling as if I had been under water all night, cooing softly. When I turned over, I saw that Eric slept with a stupid grin on his face in stark contrast to his signature smile. It was eerie to me in a way, but I did notice this warmed my black heart, even though I tried hard to ignore it.

I went to shower and when I came back, I noticed Eric wasn't where I had left him. There was a woodsy scent in the air, like freshly cut cedarwood, an odor that now was strongly associated with Eric. I followed the odor to the outside of the house, where I noticed what appeared to be a heavy fog. At first I thought this to be an extremely unusual climate for Miami, Florida. I was able to distinguish a dark, tall figure through the dense smoke. It had a rhythm plugged into its movement that both seemed organic as well as ethnic in origin. The scent of cedarwood was stronger, but it was also intermixed with something of a more suspicious origin. I heard some strange chanting and couldn't help but have mixed feelings of curiosity and fear at the same time.

I hung out for a moment, trying to decide if I needed a weapon, should just go back to my room and pretend I didn't see anything, or simply confront the situation head-on and see what developed.

Before I could decide for the most exciting route possible, the dense fog started to dissipate, and it was officially too late to make that decision. I was caught awkwardly staring at Eric making a strange dance around this fire pit to some unusual-looking kindling.

I felt as though I looked like a deer with a luminous glare about to be ambushed by an unknown prey.

Eric paused in the middle of whatever he was doing and gave me a stare down. Could this possibly be the same man I slept with the night before?

"What are you doing?" he asked me as if I was a child who was about to eat the last cookie in the jar. Trying to conceal the oddness of the moment, I gave him the only answer that would appear to lift the weight off the situation.

"I…I was just looking for you."

He looked at me and pretended to make some type of leg stretch. I decided to join in on this quasiwestern duel and went for it all in by returning the same question.

"What were you doing?" I asked this dramatically just because I could, even though that may have not been smart. Just to intensify the moment, I lifted my eyebrow and stared him down too. He paused before giving me a response.

"I…I was exercising," he said, pretending he was doing something totally normal.

I nodded, and we both silently agreed to make no big deal out of this. He told me he was going to the gym (to work out some more?) and then working on his case but that he would be back that afternoon to go to the long-awaited block party. I didn't feel that enthusiastic about going. It was just such a "gringo" thing to do. I couldn't help but feel suspicious, but not having any real reason for anything, I simply brushed the feeling off.

When he left, I set out to take care of my other business. I went and got a PO box, a bank account, a safety deposit box, and a storage unit, all of them with my new ID. Most of these things had an ulterior purpose other than the obvious. The storage unit was a place to establish my base of operations for those things that I didn't want Eric to find out about. I stashed Emilia's jewelry there, unloading it to a pawn shop or other could easily be traced back to me. It was smarter to keep it for a rainy day. I needed a PO box to have certain pieces of mail delivered, like my alternative identity and anything pertaining to the future life I was trying to make for myself. This in the event things with Eric resulted being only temporary, and that was something that could very well happen. I needed a bank account that I was able to have access to from any state easily and a safety deposit box with my getaway package, passports, money, leverage, and anything that would help my cause for the future. I needed to look for a big score. Something so big I would never have to work and live the rest of my days however I pleased. Whatever that was, it needed to be a lot of money. I just needed to keep my eye out for the right opportunity. The easiest way would be to get to Eric's money, but so far, I didn't really have to do anything devious to have access to his money. I just had to keep him happy, and that seemed effortless at that point. The only issue was what would happen once he got tired of me. I guess it would be the same fate all the others suffer through in my path.

I set off for a duplicate birth certificate; the alternative would be to go to Emilia's, break in, and steal it, but that seemed like a lot. I wasn't ready to leave a bloody trail quite yet; besides, I could easily go to another state and live as a duplicate Emilia without a problem.

When you're prepared to seize the moment, you are quite more capable to gain the upper hand on anything and everything. That is the power of flipping your own tortilla!

I decided to become a member of the local shooting range. Membership just required a generous fee and to sign up for classes if you were an amateur, unless, of course, you were in some way affiliated to a member already. My instructor was a very quiet man who, by all accounts, seemed to have many secrets of his own. His name was Kyle.

That first day, I couldn't say that I had learned too much. He told me simply to spread my legs to gain balance and aim at the target. It sounded very suggestive and, in a twisted mind like mine, maybe even sexy in a commanding sort of way.

The target was a regular bull's-eye, and my gun was a Colt Delta Elite. Holding the gun or maybe just the name made me imagine that I was at war gunning down the enemy with fierce confidence. That was what holding a gun for the first time made me feel like, that was of course, until I actually shot and missed the target, and then suddenly I felt my mortality escaping me like a coward behind a bush. In combat, missing your target could mean delivering your life to the enemy wrapped in a bow.

"Don't sweat it," Kyle said. "Everybody misses on their first try. It takes practice."

"I want to be good now," I said like an insolent teenager who feels the world should fall at her feet. Kyle shook his head as if I was to be a lost cause.

"What made you decide to learn how to shoot a firearm?" he asked.

"It's a long story, but in one sentence, I want to know how to protect myself if I need to."

"Well, maybe one day you will tell me the full story," he said.

I aimed and shot one more time, missing my target again but I got a little closer that time. I looked at Kyle and noticed how his emerald green eyes were looking away from the target to something more prominent: the backside of my tight jeans. I smiled at him so he would notice I saw him, and he blushed slightly.

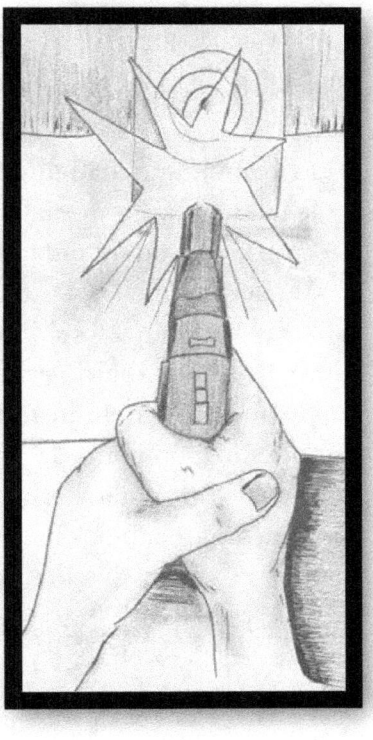

I brushed it off, saying good-bye for the time being. He had dirty blond hair and a very dark stare for someone whose eyes were so bright. He was not my usual interest, but nonetheless, he seemed rugged and disturbed despite his light features. His attitude was as if he had to keep you at arm's length because he was damaged goods. It was nothing he said that made me think this; it was simply his vibe. As I left, I found myself thinking about him; inevitably he was a mystery, something that peeked my curiosity as wanting to solve.

When I came home, the house smelled like woodsy incense again, and Eric looked uneasy. I wasn't sure I wanted to open a conversation with him and decided it was best to get some things from my room to get ready for the block party.

Eric sometimes had unpredictable behavior, and that made me nervous, especially after that morning.

"You know you should move your stuff into our room," he said, letting me know he perceived my presence. "You don't say hello anymore?" he mocked, being affronted, but really he was showing me manners.

"I thought I could just sneak by and get ready really quick before you noticed," I said.

"Sneak by? What were you doing today, oh sneaky one?" he said in a mock banter tone that made me giggle nervously as if his instinct was on to me. Did he really have a crystal ball?

"I needed to change my address, stop by my bank, and sort things out. I owed some money, and thankfully, I had some to take care of things," I said.

"Glad to help," he said with a strange inflection. I got an eerie feeling down my spine, as if he no longer was the sweet old man I had in bed the night before. He simply was another man altogether.

"Is there something wrong?" I asked, sensing a mood in the air.

"I just don't know what you do all day, and when I sit and think of it, it kind of drives me crazy," he said, tapping his foot.

"I know you have a lot of questions, but would you rather me tell you about it myself when I feel comfortable or tell you a lie just to comfort you right now?"

"I suppose I'd rather you tell me the truth when you are ready."

I began to wonder how this arrangement would work out. Eric was not busy enough to mind his own business, and soon enough I would have to create more things in my life to cover for my extracurricular activities. Eric was going to challenge me, and I definitely did not like it. I needed my privacy, and moving in with a man right away kept me from having it.

I went over to the couch where Eric was. He was still tapping his foot like an impatient rabbit. I sat on his lap and attempted to give him more magic, since it clearly seemed to have been wearing off. I looked at him in the eye and caressed his chin with my fingertips. His dimple seemed like a sad wrinkle when he didn't smile and was this upset with me.

"You have to stop being so possessive." I trailed my little finger down his dimple, through his neck, and onto his chest, playing with his gray hairs. They felt like a Brillo pad that day.

"I'm sorry. I'll try and work on it," he said.

"I feel maybe I have been a little too mysterious to you."

"Yes, you have!" he blurted out.

"I didn't expect you to say that with so much enthusiasm."

Eric shrugged his shoulders as if to tell me it was inherent in his nature.

"I will tell you what I am doing so that you don't think I am out being bad. You have trust issues, don't you?" I said.

I got an uncomfortable silence from my love. I leaned my head toward him and continued to circle my fingers through the coarse wool and changed the subject. I didn't want to make him more uncomfortable than he was already. I doubted that would have helped my cause.

"How is your case going?" I asked him.

"I feel it is a little frustrating," he said with a sigh.

"Why is that?"

"I'm defending a man who flashed a little girl in a public playground."

"What did he flash?" I asked.

"Everything!"

I must admit this did shock me.

"He was already a convicted, registered sex offender, and after serving his sentence and doing some community service, plus therapy, he decided to up the ante and masturbate in front of a five-year-old," he said in a highly discouraged and disappointed tone.

"Why are you defending him if he clearly is not showing signs of reform and he is doing worse by committing a bigger offense?"

"This is exactly why I am frustrated. I like to believe in second chances and making amends. When I first defended this individual, I managed to work a reduced sentence because it was his first offense, and he showed signs of remorse. I convinced the judge for leniency. Now this dirt bag commits a worse offense and comes back to me, expecting me to work some magic, but the issue is, I kind of want him to get what he deserves," he said, sounding so righteous.

"Why don't you just refuse the case and tell the guy you are retired or whatever?"

"It's not that easy. This individual is connected in a way that if I refuse to represent him, I would worry constantly about you."

"You mean he would stalk me and rape me?"

"It is within the realm of possibility. He may have you killed instead," he said in an alarming tone.

"Well, what would stop him from doing that even if you do manage to get him off?"

"He is too guilty for me to be able to get him off," he said, lamenting his fortune.

"I like that phrase. I might use it with you sometime—too guilty to get you off..." We both giggled heartily, brightening up the room to our usual tone.

"The more I spend time with you, the more I realize I needed someone like you," he said with nostalgia and longing.

I puckered up and shivered like a witch who got thrown into some acid. His comment was so sweet it threatened to warm my heart, and I certainly wasn't having it. It just is way too painful to have feelings; they are just a nuisance that get in the way.

He simply looked at me as if he thought my refusal of sentimentality was cute and chuckled.

"I feel like I have known you all my life," he blurted out, paused pensively for a moment, and then rushed me by saying. "Get ready for the block party." He smacked my ass, and I looked back at him in mocked surprise at the bold gesture. He retorted back with his usual dimpled grin of delight.

I decided to wear an American flag bikini under my short white shorts and solid mesh red tank top just to finish my new signature Florida style. I placed a pair of flip-flops on my feet. Eric wore another Florida staple style, khaki shorts, and a T-shirt with leather flip-flops. We strolled down this little cul-de-sac where all our neighbors were wearing variations of shorts and T-shirts. Some women decided to vary the style with floral dresses and sandals. The humidity was at an all-time high, making it feel as though it were over a hundred degrees outside. In a way this was good, since I was always very cold; it helped keep my blood warm.

There was a table set out with many dishes of varied foods, with a few awnings and patio chairs. Some of the children and neighbors were by the pool of this particular neighbor's house. Guests went in and out of the houses, using the bathrooms, changing, and grabbing more food and drinks on their way.

I dived into a table of food. I was starved and chowed down, perhaps with a little too much enthusiasm.

"Whoa, slow down. Leave some for the rest of us," said this young man who was as toasted as a walnut by the almighty sun.

"I'm hungry. Am I not supposed to eat?" I chuckled a little to hide my embarrassment. Eric was talking to the Gruebers and another couple, the Murphys. I could see him from afar. He looked as though he was squashed in the middle of conversation.

"I'm going to the pool!" I shouted out, waving off as I went into our neighbor's home to change and get a towel.

When I reached the back door to go in and get changed in the bathroom, I noticed the screen door was slightly open. I stopped entering the room, as I could hear two people speaking. I wanted to hear if there was anything juicy being said, because, of course, "juicy" was my middle name. If I found out some good info, I would hope you wouldn't think I was above extortion because I would hate to disappoint. I was all about it!

"You didn't forget to put the good toilet paper out?" the woman said.

This bewildered me. The good toilet paper? So these people would rather use newspapers to wipe their asses and leave the good plushy stuff for the guests? *Nah, that couldn't be*, I thought. My ears were probably waterlogged.

"No dear," said a man's voice with the solemnity of resignation.

"You changed the kitchen towels to the nice seasonal ones?" asked the woman again.

"Yes, dear. The ratty ones are tucked away in the laundry basket where no one can see," said the man, again with a tinge of annoyance but knowing better than to express it too loudly.

"How about the couch cushions? Did you put them out?"

"Yes, dear. I took them out of their plastic zipper bag and fluffed them up like you like people to see. The house is in pristine shape and fully ornamental," said the man, reassuring his wife the same way a dog would when reassuring its owner thus: *I'll be good now. Let's play Frisbee.*

I began to think this was a strange neighborhood of pretense. It was just so perfect in a strange way.

I did a small pause, as I usually always do before any dramatic entrance, and suddenly the owners of the house paused abruptly and greeted me cheerfully.

"I just needed to use the restroom."

"It's over there," said the woman.

"My name is M," I introduced myself. "I'm staying with Mr. Lieberman," I said, holding out my hand.

"We are the McEvoys, Alice and Ed," said Ed, pointing at each other, respectively.

"It's a nice home. You guys have great decorations," I said as I moved along toward the restroom.

"Thanks," said Alice, clearly overjoyed by my comment.

I used the restroom and took careful notice to look at the toilet paper. It was white as snow, and it did have a velvety feel. When I took a big glob to wipe my little self, I did notice it felt like soft cotton against my pussy. I wanted to thank Alice for putting out the good toilet paper, but, of course, I didn't want to give myself away for eavesdropping. I grinned maliciously in the mirror at that thought.

When I was ready to leave the bathroom, I peeked out. I wanted to make sure no one was looking. I made a clear attempt to look around without being noticed. A little risky, I know.

Alice was a dark-haired woman with a tan, and by all accounts, her image would be easy for me to pass as, as long as I got brown-colored contacts for myself.

You're probably wondering why I thought of taking another ID. It is a great precaution to have multiple IDs on hand just in case one of your IDs gets burned; you just as easily could use the other as backup. Plan B is just as important as Plan A.

I debated whether it seemed like a good moment to go scavenging through the house, but too many people were going in and out; besides, the air felt too open to do such a sneaky deed. It would have been too bold and daring. If I got caught, I certainly didn't want to have to answer as to what I was doing, only to later be handed over to Eric for cross-examination and then possible exile. Uff! The humiliation alone might kill me!

I went outside to the pool before the McEvoys or anybody else thought I was using too much toilet paper. I shook my head at this thought with a half laugh. Maybe I should just steal the toilet paper just to annoy Alice!

I was about to enter the pool, when I noticed Eric all chummy with a young woman. They were roaring with laughter as if his jokes were better than mine. I clearly saw what that old saber-tooth was up to with these usual antics. I guess you can't change the spots on a cheetah, no more than you can cure the coquettish ways of an old man. It would be too much to ask for him not to look, not to flirt, no more than it would be for me not to lie, I suppose.

I feigned a smile and dived into the pool next to Eric.

"Boy, I can't leave you alone," I said with my best attempt not to stab him and then her.

"It is I who can't leave you alone," he retorted with charm. "You are just that wonderful," he said, trying to pacify the comment and brush it into insignificance.

"Ah! Such soothing words, my love," I said, gritting my teeth and going along.

Eric introduced me to Mia and a few others at the pool, all who were too well mannered and polite to ask us about our relationship. They all held their illicit thoughts and their curious impolite eyes with hushed cornered words about Eric's new romantic liaison.

The water felt cool in its overchlorinated composition. Some children played in the pool. We all watched their innocence and playfulness, and that became the favorite pastime of this neighborhood during the party. With them around, the adults were allowed to daydream and run free from their self-imposed propriety. Watching them reminded the adults of the freedom of action they once had but now somehow didn't or couldn't. They were forced to pretend or uphold something that really burdened them for fear of judgment. The older the children got, the more they appeared to mimic their parents, leaving the carefree happiness of their true self behind. I watched this in amazement; as adults, we all fall prey to a game of make-believe.

I noticed how the McEvoys fell careless to their home, mingling with the crowd. I slipped in quickly behind another who was about to enter the house.

As that neighbor went inside the restroom, I ventured upstairs, looking for a second restroom and quickly went inside what appeared to be the master bedroom. My black heart thumped with excitement; it was the rush of being alive that only a devious deed can do for the soul.

It was decorated in a rather barren minimalistic style, something that, to me, appeared odd as opposed to the main level. It was just a bed with two nightstands and a dresser. It appeared as if the McEvoys had just moved in, that they really hadn't lived there at all, or maybe like the house had been staged for sale. When I attempted to look for Alice's purse, it occurred to me that something was wrong and unnatural about the McEvoys. I opted to look for the purse, and in an attempt to find something I really wasn't supposed to, I couldn't find anything at all. What had started as a good idea suddenly appeared to be too close for comfort. I looked into the closet and noticed that the big spacious closet was rather empty, with only five pieces of clothing. This was even more bizarre, considering that Alice appeared to be the typical woman who liked to shop. But why didn't she? I saw her designer handbag and quickly went to open it. The wallet had cash but no ID or credit cards in it, nothing personal, no health-insurance cards, or random receipts. Nothing.

I heard steps coming up the stairs and panicked. I felt as though I had made a really bold and stupid move, and now I was rushing around to recover and save my cover. I stashed everything back in the purse and dived madly into the restroom, trying my best to be light in step so whoever was coming up the stairs wouldn't hear me shuffling around. My heart began to race again with the excitement of getting caught.

The feeling of being alive! Public humiliation! Oh no! I closed the door lightly and turned the light on. I held my breath with a pounding heart whose disjointed beats were caught up in my throat as if my heart was being regurgitated. I flushed the toilet as those steps entered the bedroom. I opened the faucet water and pretended to wash my hands. I pretended because at a moment like this, who cares about real hygiene. Once I felt composed enough to open the door, I saw Alice there. I felt I should offer an explanation as to why I was in an area of the house I previously was not allowed, and the expression on her face also demanded such, even if by all appearances Alice might have been too polite to ask me.

"I'm sorry I invaded your private space, but I just really needed to go, and the downstairs bathroom was occupied," I said before she even asked anything. This appeared to ease some of the tension in the air.

Alice tried to hide a sentiment of alarm and brushed the moment off, using the regular facade she now seemed to have practiced before.

"It is all right. When you gotta go, you gotta go, right?" she said, clearly going along with me.

"Right," I said, trying to ease the awkward feeling in the air, and then changed the subject. "I love the décor. So modern and minimalistic." My words sounded so false it would take some type of miracle for her to believe me, or so I felt.

"Oh, thank you," Alice said, suddenly sounding so delighted as if those were the words she had been waiting to hear all her life.

Seeing this made me think there were more to the McEvoys than I had originally anticipated. I had to find out as to whether or not they would pose a threat to me, but even then, what exactly were they up to?

I went back to the block party. Time was forever against me, moving as slowly as the afternoon rays. I wanted to leave this block party badly and somehow had no excuse to leave. I felt horribly trapped in suburbia, more so because I just didn't belong, and everybody with their extreme politeness made me stick out like a wild rice in a pile of regular white rice. I guess there were worse things in life, but I felt like taking someone, tying them up, and torturing them with wax for hours just for fun.

The Gruebers spoke tirelessly about PTA meetings and child raising. Alice and somebody by the name of Ellen Schmitt were speaking very animatedly about aerobics classes and diet tips (liposuction). Ed and Ted, two other neighbors, spoke about the pros and cons of landscape upkeep and how to get the perfect easy maintenance lawn. Every conversation I heard was awfully too polite or practical in some way to be of any excitement to me.

Out of curiosity, I started to observe the McEvoys for any other sign that something was quite not right. Maybe I was just overthinking things; heck, I just paddled my way here right off a raft. Maybe this was normal in South Miami.

Four agonizing hours later...

Justas, an older widower from down the road, came over to chat with me. I guess I must have looked bored and in dire need of more senior entertainment. (More than Eric perhaps!)

"I've heard about you," he said, almost making me feel like I had a bad reputation already.

"I'm sure you have. I've walked around the block a few times," I said with innuendo. Justas laughed cautiously as if afraid of some social impropriety.

"Well, Eric and I have been friends a long time," he said as if a long time was a lifetime.

"I can believe that," I said, sounding rather snarky and making no attempt to hide it.

"We go way back," he reiterated as if to cue me into asking him more or as if he had something to say and wanted me to probe it out of him.

"Oh, I'm not sure I can take that back to back," I said, using the pun in my words dubiously. He scratched his chin for a moment, not sure how to take my comment. "Well, how far back can you go with a person and still be friends?" I added, changing my tone. He appeared to think of my question.

"I think people who go far back normally stay friends because of their history," he said, slightly apprehensive, and crossed his arms, leaning back into his heels.

"I think people who go way back normally grow out of their friendship over time, like people when they go off to college or get married and have kids, suddenly staying close to friends becomes difficult because people are too 'busy' or no longer can be friends because of different interests," I said, stating my point.

Justas had an intrigued look on his face, as if this was not the conversation he wanted to have and he was regretting every moment of it—even though I was, for the first time, having fun at the block party from dull hell.

"This is true, I suppose. I can see why Eric likes you," he said.

"Oh!" I was not sure what he meant by that.

"He could never be with anybody who doesn't have an opposing argument!" We both chuckled at this, knowing how true that was.

"I assume you're a lawyer too?" I asked.

"Worse than that. I used to be a salesman, a merchant, a negotiator," he replied.

"Oh man! What did you sell, trade, or barter?"

"A little bit of everything."

"Sounds mysteriously vague. I wonder if I should grill you for information."

Justas smiled at me as if he caught a cat and it was struggling in the bag to get out.

Eric looked over, and I noticed he could tell I was having fun with another man. He didn't seem happy. I think it is funny how old men behave the same way a young teenager would. It is true that you regress in old age. Eric walked over toward us, charging like a bull defending his turf.

"I see you found some entertainment, M," he said rather crass. I smiled politely at Eric.

"I think it is nice that you found someone so sassy, especially after Emily's death," said Justas, clearly making a point. Eric looked as if an old wound was just reopened.

"Yes, M is rather nice company for me."

Emily and Emilia. It was interesting that I had a version of his widow's name. *Coincidence?* I wondered.

"Just take good care of her. Emily's death was such a shame," said Justas in a tone that bothered me. I felt as though there was something left unsaid. Emily's death was a mystery so far, but for one reason or another, up until that point, I simply thought she died of age or disease.

"I know. Well, it is getting rather late, and I know M needs her beauty sleep," said Eric, cutting his friend off.

I looked over at Eric but kept quiet and followed his lead.

I felt parched and dehydrated as Eric and I walked back to our home, leaning against one another as if we had too much to drink even though we hadn't; we were just over partied.

"So how did you like the party?" asked Eric, walking lazily beside me.

"The food was good."

Eric chuckled in a way, noticing what the lack of words meant.

"That bad, huh?" Eric said.

I laughed back at his comment. "How is it that you know me so well already?" I asked.

"It's called penis magic," he said, intriguing me.

"What the heck is that?" I giggled like a little girl.

"Well, penis magic is a certain sixth sense that comes with owning a penis and being of a certain age. What it means is that you can't stick your dick deep within a woman without getting to know her well. You get a feeling for who the woman is without asking. A woman would have to be a skilled liar to deceive a man who has developed penis magic. With such a skill under his belt—no pun intended—a man would know when a woman comes versus when she fakes it, whether or not a woman has had sex recently, when a woman is horny, and a general essence of the woman he is sleeping with," Eric said, with a wry grimace that still managed to reveal his signature saber-tooth look and wrinkled dimple. It was interesting how his dimple looked like a tired asshole at dusk, something that admittedly was kind of gross. I had to stop staring at it because sweat was collecting there, making it the first asshole that cried in your face. Uff!

"You can't be serious!" I said in disbelief.

"I am." He gave me the same expression, and I was still uncertain as to whether or not he was kidding or actually being real.

"You have developed penis magic?" I asked with the same tone of disbelief.

"Yup. I patented the thing!" he said with an exaggerated amount of hubris.

"Well, why don't you make an infomercial where you wave your magic-dick crystal ball with an added bonus—a rabbit toy! Oh! You can brand your own line of sex toys! I am seeing the vast possibilities past the deeeeep horizon!" I moved my hands theatrically as I opened them into the space ahead of me.

"I don't think my face would sell a sex toy!" he said, and we both chuckled. I thought if he just found the right niche of people with an asshole fetish, then maybe he *could* sell, and then I laughed by myself with that thought.

He slid down his hand, caressing the roundness of my bottom, and squeezed hard.

"Ouch!"

"You are being a naughty little girl. I think you need punishment!"

"Oh! I am thinking more like a reward." I smiled devilishly.

As we approached our home, I saw the sculpture of the centaur and the mermaid once more and realized how it now had a different meaning than it did when I first pulled up. It had more familiarity than ever; I just still couldn't pin down why. There was something that just felt very mine when I was around the house.

When we walked in, the door was closed quickly behind us, and Eric pushed me up against the door, kissing me with such zest that I was left gasping for air.

"Hungry, aren't we?" He gave me his signature grin with a lustier tinge. I had no idea how that was possible, but it was. He gave me a playful bite on the shoulder as I gave a low playful scream back and jogged behind the couch.

"I doubt you can run fast enough!" he said.

I smiled, knowing that I could. I pulled the string behind my neck that held the top of my bikini up and allowed my breasts to bounce out. I groped my breasts together, mocking Eric to come and get it. Eric, in turn, petted his growing cock on top of his khaki shorts as if to lure me toward him.

"Nice try, but you won't win me over that easily!" I said.

He made a corny and seductive dance that looked like a dancing cobra with a bad stomachache. If that was so, then I was the fakir playing a bad tune to hypnotize it. I laughed at him, making his aggression grow as he dropped his pants to the floor in a quasi-striptease. I was laughing so hard I was having second thoughts about being able to outrun the old man. It was our version of the timeless tale of the tortoise and the rabbit. He jumped over the couch with surprising stealth and grabbed me. The sudden movement of an old man astonished me. I had underestimated his physical abilities and was now lying on the floor with his cock in my mouth as proof of it. He choked me with his chicken, keeping me quiet! His cock throbbed as the blood pumped through his veins. The more he fed me his cock, the more aroused he grew. He stopped himself almost short of his zenith with a loud groan.

"I want to be inside you," he said, panting, and with this I knew he wanted to exercise his penis magic. He bent me over the couch, with my hands held behind my back like a prisoner. He then entered me. I struggled to take him in inch by inch as he thrust deep inside me, claiming all the woman before him. He gyrated slowly with little space to move, moaning in pleasure as the slick walls of my vagina warmed to him, tender and feverish to his touch. I could not move, but I did not want to. I could feel the angry desire that plowed in me all through and through.

I felt like the mermaid in his story, conquered by a love she was not supposed to have, and he was the archer who had aimed for my heart. Perhaps this story was still too fresh in my mind and longing in my imagination. I already loved a man who only existed in fable. I longed to feel that way, and with an unlikely man between my legs, I felt like a woman really should. The desire and lust was palpably interchangeable, and the way he felt, I felt too. It was this intoxicating feeling that excited me further into climax, building me up to the delicious pleasure. My insides burned and ached in installments, each bringing me closer to a culmination, until with one more stroke of his penis, I unleashed the fury of my passions as he held me closer to his chest, taking it all in for himself. He endured longer, mostly for the pleasure of seeing me tremble beneath him, until he no longer could withhold his release any more and exploded inside me. The warmth from his juice poured in me as he hugged me tightly when he came. We stayed united like that for some time, enjoying the postclimatic glow that comes only from satisfied lovers.

"I thought you were tired?"

"For this I am never too tired," he said, and I knew it was time to shut up. Any further comment would only insult my lover's age and draw a wedge between us that I felt was inappropriate for our arrangement, but also for these affections, I didn't want to admit I had.

We went to bed that night. I was spooning between Eric's arms, as the fan over our bed laid a breeze that comforted more than any blanket. The night went on, raising our closed eyes to the clouds, as consciousness awaited us at the other side by the sun. The next morning, a horny feeling awakened me. I felt and smelled like sex and cedarwood. Eric lapped gently between my legs, tantalizing my lust sweetly with his adoring tongue. The feeling of being seduced by velvet was intoxicating. He licked with the gusto of a culinary expert. I felt too sleepy to climax yet but not enough not to enjoy it.

"I could keep you there all day, you know?" I said. The shameless confession of a sexual woman! I grabbed Eric by his gray hairs and pushed his face into my pussy as my arousal grew. I felt raw as he used his tongue and free in my abandon to it. I imagined I had a big cock up inside me as I sucked on another; the images of phallic flesh invaded me. For a small instance, I saw Kyle in my imagery, feeding me the sensations of his cock with his kiss and the deep penetration I was getting from an eager new lover. Considering the deep, loving sex I had the night before, I felt I needed or wanted to numb my emotions with another, even if just in thought. It worked;

it was just like having a new and exciting man in my bed, someone I didn't quite know.

I quivered as I greedily escalated toward my orgasm. I wanted to come hard as one does when the buildup has been prolonged and the climax echoes through the body. I replayed my thoughts and even had secret thoughts of having my ass fondled as a precious gift few get to enjoy. All my thoughts flashed as my heart quickened, and I contracted and suddenly unfolded into climax. Eric lay next to me, not expecting any loving, just cuddling next to me with the pungent smell of my arousal and the cedarwood that came whenever he touched me sexually.

"Are you satisfied?" he asked.

"Yes, but now I am hungry for food!"

We sat in the kitchen. Apparently, Eric decided he wanted to show me he was an accomplished egg maker.

"What are you doing today?" he asked.

"I think I want to enroll in classes and get a degree. I don't want to feel I am home all the time, and it will give me something to do while I get a job—a hobby or something. Besides, I need to do something. I can't expect you to support me for the rest of your life like this. What happens if you tire of me?" I spoke my mind too much, and Eric looked troubled by my thought.

Chapter 12

LOOKING AT THE HORIZON

Where am I? And why am I here? The thoughts circled in her brain over and over.

The familiar feeling of being an outcast started to grow within her. Everywhere she went, in life and after and even in her new life, it was simply something that couldn't be outgrown. It followed her like a friendly enemy—one she knew too well and was always passively waiting for the final confrontation, one that Acaricia would seem to always avoid, yet always endure.

"What is this place called?" she asked, looking at the horizon from the window, like the women would do when they expected their men to return from a long, sea-faring voyage.

"Atlantyda in ancient form or Atlantis," said the sage with the dog as he sat down for more conversation. He was expecting the talk and inviting it in.

At the time, neither of them knew how big of a myth their civilization would one day be. The thing about myths is that just like a lie or even a fable, they all have a modicum of truth behind them somewhere. Believing in something must never be the same as lying to oneself; if and when you do, you may be walking a gray line between the little lies we tell ourselves or the big lies we get stuck in.

"Do you know why I am here?" she asked, still looking out the window.

"I do," said the sage, making it apparent that he was not going to give her the answer she was looking for.

"Well, why am I here?" she pressed on, still avoiding to look at the sage.

"Well, because we both need each other. The gods sent you here to redeem us or to be our doom. We are supposed to help you achieve enlightenment or fail in the process."

"You know the future, Sage. What is to happen to us? Will I achieve enlightenment? And how am I supposed to redeem an entire island that seems to do very well on its own?"

"The future is always changing, Acaricia. If something is supposed to happen, it will, one way or another. However, change is one of the hardest things to achieve. To change the course of something, to change a life, to change anything for that matter requires a tremendous amount of strength and energy, and it is something that must come from the heart, and only there can a positive permanent change take place. If we, our island, and you do not change, then we are doomed. So you see, this is a big challenge."

"We are called the people of light. We all seek enlightenment. We are the favorites of the gods, but we have been given so much power that some of us have become godly or godlike. We not only reached enlightenment but also superseded it. This has angered the gods because even though we are made in God's image, and we aspire to be like him, we were never meant to be superior to him in any way. We were never meant to overpower the gods or defy them in any way, but this is what has happened."

Acaricia looked back at him, deep in thought. She wondered if by taking her own life she was defying God and overpowering his will. She was angry and refused to believe or give worship to an entity that had done nothing for her in life. God was not the protecting loving father, she sought. God had abandoned her, and she was not going to worship or place faith in a disappointment.

"I suppose that if I could become my own god, I would," she said with a tone of empowerment.

"Unfortunately, many feel like you, and that needs to change," said the sage in complete disappointment.

"If change is not in my heart, why would I do it?" she said, apprehensive.

"You must look past that and into the horizon," said the sage, trying to be optimistic. "When you look farther than where you stand, you can start to see the future around you. All those things that may come in time." He paused, allowing a moment of reflection to come through.

"Wouldn't you like to feel love and caring, those little meaningful moments in life that make a difference between living and being alive? When you become your own god, it gets very lonely there, and things tend to be bland. All true meaning is drained, and little to no satisfaction is ever felt. There is only a darkness to the soul that continues to grow and overtake it all."

The sage continued to drink from his lemon grass tea infused with fire fruit.

Acaricia stood by the window; her solemn silence was a clear depiction of her mood. She did want those things and had given up on ever finding them when she walked into the sea. Was this a second chance at a clean slate? Would she be able to overcome her sadness and be happy? Or was her black heart more powerful than the purest of love?

Chapter 13

AWKWARD MOMENTS

After a few moments, Eric responded. I was not sure if his pause was due to a lack of things to say, a need to think through his thoughts, so as not to seem too blunt, or because he was thinking of a story to say to appease my queries.

"I don't want to scare you away or jump into things too quickly, but I would like to think of you as someone more permanent in my life. This is the way I have been approaching you so far. Take as long as you want to find something that makes you happy. If that is school for now, so be it. You are very young," he said, sounding very convincing.

If he only knew how old I really was, but that was a fact that was better left alone; since he seemed to like them so young, it was best to keep up my ruse. I sensed that Eric had plans for me that, even though I felt I wanted them, made me very uncomfortable.

I still debated the possibility of leaving as soon as I was done with him. But every day that passed made me feel more conflicted about this. I couldn't fall in love. Besides, he was only getting older, I thought. What I failed to realize back then was those things that I actually wanted to believe that I didn't like about Eric because he was older were, in fact, me lying to myself. He was just what I needed and wanted. I was afraid to be happy. I was afraid of losing him to death or otherwise, because he was not immortal like me.

"Thanks, honey. I just feel sometimes that I need to do something. It makes me feel independent. I hope you understand that."

Eric nodded, looking away from my eyes. "I will give you my support just as long as you don't get so stressed that you have no time for enjoyment with me. Understood?" he said in a very demanding tone of voice.

"Yes, honey." I gave him a convincing look, and he shot back a very assertive one.

A month later…

I was taking the time to assess the future I really wanted, one with a financial security that would render me independent. I had to look for a more conclusive way out; right now that seemed to be narrowed down to Eric. *Stay with Eric as is,* I thought, *and secure a life together that would hopefully end in "death do us part" and you inheriting his money.* But that very well could take up years of my own life, years that I wasn't so sure I was willing to give up. The other option was promoting a situation in which I became a black widow quicker, and that was more likely up my alley.

Another scenario was me planning a big steal—rob a bank, for example. The research I had done on this scenario was hugely disappointing. To rob a bank as a one-woman show would be too risky for the payoff. Most local state and federal banks only carried seven hundred fifty thousand dollars (or less) in the vault at all times max. This was partly due to regulations involving consumer consumption, the current economic depression, and, of course, liability of theft. This amount of money, although nothing to scoff at, was not enough to ride into the horizon happily ever after. To go guns blazing into a bank was a ballsy move. I might have gotten away with it once, or maybe twice if I was lucky. Most banks I had staked out were in high-traffic areas, making the getaway more cumbersome. Police response time on average would be five minutes or less; then there were cameras, disguises, and the getaway vehicle. I needed to steal a vehicle for this scenario. Any purchase would be too risky to be traced back to my current identity, and I didn't want to throw mud on my new identity quite yet. It was a plausible scenario, but I needed to rob at least ten banks before I'd feel satisfied moneywise.

Any other scenario just seemed too rudimentary to pull off at this time. I needed to develop more skills that, quite frankly, I hadn't yet mastered. So I saw myself humbled to a petty life of quasicrime. For an evil person, this type of crime was just sad.

I had decided to keep tabs on my neighbors, the McEvoys. Something in my gut told me they were out of place; perhaps it was paranoia, but you can't be too cautious of people who appear to have the cookie-cutter life. They'll end up sideswiping you with a smile and a fresh batch of cookies.

I met up with Kyle at the shooting range for more practice. When was I actually going to shoot someone? I wasn't sure. My life had already been threatened quite a few times, and I felt I needed to be prepared for the worst-case scenario: my enemy or me. You see, dying for a woman like me is different than it is for everybody else, and I most certainly hate being sideswiped.

I was starting to have a nice getaway setup. I had invested in clothing that was easy to wear and blend in any crowd, like jeans and a T-shirt, sweats, sneakers (the run-as-fast-as-you-can-in-the-face-of-adversity type), and that sort of thing. I was also making sure to pad my bank account, and even more than that, I was making sure to keep the cash handy in case my account was...let's say "unavailable."

I was plotting these things as I aimed with my gun, when I felt Kyle was just a little too close to me. He seemed a little nervous but was still hovering over me anyway.

"I think my aim is improving. Do you think you can also show me how to shoot moving targets?" I asked eagerly, not realizing how overly optimistic I was of my skills.

"Whoa," he said with alarm, raising both hands as if to say, "Caution—Red Alert!" "You are not at the point where you can just take off waving a gun and shoot a moving target. You learn quickly, but you are a far cry from being a good gunman," he said, clearly feeling threatened.

"You mean gun lady. You want to be politically correct," I said.

Kyle cracked the corner of his lip in a half smile as if my comment was cute to him in some way. I was quite confident my charm was working well on Kyle, and pretty soon, he would be ripe enough to savor in the throes of my bed. I smiled wickedly at this, and almost as if Kyle could read my mind, he blushed and took a step back.

"Well, then, gun lady it is," he sighed. "Truthfully, M, if you wanted to be good, I would recommend practicing every day. I am not sure if your schedule or money permits such a thing as I do charge by the hour."

"So does every other whore," I blurted out, interrupting, to which luckily he cracked up as if this was the funniest thing he had heard in years. His laugh was quite unbecoming of his normal dry self. His laugh showed me there was someone more fun and lively underneath the "I have a dark past I'm not telling you about" exterior.

"What I was about to say before you called me a whore was that if you wanted to, I would dedicate some time to training you for free," he said.

"For free? What's the catch?"

Kyle looked a little embarrassed as if I had put him on the spot or something.

"Listen, there is no additional reason. You clearly look like the type of girl who likes this type of stuff and wants to get good at it. You also amuse me. I like to hunt, I do crossbow training, and also can teach you how to defend yourself and fight." The inflection in his tone was as if he knew where I wanted to go with this. *He can't possibly be psychic*, I thought. But part of me couldn't shake the thought that his intuition was better than he actually was showing me.

"So you want to teach me to defend myself so that I am never a victim again?" I asked, alluding to my past.

"I suspected you have been some type of victim, but I would be happy to help you feel unafraid of walking alone at night anywhere and at any time," he said, as if he too knew that feeling of always walking alone.

It is basic psychology, to bond with another, to make them feel we've gone through the same things. Individuals like Kyle normally don't trust people easily, so it was best to cook him slow, like pulled pork. I felt I wanted to savor every encounter and peel off the layers slowly. The harder they are to seduce, the harder they fall in love. I felt Kyle would look nice on my trophy wall; let's just see how much of a fight he would put up with.

"I like the idea of being a badass. You really think you can make me one?" I asked naïvely.

"If you wish upon a star, do a magical dance under the fool's moon, and call upon a miracle, sure," he said, goading me. "Besides, I like special projects." His inflection was intriguing, and I couldn't make anything of it quite yet. But I did suspect there was an ulterior motive to this.

"I see you have a sense of humor, but fine, I will take you up on your offer for 'free' training, even though they say nothing is really free," I said.

"Well, maybe you will do something for me later," he said, not meaning to sound as if it had any innuendo but all the same made me laugh as though it did. He flushed a little, looking at the ground shyly. Despite his good looks, Kyle didn't quite strike me as a ladies' man. I had a feeling about him, yet I couldn't quite put my finger to it.

"I can't wait to find out what this something is."

Then suddenly, like a psychic vision or more like dramatic imagination, I had a flash of camouflage pants dropping as this big hard-on bounced out, and his hands and hips swayed together, doing a little tiki dance around a tree. I laughed by myself as I walked a few paces away.

I was engrossed in my own thoughts, supremely enter-
tained by the possibilities, when I began to feel a chill
again. I was usually always cold, even in ninety-degree
weather; however, this was the feeling I normally see in
my victims just before I strike, so now feeling this twinge
was odd. I looked around, trying to see if I was just paranoid or something was actually lurking in an unsuspecting background.

I got in what now was my car, the Grunge Rover. I had
to talk to Eric about this; I needed a car that was more my
style, something sporty and fast. I made a mental note to
bring this up in our next conversation.

The feeling that was troubling me took over, and I
decided to leave my emergency preparedness plan on
hold for the rest of the day. I looked over at the built-in
GPS and thought about all my movements being tracked
by this device. Was Eric the type to do that sort of thing? It
was definitely within the realm of possibility. I had noticed
how modern his Miser-ratti was; it practically drove itself.
So he could be watching without me really knowing.

I pulled up into the garage. When I got out, I touched
the hood of Eric's car. It was warm; he too had just come
back home. I snuck into the house half expecting to find
something—call it woman's intuition. My mind was racing; maybe I was to find Eric in bed with another woman.
Oh! I had to push the thought out of my head; the image
was too much to handle, and I was already getting mad
thinking about it.

I walked throughout the living room, the kitchen, and went up the stairs to the bedroom. Eric jumped when he saw me. He was startled to see me as if he wasn't expecting me for a while.

"What are you doing?" I used my authoritative voice.

"I'm sorry," he apologized. I had just caught him in the act of going through my things. His hands were on the dresser where I kept my underwear.

"What is it that you think you are going to find?" I asked in an accusatory fashion.

"It's just that I know so little about you that I...I don't know what to say."

I sighed. "You really don't trust me, do you?"

"It's not what you think," he said just like any man who gets caught with his pants down.

"Well, it looks really clear to me that when I am not home, you look to see what little I own in an attempt to find secrets about me or something." My tone grew a little louder as the anger rushed through.

"I missed you, and I wanted an article of clothing to smell before you returned," he said, admitting to a degrading pastime.

Could that really be? I thought suspiciously.

"You think that by smelling my clothing you will get to know me better," I said, holding high on my moral ground. The thought was ludicrous and sounded like the most stupid lie I had ever heard. "You insult my intelligence by telling me such a bad lie," I said, still berating him like a misbehaved child.

Eric, who was well over six feet tall, looked as if he had shrunk to the size of a midget.

"You are shriveling worse than a battered penis. What happened to penis magic and knowing me intuitively?"

My words were so lame that I almost burst out laughing, but I needed to remain angry if I was to be taken seriously. Eric was about to laugh, but he didn't seem to want to risk making me any angrier by doing so either. He turned his face to the side, trying to let out a little laugh. I purposely faced him so that he couldn't and, in doing so, made him burst out in laughter.

"I'm sorry," he said, putting his hand out defensively, as if expecting me to exercise my right to physical violence. Yes! I am not above violence against the elderly; in fact, I was starting to feel I was all about it.

"I know you are mad; I just can't help but laugh. That was funny," he said in a twist of conversation.

"Grrrr." I was still trying not to laugh with him, but I managed to get a meek smack across the face. "I hate you!" I sighed at how childish that sounded. It was awful. I knew I was supposed to be a young woman, but now I was regressed to a resentful teenager rebelling against her parent.

Eric took advantage of the moment to grab me and hold me in such a way as to prevent further harm against him or myself. Great!

"Listen, I know you're upset, but I mean no harm. You have to believe me. What do you say I eat your pussy real quick?"

"That's not enough!" I said, affronted about his bold response.

"Well, what would make this better?" he asked as if grasping at the air for ideas that eluded him.

"I want my own car!"

Eric let out this huge outraged chuckle of disbelief. "What kind of car?"

"Something fast and sporty."

I gave him my best-child-at-Christmas voice and matching pleading little angel eyes.

He looked at me as if he was thinking about his offense and whether or not it was worth the price of a new sports car.

"So let's see…I get caught going through your drawers and attempting to smell your panties because I miss you when you leave the house, and rather than understand me—your faithful yet incorrigible lover—you abuse me and emotionally extort a brand-new sports car out of me? This is classic and priceless."

I pouted a little, not thinking my saber-tooth lover was stingy, but he definitely looked like it now.

"I'll tell you what I will compromise with you. I will get you a new car, register the vehicle under your name, and take care of everything, but you, in turn, must let me know what you're up to all the time. I worry about you, and I certainly fear what my client may be capable of if he finds out about you." Eric sounded genuinely concerned. What a manipulative double cross!

"Is he the only client who has threatened you?" I asked, not really thinking about how he countered this attack.

"No, but somehow all the other threats seem far away, and when they were issued, I guess I felt fearless in the sense that I had nothing to lose but myself. Now that I have you in my life, I actually want to live to enjoy you," he said, sounding really genuine.

"Wow, that is actually sweet. That is so sweet I feel my little heart melting," I said this involuntarily with a snarl, almost feeling allergic at the thought. The pang in my heart started to feel like a stroke; this caused me true physical pain. I paused to regain composure so that Eric wouldn't notice.

I also began to think that Kyle was going to be good for me because if I could easily be overtaken by an old man, maybe I should be afraid to walk the streets alone at night.

"Eric?"

"Yes?"

"How did your wife die?"

Eric looked away at space almost as if this was a taboo subject but also thinking carefully about what he was going to say.

"I just couldn't protect her."

"From what, Eric?"

A mournful silence chilled the room followed by an uncomfortable silence. I continued then with another subject instead.

"The other day at the block party, something kind of bothered me about the McEvoys," I said.

"Really? What was that?"

"Maybe it's nothing, but how long have they lived here?"

"Not long. They moved in this year. They are a fairly young couple with no children."

"Do you know what they do for a living?"

Eric raised his eyes as if trying to recall a forgotten memory. "I think Alice does real estate, and Ed, I think, is an investment banker. Why do you ask?"

"Well, it's just...I was inside their home and ended up going in the bedroom bathroom and couldn't help but notice how bare and unloved it seemed, especially since the downstairs seemed so decorated and well put together."

"Well, maybe they are just getting situated still and made the downstairs look better to receive guests," he said, providing a logical explanation.

"Well, that makes sense," I said, still very unconvinced. I also realized that Eric, in his own way, was the type of person who believed the best of things and people. He refused to see there could be any evil, and perhaps that was why he refused or just couldn't see me for what I really was.

"Oh, by the way, I was talking to Pike this morning when I got to the gym, and he said that one of the girls was attacked in the parking lot at night. He said she was in a coma and with some minor injuries but that her purse was stolen," said Eric as if he was talking about an event on the news.

I shifted a little.

"Really? Wow, I thought that was a nice neighborhood. It seems like there are hooligans everywhere these days." I made my best attempt to sound concerned.

"I would just rather you avoid going to the gym at night—or maybe it would be best if we went to the gym together," he said.

It was interesting how Eric used every situation to his advantage in order to control yet another aspect of my life. I was uncomfortable with this but went along for the time being.

"Well, we can go together, but I think as an extra precaution, maybe we should think about becoming members of another gym." Eric immediately frowned at this. I guess he was just not used to change. Maybe he was midway through the ass challenge and wanted to own the bragging rights that come along with bouncing a coin off your glut! In either case, changing a gym didn't seem to be in the cards.

"OK," said Eric in a low voice, barely audible, not wanting to argue, but that made me realize that it was best to just leave things alone.

I opted to go for a run out in the neighborhood; I needed a way to work off all those calories I had been digesting.

The sun was beaming the brightest just before going away to its nightly slumber. All the shadows crept out and stalked in an ominous fashion. I noticed that most of the houses had a tranquil feeling around them with the low umber lights flowing on the walls, encasing them with some security.

I wanted to spy on the McEvoys, since I was not completely convinced they were what they appeared. I ran a couple of laps, getting the feel of the terrain, and opted to approach from the shrubbery on the side of the home. It was dark enough that I could easily blend into the shadows and scurry along the side without being noticed.

Part of me was expecting Alice to be sitting down, watching TV, and Ed to be curled up on his lazy chair, reading a book, or maybe Alice would be in the kitchen whipping up a snack, while Ed relaxed, watching a football game. Any homely scenario would have appeased my curious nature and put things to rest at that point; however, there was a different part of me that expected them to be hiding from the law in a makeshift life cooked up to lay low, or maybe they were plotting a heist against one of our neighbors, but in a way, that may have seemed too far-fetched. Even though most of our neighbors were well off, it didn't seem to hold any logic as to why someone would go through the trouble to have such an elaborate setup just to steal a neighbor's belongings. The only thing that would justify such a thing would be spying on a neighbor for some type of state secret or some type of surveillance themselves for some reason. Quite honestly, the block party had proven so boring that scenario too seemed out of place. They couldn't possibly be spying or have anything to do with me. They had been living there longer, and besides, nobody really knew who I was or where I came from, so that was too much conjecture to have.

I crept up closer to the window where the lights were on. Alice seemed to be dressed in an out-of-character garment. She didn't have the cookie-cutter Florida-lifestyle getup. She wore a pantsuit. Eric said he thought she worked in real estate, so this was not necessarily out of her line of work, but why so stuffy? Her walk had a distinctive authoritative demeanor to it, not the same type she had before when she ordered Ed around. Perhaps she was making money and felt the power under her heels. Who knew? I must admit it was interesting to watch her converted from an uptight housewife into an authoritative businesswoman.

Ed, the supposed banker, was coming home wearing a navy-blue solid suit with the typical white collared shirt and a boring dark tie. In a way, his unassuming look helped his facade because it made you not suspect. If I think hard enough, the only reason I suspected something was wrong was the stark contrast of their bedroom to the rest of the house. It was as if nobody had slept there, had any type of sex, nobody dressed, changed, or done anything in that bedroom. It begged the question, *Were they a real couple?* In a sense, even the conversation about putting the good toilet paper made sense as if their job had a budget to contend with or something. It did seem a little extreme to save on toilet paper, though. I just couldn't fathom why two unsavory characters would come into suburbia to plot something; there had to be a real reason, and to make matters worse, they were thrifty criminals. I shook my head at these thoughts.

After a few more minutes of uneventful and unsuspecting behavior, I was about to leave, when I noticed something. For a split second, as Alice put her hand on her hip, she pushed back her jacket, which must have kept her hotter than necessary in this weather, revealing a holster and a gun. At the time I was unaware of what a berretta was, even though now I am familiar with it. I was shocked in a way. I wanted to look closer at the upstairs, but this would involve me climbing on a tree like a monkey, and of course, that was just not my thing. I wanted to listen in on what they were saying, but that required me to quiet down my heart. Somehow knowing that I stepped in on something had me on edge.

"Any new movements?" asked Ed.

"Nothing out of the ordinary," said Alice.

"How long do you think we should do this for? I'm getting tired."

"As long as it takes."

Silence grew between them as if there were nothing else to say. Alice drew her laptop and appeared to be reading something important; more of this went on until decidedly there was nothing else for me to find out that night without risking being caught snooping or even worse...

At dinnertime, Eric decided he was going to show me his prowess in the kitchen. He was making me his ultimate gourmet meal. He went and fished the ingredients at the market, taking care to get the most prized, the most revered of all ingredients to serve a woman such as me.

It astonished me that after such a formal introduction, it took him all but thirty minutes to prepare his lavish meal and, when served on the table with a goblet of wine, was nothing more and nothing less than mac and cheese.

"This is the best meal I have had," said Eric as if feeding me lines.

I simply nodded as a polite gesture of gratitude, hiding behind my disappointment. "Eric?"

"Yes, my love?"

"I've been thinking a lot about your case—you know, the repeat offender."

"Uh huh?"

"I've been worried about what would happen to me if you lose his case or in some way upset him. Does he know where you live?"

"I haven't told him where I live, but nowadays if someone wants to find you, they can. There is no hiding under a rock or running away. Running away only works for a little while," he said as if this was something he had given careful thought before.

His words resounded in my brain: *Running away only works for a little while.*

"I assume you have a plan on how to neutralize him."

"You make him sound like a bad odor," he said, chuckling as if my life wasn't anything to be concerned about.

"I'm happy you seem to be quite lighthearted about the matter."

"I've been threatened before, so I am not afraid."

"How did you resolve it in the past?"

"I didn't. They killed my wife instead." Eric dropped his fork abruptly as if the conversation needed to end. He chugged his glass of wine as if it were a cold beer and changed the topic of conversation.

I pretended to go along with him, knowing I touched a painful subject that needed lulling.

The night progressed without further incident, although at nighttime I did notice the absence of Eric's devoted touch. I felt as though he still, in some way, mourned the love he had to his wife and the regrets that laid with his past decisions. His distance that night left me feeling cold and unwanted. I worried I had done something wrong, and it mattered to me—not just because my stability was threatened but because my heart was engaged with him.

That night I tossed and turned, unable to sleep, from worrying an event that normally didn't happen to me before.

The following day, Eric left early before I awoke and said nothing of his whereabouts. I felt cold—very cold—in the morning, as if the air was frozen, clearly an impossibility with the staggering heat. I assumed he would be at the gym or perhaps checking up on his case. I gave myself excuses because I didn't want to think that Eric was growing distant from me. In my black heart, the pain was twisting it to pieces, but I forced myself to go back into its normal state and once more brushed my feelings away.

As I left in the morning, I did notice a car with a man inside, reading the newspaper. He seemed to be waiting for something or someone.

I walked across the mason work with the sign of the archer and got in my Grunge Rover. I was beginning to feel paranoid about simple things that could be anything or could be nothing. I slowly drove past the McEvoys' home and watched as they both appeared to go to work. An elaborate facade or their true nature?

I checked my rearview mirror; nothing seemed to appear behind me. I relaxed for a moment, feeling that I was perhaps overworked in my machinations.

I went to see Kyle, but as a precaution, I parked on the street in front of a lingerie store and walked in as if

I was a regular customer. I browsed the store that was decorated like a French brothel with a dim light and in all shades of pink and deep fuchsia. The pictures on the wall had women ready to be taken. One step further and this could have been a sex shop. I looked for an Employees Only door. When everyone was distracted, I walked through it and began to look for a posterior exit. The room was a place for excess merchandise to stay put, while the ones on display be sold. There was a bathroom and a small lunchroom for the employees' belongings, a microwave oven, a small fridge, and, of course, the water cooler. There was no one in sight. It seemed like a golden opportunity to get another spare ID for my final getaway; however, I was on camera. Somewhere in the store there was a camera, and I was sure to be on it; if I took a purse, then I was closer to being found by someone, most likely the authorities. I left it alone for now. I found an exit in the back, as I knew there had to be one. Every business store has to have two exits as a fire precaution; otherwise, they would be in violation of code. Besides, businesses need to load the merchandise through the back so as not to disturb the clients while they shopped. I escaped through the backdoor like shit through an asshole and lost anybody who dared follow me. Or so I hoped.

After that, I went to meet Kyle. When I saw him, he said he wanted to give me a different type of training because, obviously, I was a lousy shooter. This seemed abrupt to some degree, but I saw in his eye that he had something in mind for me that I didn't plan for.

"What type of training?" I asked.

"It is hard for me to tell you not to ask me any questions and just trust me and go along with it, but this is exactly what I am asking." Kyle clenched his teeth, almost as if crossing his fingers and leaving Lady Luck and fate to do their thing.

I narrowed my eye and gave him an x-ray look. "So you are giving me free training? For no reason at all?"

"Let's just say I recruit people with certain capabilities, and I think you have them. I just need to prove it with some training." Kyle had alluded to this before, but I suppose now was the better time to put things into action and not just talk.

"Hmmm...well, what if I decide I don't want to be recruited?" I asked.

"We all have free will, but I doubt you would refuse."

"You speak as though you know me well."

"I pride myself in being a good judge of character," he said, winking at me in a way that seemed unnatural for his persona. It made me uneasy to see that perhaps I hadn't judged his character accurately.

I got into his car; it was a black Korvette that had a plate that read "Blklisted." It was a nice car, but it made me wonder why all the men in my life all of a sudden needed to own fast cars.

"Is this a South Beach thing?"

"What is?"

"Owning a fast car," I said. It was no big surprise that Kyle's response was his signature gloomy silence. In a way he didn't want to acknowledge he was one big cliché. Blacklisted, huh? I guess he felt he was an outcast.

Kyle took me to this big, abandoned-looking industrial area by the docks. He parked by some warehouses and didn't even bother getting my door. When he saw me walk out on my own, he said, "Oh sorry, I was going to get that."

I nodded with a glare, in a gesture that said, "Yea, right."

"Charming. I bet you are single," I said.

"For your information, I get a lot of pussy," he said, not sounding too convincing.

"Sure, if by pussy you mean your hand covered in a goop of Vaseline," I said.

Kyle cracked a half smile as if this amused him. He looked as though he wanted to say something but was perhaps too shy to say it.

He resumed to his usual annoying silence once again. He opened the door, which made a creaking sound as it flung open. It was dark, but then he switched the light on, and it looked like a huge personal gym and training camp of sorts. There were floor mats, punching bags, wooden Chinese dummies for martial arts training, and various equipment for working out. The question, though, was this: Was this all just for self-defense?

Everything in sight looked worn with use, perhaps even an obsessive type of discipline, but then, again, that could just be my dramatic imagination at play and not an intelligible observation.

One of the walls was covered with all sorts of knives, a bow and arrows, nunchucks, fighting sticks, swords, and things I didn't even recognize to be used as weapons, but I could only assume they were, since they hung together.

"Nice toys." Kyle gave me a half grin, so as not to show me full satisfaction. My original thought that he was shy and secretive seemed to evolve into some type of obscure pettiness that he had with words, facial expressions, and in his overall persona. It was as though he didn't want you to know what he was thinking.

"We're going to start on the floor mats. I want to show you some blocking techniques, but first I want to tell you some self-defense basics. Self-defense is not about kicking ass. It is about survival. Many times, survival means running for your life." He used a tone of alertness and waved his hands as if by doing so he would make his instruction stay on the top of my brain.

"You're going to teach me how to be a coward then?" I chuckled.

"The coward's way is always the first line of defense. There is no shame in it as long as you live another day, even though there is no real honor in it either. But leave that to other people who like to die fighting."

"It is always better to say I ran than to say I died, I guess."

"True. If you are to be attacked, the first thing is to avoid or avert your attacker. Do not let them touch you or ground you in any way. You need to leave your attacker injured enough to run and get away to safety."

Kyle showed me the immediate vulnerability points on the human body: the groin, the neck, the solar plexus, the eyes, the lower back where the kidneys rest; curiously enough, he said that if I hit that area hard enough, I may be able to kill a man. He showed me attack sequences easy enough for any idiot to execute on a common attacker, but a true fighter would recover quickly from minor pain, so to move quickly was the idea to get a big man down.

I tried some of his sequences, mocking a strike, as Kyle faked going down by the blow. I pretended to kick toward the testicles and then aimed my knee to the stomach and elbow to the back as my opponent was holding his groin. In most cases, this would make a man go down and would disable him enough to run away.

"The elbow is the hardest point in any body. Use it to strike as much pain in your opponent as needed, and throw the weight of your body into any strike you take," he instructed.

We practiced a few more moves, including how to get out from under an opponent when on the floor. He came at me too quickly for me to react and took me down. He held me down against the ground. I felt the weight of his body against me; the feeling caused an involuntary arousal, something I felt in his crotch too, as he got up quickly, trying to avert a hard-on, or so I thought. He gave his back to me, and there was an awkward moment between us that I couldn't quite explain. It was not the usual sexual tension I was used to, and this too made me uneasy.

"You need to learn to react and not freeze. Many people are not used to being in a physical confrontation, so they fail to react in the face of fear. I can give you all the training in the world, but you need to overcome the fear to act."

"I thought that was what adrenaline was for," I said.

"Even if you get your adrenaline pumping, it doesn't mean you will react quickly enough. Some people do, and some don't."

We trained for a few more hours in a similar capacity. Kyle was very skilled, and this he knew well about himself. He carried himself with confidence.

"Were you military trained?"

"I train in many disciplines," he simply said, averting a direct answer.

"Why won't you tell me?"

"One is most vulnerable to those who know them well. We all keep things for ourselves for this reason, don't we?"

I looked at him, pensive for a moment, realizing how true this was and how I myself did this as well. "Being vulnerable is not a sign of weakness. It can be a sign of strength. To let go past the barriers and walls that one holds for protecting oneself and not be afraid is liberating," I retorted.

Kyle glared at me as though this was ill received, but he again gave me a curt silence and said to meet him there the next day.

"Take me to my car then." I smiled. Kyle had forgotten we came in his car.

Kyle dropped me back at the shooting range.

"Where is your car?" he asked.

"I feel I am being followed, and I don't want anyone to know I am seeing you or why. So I parked it a few blocks back and went about a wayward way to get here without being seen."

"Why are you being followed?" he asked, intrigued.

"You tell me your secret, and I'll tell you mine. Then we will be vulnerable together," I said.

Kyle grabbed something from his glove compartment and handed it to me. There were two things in his hand; one looked like a regular quarter and the other was a pair of sunglasses.

"This looks like a regular quarter. If you press the head down, it will activate an alarm and a tracking device. If you come into trouble, press it, and I will come for you. This is a pair of sunglasses that will allow you to see if anyone is behind you."

"You would come for me? Risk your life?" I asked, almost touched.

"Don't kid yourself into believing I would only do this for you. I take pride in this sort of thing. It's what I live for. I would do it for anybody." I shook my head at him, leaning over the window in his Korvette.

"It won't kill you to show me affection, or is that considered to be too vulnerable too? However, I am not sure you are executing the first line of defense by honorably laying your life down to a fight that isn't yours."

Kyle gave me a coy smile, one that seemed to tell me he knew more about me than he was saying.

I walked over to my PO box to recover my mail. Most of it was bank stuff and a few bills from my storage unit, but between these things was a letter that was square and red and addressed to M. I opened it, and inside was a red card, and in black ink it read, "I know who you really are."

Chapter 14

THE VALUE RING

"What is this?" asked Acaricia, staring at a round piece of gold on the table next to her.

The sage with the dog was quiet, as if he had not heard her. Out of standard curiosity, Acaricia grabbed the round piece of gold and placed it on her bare finger—her middle finger, to be exact.

She spread out her hands before her and admired her skinny, long, delicate digits. It was a simple piece of jewelry, but in a way it was singular, because it was the only piece she wore. For the moment it appeared to be the only item of value she had.

The sage walked toward her with a cup of tea, which was the color of crimson. It was scalding hot and had a pungently sweet taste.

"It is a value ring or a ring of value."

"Isn't it the same thing? It looks so simple," she said, still admiring how it looked on her hand.

"Perhaps it is," said the sage with an intriguing voice. "If you believe it to be a simple item, you can take it off if you like," he said, using an ambiguously affronted tone.

"It is not that," she continued, mesmerized by the ring. "It simply looks modest for the value you say it has."

"Many times it is those things that appear to be unassuming. Those are the ones with most value. Never underestimate things by their appearance, or overestimate them for that matter, either."

There was a moment of silence as they both reflected on what had just been said. It was one of those moments intended for wisdom and insight; however, neither party was getting it the way it was meant.

A few uneventful and average days went by after that day. Acaricia often felt the watchful gaze of the sage, and when it was not the sage, it was his dog.

On one particular day, Acaricia roamed through the town, exploring, when she found an open amphitheater. There were several people playing instruments for the fire day celebration, but one in particular had caught her eye. It was a golden young man playing the trumpet. As he played, the energy in the ambience was filled with such delight and pleasure that only a true artist could be said to have played. His tune was a gaily yet whimsical sound. The melody carried such euphoria within its compass that it drew in a series of spectators; one of them sat closely in the front—it was Acaricia. As the music played, the ring on her finger grew warmer; it seemed to parallel a similar warmth in her heart, and inexplicably she felt the need to place her hand on her heart.

When the men took a break from playing, Acaricia took a moment to ask the golden man a few questions.

"Have you always played this way?"

"No." He chucked as if she were joking.

"You played as though you felt it. It was not just a mechanical way of playing a tune," she said, surprising herself with this new emotion.

"If I didn't feel it, none of my work would have had any purpose. It is because I feel it in my heart that I play the way I do," he replied.

Although his words were spoken sincerely, they were taken with a slight annoyance. Acaricia felt as though his words burned with recrimination for not having a purposeful meaning herself.

She wanted to continue the admiration she felt at first, but there was a more powerful shift inside her, preventing her from doing so. The ring and the warmth in her heart both faded in unison, growing dank.

The sage had sent his dog to do his bidding, and he had already seen this failure. The sage worried that darker feelings still brewed within Acaricia, and without any purpose to increase the value of her soul, she would inevitably be their doom.

Chapter 15

THE BRIEFCASE

"I know who you really are!" I felt utterly bewildered. Who could possibly know who I really was? Not even I knew the answer to that. Some anonymous coward wanted to think he could get the upper hand on me! I was starting to feel I needed more than just a coin and sunglasses at that point. I really needed to get to know my opponent.

Who was following me and why? How did I get on someone's radar? I needed to avoid being followed. Was someone back at Cuba, having me hunted? Why? Truthfully, I could just have been shot, and life would go on without torturing me with this lame stalking. Considering I had so little life established out here, the only possibility that made any sense to me was this had something to do with Eric. Did his wife come back from the dead to haunt me for screwing her old man?

The fact is this, I didn't know enough about my surroundings to be a competent criminal or even to make a good assessment of what the hell was going on. This letter was a wake-up call that I needed to do my homework and stop goofing off with my men and sharpen the knife.

First things first: I decided to go back to the scene of the crime. At the gym I saw Pike and decided that I needed a personal trainer.

"I need you," I said, using my special seductive voice.

"I haven't been able to stop thinking of you since that day you were here. It's been a while," he said.

"I'm flattered, Pike. Eric told me something happened the other day in the parking lot. That's why I haven't been back. I've been scared." I tried my best to sound as convincing as possible; however, I didn't need to try too hard, since you combine a very plausible explanation with general expectation, and good lying need not come into play.

"Yea, a girl got mugged while she was trying to get into her car. She had a pretty bad head injury, and her family is suing the gym for lack of protection and bodily damages."

"Wow, really? I had no idea people could do that. Isn't the parking lot not a part of the gym? What does the gym have to do with her attack?"

"Well, the parking lot is part of the gym like a sidewalk would be to a homeowner. It's really the owner's responsibility to keep the lot in order—weeds, holes, and maintenance—and in this case, our gym doesn't rent to a landlord; the gym owns the land. Emilia, that's the girl's name, is in a coma and has not been able to name her attacker, and there are no cameras pointing at that location. So we really don't know the perpetrator."

Pike started to spot me on my squats as we continued the conversation. I began to think I underestimated my strength; it took one blow to put her down. What a pity that this wasn't even my best attack!

"Wow, I can barely believe it."

"I thought you would know all about it since Eric was planning on taking the case."

"He is?" I asked with genuine surprise.

I practically fell on my ass on that last squat. I didn't like the idea of Eric getting too close to my true identity or even finding out what I did to get it. This was a problem. I changed the subject to divert attention from my true feelings. Thoughts, feelings…I guess you can pretty much lump them together into the same thing at this point.

"Is Pike your real name?"

"It is. My grandfather loved to fish, and in his honor, my father named me after some ugly South American fish that he loved."

He used such a self-loathing tone that I couldn't help but laugh at his disgrace.

"I thought it was a nickname for being or looking like such a touch guy."

Pike chuckled loudly at this as if I was the first woman to ever really think this of him.

It was well into the afternoon by the time I was about to get home. I had driven past the McEvoys' home, and they still were not home yet; not much to report on that end, or so I thought.

As I was pulling up to my new home, I noticed Alice walking in our driveway. When she saw me, she looked as though she wasn't expecting me for some time.

She walked over to my car, saying her polite hellos, and asked me about Eric. I told her I wasn't sure when he would be home but that if she wanted, I would have him stop by her place or give her a call. She smiled, said good-bye, and walked away.

I noticed that to all this, Eric was still quite absent all day. No car, no word, no letter, no nothing. Was this some strange way to tell me to leave his house? I wondered this with deep insecurity after the cold night we had had the previous night. There was an odd, empty feeling in the house without him. The scent of cedarwood was gone, or most of it at least. I found myself having this odd feeling of longing, perhaps even possessiveness. *Where are you?* I thought, tapping my foot. Suddenly, I saw myself be just like Eric was the other day when he waited for me.

I waited a whole five minutes—five minutes too long if you ask me—before trying to look for something. I needed to know more about Eric—more about my friendly, flirty host with a troubled emotional past. It was funny how, earlier, I was all over Eric's case for going through my things, and now I seemed to be doing the same, but rules don't really apply to me, so why follow them?

I went through his rooms, most of them guest rooms, with nothing of interest, and then I finally reached his study, a foreign area of the house up until now. It was full of bookcases with books of all sorts of designations, everything from science to fiction, but one thing stuck me as odd: he had a New Age section. Some of the books in that section were very old, as in centuries old, and others were just very used, as in, read over and over. There were some scary thoughts that crept through my mind, such as what kind of stuff was Eric into on his spare time. Did he practice witchcraft? Was he somebody like me and I just hadn't figured that out yet? These thoughts come into your mind when you are prone to jump to conclusions, make educated guesses, and have wildly vivid assumptions, but was this simply my overworked perception or a reality? Reality can be very harrowing, to say the least. I was looking around an uncharted territory, thinking of an old man dressed as a half-naked shaman, conjuring up spirits in the backyard, making human sacrifices perhaps. Then another thought crept in. *Am I really here as part of his generosity, or is this some type of ritual where he gets rid of me in the end, offering me up as some sacrifice to some secret cult?* Far-fetched, huh? Let's just hope that wasn't the case.

I twiddled my fingers nervously as I read some of the titles, such as *Raising the Dead, Talking with Spirits, Conjuring Souls, Mind Control, Meditation for Gurus, Where the Soul Goes After Life, Warlock's Manual to Everyday Spells.* Then there were books with names written in a dialect resembling hieroglyphics: *Palmistry for the Average Reader, Alchemy for Beginners,* and so on—I hoped Eric knew how to use these better than his average cookbook! I must admit these books were not what I considered your average bookstore read.

I looked around some more through the drawers, finding mostly files on old cases where he defended some lowlife bottom feeders. He had a few bills, mostly utility, in another drawer and some random mail hanging out. One thing that caught my eye were his bank statements; Eric had several hundred thousand in just a simple checking account, a Roth IRA with several million, investment accounts with a few more million, and a few savings accounts, all averaging around five hundred thousand each. Comparing his assets to my weekly allowance, I was beginning to think Eric was really cheap with me for what he really could afford. This was an interesting thought that was getting Eric closer to the edge of dear death than to my heart, although in truth, he needed to go through one to get to the other.

I noticed a small, leather, brown-colored briefcase at the side of his desk. It had a combination lock, and it did not just pop open, so whatever was in there was of some value to someone, most likely Eric.

I looked at the clock: it was almost six. It was rare not to hear from Eric all day. I don't believe there was one night that had gone by without me having dinner with Eric or seeing Eric early through the day. He usually said where he went or what he was doing or left me a note to be ready for dinner or something. So where was the old bastard?

I popped the lock open using my keen abilities and discovered a volume of his uncle Bernie's diary. I browsed through it briefly; it had several images of a bewitching mermaid inside and some tales and warnings about her. I sighed deeply, knowing what this meant. Inside the briefcase were also special stationary in red with gold lettering on the top. It was a specially made paper with elegant embossing. The header read "The Atlantyans." It also had a watermark on the paper just below the header representing them; it was some sort of an emblem that I recognized well because I carried it on the palm of my hand. The three wavy lines embossed on my hand began to throb like a heartbeat, and my ring began to burn on my finger.

I fell into the leather seat, feeling vulnerable. I wondered how long Eric really knew about me. I wondered why I was still there in his home. What was he going to do with me?

Was this the reason he wasn't home yet? The pain and anxiety gurgled together in the pit of my stomach.

But after a few minutes, I resolved to continue looking for anything of value that may be in his home.

I went through his bedroom drawers, not finding much except strange panties (augh!), unused lube, and a dildo. The panties were crumpled up at the crotch with a clear smear of something I didn't really want to think of. I looked under the bed, took a peek at the attic, but did not feel adventurous enough to go to the basement. I looked behind most of the paintings in search of the proverbial safe in the wall. I guess that was sort of outdated. I searched hard, but whatever dirt or secrets Eric was hiding, clearly I wouldn't get to quite yet.

Nighttime fell upon me, and nothing else seemed to be found. I was feeling very uneasy about not seeing Eric so that we could talk or something. I began to grow uncomfortable not having him around, and I would even go as far as to admit I missed him. I worried what he was going to do or say now that he knew the truth, or so I thought. It was now nine, and I had pretty much rummaged through every room and space in the house, and now I paced impatiently to the chime of the clock in his study.

Eric was gone. Was he spending the night out? Did something happen to him? All these thoughts were gnawing at my hemline. I felt like a porched cat looking out, waiting and expectant. The minutes tinkled on my skin, and every thought I continued to have buried me more into the ground of desperation.

I wondered whether this was some type of payback from Eric for me always coming and going without much word. Was he really that petty? Just the thought of him sitting on the couch, waiting and tapping his foot, reminded me of his reproach and how crass I had been walking in so debonair. Now it was I who waited. Eric was my benefactor, my lover, and, at this point, a big chunk of my life and the possibility of my future life as well. Could he forgive me for our past?

With him gone like this it would mean that I needed to get another life quickly…

I sulked on the couch, digesting and regurgitating these thoughts. What would be my options at that point? *I hate this*, I thought. Starting over again, moving around, taking life's mishaps, and cleverly spinning things around with a smile—it all gets old! What would happen when I ran out of wit, when my little sparks turned out and there was no more magic to be played or stories to be told? I was clearly uncovered and outsmarted.

I needed a permanent life so that the unexpected wouldn't always come to knock me down. I ticked lightly back and forth on the couch. The clock struck another hour. I left most of the lights out in the house, and I was glad I did.

A car pulled up across the street. The lights were too dim to make out any details; however, the vehicle was dark and had tinted windows. I saw two people climb out. By the way they walked strutting their shoulders, their size, and overall figure, they appeared to be men, although one figure was substantially smaller than the other. I saw them walk across the street toward our house. When they reached our house, they didn't knock like a stranger would; they walked right in, holding a key to the door like they owned the place. They didn't look for an alarm or stumble onto anything. They walked in as if it was a stroll in a familiar park.

I scurried away into the study, trying to hide from sight. I suppose Kyle was right; it takes a certain person to confront an attacker head-on. Clearly I was the second type: the person who would cower when confronted. The men seemed to be coming specifically to the place where I chose to hide, leaving me no choice but to confront them.

My heart pounded loudly, and in an effort to make no noise, I was trying not to breathe. I began to feel my body throbbing to the rhythm of my heartbeat. I was painfully aware of my presence in that particularly small place in the world. I preemptively was already kissing my life good-bye, but then I thought, *I may be a coward, but I will not go down without a fight!* I looked around quickly for a weapon. The footsteps got closer. I went toward the chimney and grabbed the fire iron. It was particularly stuck on, so I yanked it, making a loud noise, and as I did, a small opening in the wall in between the chimney and the bookcase appeared. I stepped in quickly, pushed the wall back into place, and sighed. My thoughts were racing, as were the men into the room, realizing that was where the noise I made came from. I observed them from where I stood. I could see them from the two-sided mirror that, on the other end, appeared to be just regular chimney tiles. The men looked bewildered to find nobody in sight. Their ears had deceived them, their body language said they heard something, but their eyes said *Where?* A man is a fool to what eyes can see. The two men looked around for a moment and quickly found what they were looking for: the brown briefcase. Without any further incident, they grabbed it and left.

I stayed where I was for, maybe, another ten minutes. I wasn't quite ready to move yet; in a way, I was stoic from the entire event. Why would two men come to pick up a briefcase? That was really a one-man job.

I stepped out carefully. I wanted to make sure I was in the clear. Knowing someone other than Eric had a key to the house made me very uneasy. I closed the opening on the wall and placed the fire iron back in place. *How unsuspecting*, I thought. It's very common for people to own chimneys and have one in a study or library; however ornamental, I never stopped to think how odd it was to have a chimney in Florida with all the heat. When the hell would you use it? Yet, with its classic look, you would easily fail to see how out of place it was. It made me wonder if there were other things in the house I had missed because I never really stopped to pay attention.

I gathered whatever small possessions I had and placed them in a bag. I wanted to use the phone to call Kyle. He seemed like the only person who would help me right then. I desisted from using Eric's phone because I wanted to leave no traces as to where I went or who I was seeing, so I pressed the head of my quarter instead and waited to see what kind of response time Kyle had before getting me.

Not ten minutes had passed, when Kyle snuck through the back so silently that it wasn't until he was right behind me that I knew he had arrived. Scary!

"I told you to use this in an emergency!" he practically shouted as if I had wasted his time. His green eyes had a nasty glare.

"I guess your idea of an emergency and mine are different."

"Why am I here? You seem perfectly fine."

"I am not fine. I've been living with an older man who has been supporting me, and I have not heard or seen from him all day—something that has never happened," I said, distressed.

"This is why you called me—to say an old man was missing?"

"I am just trying to explain the strange day I've had. I waited for him all day, and nothing but two men came in the house. They had their own key, and they stole his briefcase."

"Well, how do you know your older man didn't give them the key and that they were doing something expected? Why did there have to be any treachery involved?"

I never quite stopped to think about that, but my gut told me there was an evil beside my own present.

"They were dressed in black," I said, as if being dressed in black was a prerequisite to wrongdoing. Eric gave me a sideways look as if my remark was childish or clichéd in some way.

"Anything else?"

"I received an anonymous letter."

"What did it say?"

"Something about my past. I am not trying to be coy, but I am not ready to be vulnerable. Can't you just trust me when I say I need your help?"

"So you're scared?"

"Listen, I am not the tough girl you think I am."

"I never thought you were tough, M," he said and laughed as I pouted.

"Listen, I also have a kicker. I have these strange neighbors who try to appear like they're regular suburbia, but I suspect they are here for other reasons. They pretend to be something they are not." I felt I was ranting and sounding severely paranoid, and the look on Kyle's eyes confirmed it.

"Listen, I'm scared, and I don't want to be alone. Can I just hang out with you until I figure out what happened to Eric? He's the old guy," I said.

"I hope this is not a ploy to come and live with me, because if there is one thing I hate, they are freeloaders."

His comment stung me. I felt a rush of violence come from my core, but rather than hit him, I simply gave him his quarter back with a look of disdain and, with my bag of clothes, walked away toward the door.

"A couple of days, but you try anything funny, you're out."

Anything funny! I was outraged!

I followed Kyle to his car. It was parked up the road in front of a house that apparently had company, so it just looked like he was part of the party. We got into his Korvette and drove off into the night.

Kyle took me to his house. It was a really small place. Part of me was expecting him to have this huge mess lying around; instead, everything was neat, barren and essential. He had a seat and a TV, and that was his living room. His TV was old, not like the new flat screens; and I hadn't seen a vintage TV like that since the slums in Cuba: it was practically a black-and-white TV.

The next room had a computer, a desk, and a wooden chair, all very stark and clean things that felt almost empty. His bathroom too carried only the bare minimum: soap, deodorant, a first-aid kit, two-in-one shampoo and conditioner, a razor, and a towel, all in the cheerful colors of black or white. When we reached his bedroom, it was just a mattress on the floor, one night-stand, and a lamp.

It made sense to me why he had this decor; it reeked of practicality and lack of money. His kitchen consisted

LONNY LEE

of a mini fridge, a microwave, a toaster oven, a hot plate (yup, no stove), and some scarce dishes. He had a bowl, one plate, two glasses, one cup, and two sets of silverware. Nothing more. It was apparent he was used to being single and never entertaining anyone, not in a stylish fashion at least.

I was hungry, but I did not want to complain. I felt like a child who had been punished to go to bed without a dinner.

Kyle was not much of a talker, and he was definitely not a plushy teddy bear to curl up to late at night, either. I began to miss my old man once more, but I also was still too stubborn to admit that, even to myself.

"I only have one bed and no couch, and I will be damned if I sleep on the floor in my own home," he said.

"Isn't your mattress on the floor?" My painfully obvious question only gained me a big fat snarl in return.

I got ready for bed wearing my black microfiber nightgown, and as I lay down to bed, my stomach gurgled with a loud hunger pang.

Kyle went to the kitchen and grabbed a ready-made protein shake flavored to be like chocolate milk.

"Here," he said, handing it over like a barbarian.

"Thanks, I am touched," I replied. He gave me another glare as if I was being ungrateful.

I chugged it down, only to feel sorry for the chalky and grainy aftertaste.

We finally lay down side by side like brother and sister. It was the first time in a long time, if ever, I had gone to bed with a man without any sexual situation between us. I wondered if I should sprinkle my magic on Kyle; however, it might have been prudent to save my allure for a rainy day instead. I seemed to be having a lot of those back then.

I lay there wondering once more what possibly could have happened to Eric and what would be of me now. There were no missed calls on my phone.

"Kyle?"

"Yes?"

"I can't sleep."

He sighed, annoyed. "What do you want me to do—rock you to sleep?"

"You know, I wonder what type of man is chivalrous enough to rescue a woman in distress but give her the short hand of his words."

"I'm sorry. I am just not used to being the sensitive type. I am the doer, the action taker, and the problem solver. I am not the type who likes to listen to problems or dwell on my feelings or those of others. I was just not built that way."

"What kind of mother did you have? Did she just leave you to your luck on someone's porch?" I said facetiously. It's hard to manipulate someone when they show no weakness whatsoever. I noticed my comment struck a chord with him.

"I am an orphan, by the way. Thank you for remind-ing me that I am alone in the world with no one to care for but myself," he replied.

"I'm sorry," I said, wishing I had just laid there qui-etly. "But you are alone in the world because you make it that way."

"It's funny that you say that, M. What kind of person fears their normal life, runs away at the slightest sign of their own paranoia, and reaches out to who practically is a stranger for help? You don't make any sense to me. You are either lying or hiding something."

"Touché! But as I recall, you offered to help when you gave me the glasses and the quarter," I said.

I rolled over, pouting. I lost the battle, but really there would be no way of weakening this man, if not by using my magic. I needed him to look me in the eye; I needed to speak to him with my love voice.

"I was expecting an answer, M, which is, are you lying or hiding something?" That was a loaded ques-tion with no good answer. How do you ask someone whether he or she wants the dark pit or the sharp pendulum?

I rolled over toward him and asked him to look at me. He turned his light on and bucked up like a wild horse. My magic wouldn't work on him unless he soft-ened toward me.

"I am not lying. I am just not telling you everything, so in a way it is a half-truth. You yourself taught me the dangers of revealing oneself too much. I am surprised you now are encouraging me to be so transparent."

"When you ask me for help, I expect you to be transparent. You can't ask someone for help and expect them to just do so blindly. What kind of idiot do you think I am?"

I didn't like his tone of voice, but what I hated more was the fact that he was right. I also hated the fact that all his questions had a sharp edge.

"Listen, I have a questionable past, and maybe you are right that I am paranoid. I am trying to leave everything behind and start anew, but it just seems impossible."

"Well, if you ask me, you are starting a new life by keeping secrets. Do you really think that is possible? You will always take your past with you like that. It isn't healthy."

"Who doesn't have secrets?"

"Well, yours seem to haunt you."

"I think yours do too!"

"This isn't about me. Stop trying to change the subject, and just give me a straight answer."

"Can't you just let it go?" I said, giving him an intense teary look as I brushed my breast on his arm.

He grabbed both my arms and held me far from him as if I had offended him. This was a very odd reaction for a man to have from a beautiful woman.

"Listen, I am not like other men. You can't just seduce me into helping you. It just won't work."

"Well, now that you have me figured out, now what?" I was seriously affronted by this. How dare he call me out on this and still dare pretend to be a real man?

"Your only way out is telling me the truth," he said, flushing me out like a rat through a cracked hole.

"In my experience, those who resist seduction the most are the ones who fall the hardest, but you will prove me right on that another day. All I can say is that I am not who I try to appear to be, but I am trying to live a normal life. I escaped from some bad people, and I think they are looking for me to kill me. I suppose that is what happens when you escape. You always live life looking over your shoulder, believing there are monsters when, perhaps, there aren't any. All I am asking you is to help me see if the monsters are really there, or if I am just imagining them. Help me find Eric, and see if it was all just a bad dream. You said you were going to give me a couple of days, and that is all I need. If things happen during those two days, I will tell you more."

"Fine. Tomorrow I will ask one of my contacts to dig up any whereabouts for Eric. We will start from there. I will play by your rules for two days just because I am curious now, but anything more that happens, you will have to give me more than just vague answers, M. I must admit, though, I do like your style, and with proper training, I think you will one day be a very fierce woman, that is, if you aren't already. Good night. I need some sleep to be alert."

"Wait. Can you tell me what you are recruiting me for?"

"M, I have been watching you and training you for some time now, or at least enough to know you will be a part of us, but I don't believe you are ready yet."

"What do you mean?"

Kyle sighed as if he had traveled this long, frustrating journey. He grabbed my right hand and faced my palm up to show me my watermark as if he knew what it was.

"I know who you are," he simply said.

Kyle turned the lamp on his nightstand off, and we both lay silently in bed. I lay still, feeling cold, my mind still racing in overdrive.

The next morning, Kyle got up and walked out to the other room where he called up one of his buddies. He had a conversation with him that I couldn't hear. I was quite uneasy and didn't feel I could quite trust him until he was under my spell, but he clearly rejected to be weakened by me; he was overcome by his logic. He also knew what I was.

I got undressed, leaving my clothing on the floor, being careless with my nudity. Modesty was never a strong suit for me; I love to show off. Kyle heard the water running in the shower, and he stood like a good boy just on the outside of the bathroom to tell me we were going to see someone and to get dressed quickly.

I cut the water and walked out all wet as he just stood there trying to look away but unable to.

"Why are you staring at me? I thought you saw naked women all the time," I said slyly.

"A beautiful woman is always a sight to see for a man, no matter how many women he has seen."

He stood and watched as I got dressed, unabashed whatsoever, but there was something different about the way he looked at me. He looked as though he was staring at a beautiful piece of artwork and not as a woman whom he lusted over. He had no desire.

"I am surprised you can just stand there," I said coyly.

"I am a disciplined man, M. I like being tempted, but I also enjoy resisting." There was something in his words that didn't sound right.

I walked over to him and gently whispered in his ear, "A man who tortures himself. How nice."

"I know the value that I hold, M. We all have lessons in life to learn. I have evolved from a place of mundanity and am not swayed by lusty pleasures. I am part of the people of light. Do you remember that?" he said solemnly like a decree of sorts.

I thought for a moment. There was something awfully familiar about what he said, and I knew it but couldn't quite remember then.

Kyle walked to the bathroom and took a five-minute shower. He locked the door to the bathroom, as if I was to invade his sacred privacy or, worse, try to rape him. I might add I was deeply insulted by this.

I thought in my mind on how he needed to relieve himself and wondered whether or not he took the time to do so in the bathroom.

His viridian eyes appeared to be lighter than ever before.

We left and drove for maybe ten minutes through some highways and then another low-class suburb. We got out of the car, and to my big surprise, I had to get my own door. I shook my head, dismayed at his lack of chivalry once more. I was beginning to think Kyle was raised by monkeys or cavemen. Maybe I just needed to let my old-fashioned values go if this relationship was going to work out. Augh!

We met a man named Paco. Paco was a skinny-looking tall Hispanic man. I was not told where he came from or why we were there, but it was very apparent soon. He walked over the wire fence, placed his hand casually on the bar as if talking to a neighbor about his last BBQ, and extended his other hand. Kyle handed him a few bucks, and Paco began talking.

"Eric is in the ICU at the South Miami Hospital."

"What happened to him? Is it his health?" I asked, assuming it was his age that landed him there, because he couldn't have possibly been there due to an accident, since they drive very slowly in Florida for anything more than a fender bender.

"He had an accident!" he replied.

Wow, I was shocked.

"Apparently, Eric ran off the road and hit a tree at a high speed. He was found unconscious by another driver who saw the fumes coming from his car."

"How did you find all this out?" I was bewildered how this very plain, average-looking person had so much information about a stranger.

"Lady, knowing things is my business. I get my info from local PD, EMT, hospitals, social media, some very mild speculation, and other unmentionable sources. I do whatever it takes to get answers. That is what I do," said Paco proudly. He appeared to be a paid snitch to me.

"He ran off the road?" I reiterated. "There could have been some foul play."

"Eric is old enough to just do that sort of thing, I suppose," said Kyle, trying to downplay all the odd coincidences.

"If I need some information on somebody, I could just ask you for it?" I asked Paco.

"All information comes with a price, lady," retorted Paco.

Kyle and I got back into the car as I wondered about this. In a way, I felt better that Eric was still around in the hospital, but then I wondered about how things really happened.

"I'm going to drop you off at the hospital for a couple of hours. I have to take care of some things. I will pick you up later and take it from there as to what we will be doing."

"Kyle, don't you think it is strange that Eric had an accident and that people wanted to take his briefcase the same day?"

"M, it could be unrelated. Just find out if it was really an accident. It would be good to know what was really in the briefcase, and it would also be a good idea to look into your neighbors."

"There is also another possibility, Kyle. Eric told me he was defending someone who was connected enough to want to hurt me or him if anything went wrong with his case."

"Do you know his name?"

"Actually, no." I felt that all the details around my life were always vague. I spent too much time wrapped up in the immediate that I failed to see the oncoming problems, the same way I failed to see Dalia as an enemy. Kyle gave me a displeased grunt as if I had given him more dots to connect without a writing tool.

"Listen, keep your eyes and ears open, and try your best to stay out of trouble. It is just two hours. Make sure nobody is following you, and if anything suspicious happens, call me." Before I could tell Kyle the obvious, that I had no phone, he handed me a disposable flip phone. He never opens doors but always takes care of my more baser needs.

"I feel like I have been costing you a lot of money," I said, thinking of his Spartan lifestyle and how his lack of resources was what made it that way.

"A man with little to no needs and wants has the ability to save money. The way I live is a lifestyle choice, not a depiction of my financial status. Don't concern yourself with a fifty-dollar phone," he said, sounding very thrifty and generous at the same time.

"Why are you helping me so much if you don't even want sex from me?" I asked, because suddenly I just didn't understand why he was offering me free tutorials, free help, and not even wanting the regular stuff an average man would want, for not wanting to say this was abnormal. Kyle was not the kind and generous type either, or at least he didn't appear to be with his brooding past of many faces.

"I already told you I have no trouble getting sex. I am interested in seeing if you have what it takes to join our group. I offered to help you once, and you asked. I also do not shy away from problems or conflict. I am a man, and my duty is always to help and protect. Besides, I only offered a couple of days at my place anyway. It doesn't seem like a lot." *He must really hate being vulnerable,* I thought. In a way I was beginning to think of him as a saint. He was a man of honor.

"It does for someone who has done nothing but reproach me and make me think that all this could be coincidence," I said, feeling mistrust for his words.

"Stranger things have happened, M. There are a lot of coincidences and ambiguous occurrences, I grant you that, but so far there is no real confrontation, no

real enemy, no blood, no threats but just a lot of speculation, and you strike me as the type of person who has
an overactive imagination. I can't go out of my way to
chase something that doesn't exist. That's just not what
I do."

"What is it that you do then?"

"I have spent a lot of time training and preparing
myself. I just don't do amateur hour. If I tell you, you will
just think I am crazy," he said, being coy.

I could question Kyle more, but we somehow always
managed to give each other these roundabout answers. I
just was not in the mood. I so wished I had him under my
power, but I needed him to ease his attitude toward me
before that would work, but I was beginning to feel like
Kyle, for some reason, was immune.

We reached the hospital, and he told me he would be
back at eleven for me and went off.

I followed the signs to the ICU and walked up to a
room that had his name. People were walking back and
forth, all distracted by the sounds of the ward, their
responsibilities, and the patients who were there.

I looked over at a patient on a bed. I didn't quite recognize who she was; it was her name on the side of the
door that stood out to me: Emilia Olivares. She was the
woman I attacked in the parking lot outside the gym.
She happened to be alone there. I thought about getting
rid of her once and for all, but she had family who would
keep fighting in court for her. It would have been easier

to take her identity and not get caught had she died, but it was the fact that social security gets notified of deaths that worried me. What would happen when I used her social security and it came back that it was a dead person's? She had to live for now. In a way it was very convenient to think that she would always be in a coma. It was the ideal scenario. She was alive and too sick to do anything.

I walked a few doors down and dangerously close to the truth was Eric. He was resting with his eyes closed when I walked into the room.

He opened his eyes softly as if he was still weak from all that had transpired.

"How are you feeling?" I asked in a surprisingly sweet tone.

"Weak, but I think I could still do you if I wanted to!"

I chuckled at his remark.

"You are incorrigible—I don't think I will ever tire of saying that. I see you must not be that ill if you are this cheery," I said with a lusty smile.

"You make me feel that way. I am happy you came. I was worried when I called the house and you didn't answer. I thought something happened to you," he said softly in a concerned tone.

"Well, I didn't stay in the house because some men came in and took a briefcase from the study."

"I was worried about that. Nothing happened to you, right? You were OK?"

"Well, I am here, aren't I? I suppose when you are this badass, you are really hard to kill. I guess that goes for both of us."

Eric chucked lightly; he was clearly in pain.

"Well, I am still kicking," he said and smiled, twitching a little from the pain of his injuries.

"I hate to sound crude, but I am happy you are alive. I don't know what I would do without you right now. I rely on you," I said in a moment of vulnerability. In my black heart, I began to feel that pang once more, but somehow it was less of a pain than it had been in days past.

"As soon as I get out of here, we should start thinking about our future," he said.

"There needs to be a future to think of it," I said, but then I wondered about the secrets Eric knew about me and how we managed to dance around them at the moment.

"There *will* be a future. I promise," he said as I wondered all that he knew about me.

"What happened, Eric?"

"I had an accident. Can't you see?"

"Really, the truth."

"I was run off the road by another driver."

"So this was on purpose?"

Eric held out his hand and reached out to mine as if he needed to feel my warmth. I placed my hand in his, and I could feel his warmth too.

"I may be old, but I am very much resilient. I am not built for strength. I was built to endure. They can run me over, beat me to a pulp, but it wouldn't matter. I will always get up and walk away in one piece," he said, with such conviction that tears started to well up in my eyes. I fought those suckers back tooth and nail, and so I was able to bottle up my feeling yet again. This was becoming harder and harder as time went on between us.

"You are a crazy old man. Do you mean to tell me you put yourself in harm's way? Or simply that you've made it this far in life by being too stubborn to die?" I chuckled at this, thinking about how my mantra was similar to his. (Evil never dies.)

"The latter, my love. I am simply too stubborn to die these days. I just still have too much to live for," he said so sincerely.

"Do you know who did this then? Am I in danger? Two men came into the house yesterday. I was scared," I rambled off my words, and even though maybe I was scared, it seemed completely unlike me to feel that way.

"Did they take anything else?"

"I hid behind that inconspicuous chimney of yours and watched as they took your briefcase?"

"So they didn't see you?"

"No, but they heard me. I left the house and stayed out because I couldn't risk anybody else coming back or attacking me."

"You did well. They took the briefcase," Eric reiterated with regret.

"What was so important that they had to take the briefcase?"

"I had some important court-case notes in that briefcase and an important volume of my uncle Bernie's diary and stories that we were doing some research on. I am not sure who attacked me. It could be my current case nut job for advising him on a plea deal, or it could be a past client whose trial went awry. I have some of those."

"Does anybody but us have a key to the house? Those men walked in with their own key, and they knew what they were looking for. They walked around the house as if they'd been there before."

"The maid. She has a key. She's worked for me for years without any incident—not even a penny lost." But somehow I noticed Eric didn't seem surprised at all. He knew something; he was just not saying it.

"You seem upset, honey," I said, trying to probe him for some answers.

"Well, it's just that my uncle Bernie's writings are extremely important. They are not just a legacy to my family full of imagination and stories. Over centuries, it has become much more than that."

"How do you mean? I know you told me one of his stories as though you actually believed they were true."

"Well, there are several odd findings in these readings, and some of them have these references that could be plausible to the beginning of life and humanity. Some are predictions of events that have happened, and others seem to be exaggerated myths like a fable. He wrote it in such a way that it remained an enigma whether or not they were more than just stories. Uncle Bernie lived during the eighteenth to the turn of the nineteenth century, and in his writings, he said he saw people with an artificial source of light at night. 'Its light was an aberration to God and his natural light. It shone through a filament covered by glass, and in a small unit, people looked as though they held the sun in their hands.' He wrote things like that," he said, sounding intriguing.

"So was Uncle Bernie psychic?" I felt utterly bewildered; this was a grown man in apparent full mental capacity believing in fables just as tall as my stories. I suppose maybe this was why he had fallen for me.

"We were never certain of anything about Uncle Bernie. All I know is that his books have inspired some sort of following among historians, believers, and researchers—those people who seek an alternative truth to what is considered popular belief. Even in life, Uncle Bernie was quite eccentric."

"How come I have never heard about this before? Are you trying to tell me that those men were probably there for your uncle's writings? Would they try to kill you over them?"

"M, it's a possibility I don't want to overlook. Where are you staying?"

"I am staying with a friend who is teaching me self-defense."

"A man?"

"Yes."

"Are you sleeping with him?"

"No, he knows I am with you. He helped me find you, and he brought me here. He's picking me up soon."

"I would prefer that you stay alone." Eric's tone was stern. Commanding. He was no longer looking as gaily as he did when I walked into the room.

"Where would you have me stay? If I stay anywhere else, I expose myself to being alone and having no protection. Until you're better, I'd rather stay with him. You have to trust me," I said, thinking about how I wasn't so sure I felt safe with Eric. Could he really protect me? The answer to that was grim...

The nurse walked in as we were holding hands.

"Are you family?"

"Yes, she is," said Eric without hesitation.

"He suffered a concussion and some hemorrhaging. The swelling went down overnight, and he is under observation. Do not strain him in any way."

"When will he be released?" I asked.

"It is hard to say. If he progresses steadily into recovery, then a couple of days, but that's to the doctor to say, not me," she said.

The nurse adjusted Eric's pillow and, by all accounts, looked rather stuffy and prude, not to say she was as sweet as a lime.

"Nurse Amy, will you be giving me a sponge bath later?" asked Eric.

The nursed stared him in the eye as if he was a devil. Her expression had a mixture of contempt and disdain puckered up in her mouth. The prevailing belief that Eric gave her a harmless yet flirtatious banter started to relieve her fears. The latter outweighed the first, and she gave him a smile as if to say "Hey, I'm on to you."

"If it makes your stay more comfortable, sure. But just beware I also do prostate examinations." Nurse Amy gave him a playful wink.

"I think I might like that! Are they free?" asked Eric.

We all chuckled. I shook my head.

"You will just have to excuse him. He is incorrigible!" I said.

"Miss, sometimes you reach a certain age where you just let it all hang out. It's OK to invite some spice to this generally grim place stuffed with illness."

I nodded. Eric smiled and gained more confidence, not that he needed it in his pursuit of the shameless art of being a dirty old man.

"Get my things that are in the closet," he said.

I grabbed his wallet and his clothes.

"No, not my clothes," he said, sounding like a grumpy old man all of a sudden.

"Is this all your stuff?" I asked.

"Yea."

"Where are your keys?"

"With the car, I suppose. Listen well, if you need anything, feel free to charge it. The pin number to my ATM is one five one five. Take your weekly allowance, and cover any expenses if you need, but do not clean me out, woman." I chuckled loudly at this. "I need to trust you. Can I trust you?"

"Can you change the spots on a leopard?"

Eric shook his head, dismayed, but with a smile. "That's not very comforting," he said.

"I've never kicked anybody when they're down. I usually take people down altogether," I cackled. "Besides, with the ATM card, I can only take out six hundred dollars a day. That's not taking you for all your worth," I said.

"Women!" he said, laughing it off.

I kissed Eric my good-byes and promised to visit him the next day. I walked away pensive, thinking of the possible attackers and the reasons why there were just too many things going on to hone in on it. I needed to rule out the possibilities. How do you fight someone when you don't know who is attacking?

Chapter 16

THE BLACK HEART

The black heart is a curse. Often, it makes a home to those who want to love, but love somehow seems to be evasive to them. Those who love you, you cannot love, and those you love move away from you, making the owner of a black heart all too bitter and angry. Many times, those with a black heart will feel a never-ending emptiness that wallows in loneliness.

The black heart festers in the soul, and every disappointment makes that heart sadder and more cynical, prone to evil as time goes on. At its best, the black heart sours to the point where true love could never be felt again. A black heart will always remain closed to the possibilities of love, and a closed heart will never let love in.

Acaricia always felt that longing. She was aware of her emptiness and the longing to fill what she felt was missing.

The sage with the dog could sense the evil brewing inside her. It was a big force that compelled an attractive allure—the need for more charitable souls to help it. The sage could not quite see clearly what this indescribable evil was, but he soon learned to suspect the power it possessed.

In the mornings, Acaricia would go up to the fountain hole to fetch water, as was now her new custom on this unusual island. Every morning she saw this handsome young man doing the same as her. He had the most absurd hematite eyes and the most fiery of hair. His skin was tanned and had the healthy glow of a good diet. She would often speak to him in the mornings as they smiled constantly with one another.

The sage with the dog often worried what love or disappointment would do to a troubled soul, but at the lack of any success with Acaricia, he decided to watch and wait the outcome in hopes of steering Acaricia into a more positive state of being. It all appeared harmless. For days to come, the young man appeared often at the door like a lovesick puppy filled with the magical enchantment of Acaricia's unusual charm. After a week, the boy began bringing the water to the sage's home with other offerings, such as food and jewels. Most of the jewelry brought to Acaricia was made by the sea—mother of pearl earrings, pearl necklaces and such—and this pleased her so very much.

The ring of value often felt hot, announcing what practices gave Acaricia value, and one of them was the power to enamor. By the third week of these courtship-like rituals, the boy had asked the sage for Acaricia's hand in marriage.

Acaricia simply said no, and the following day, the young boy took his own life by drowning himself in the fountain hole in the middle of the plaza for all to see like a spectacle of his unreciprocated love.

When the sage confronted Acaricia with the boy's death, she simply looked coldly at herself in the mirror and, with an overexaggerated sense of vanity, combed her hair.

"Do you think I should care he took his own life?" she asked.

"I believed you cared about him even if you did not love him."

"I cannot have control over other's actions. He chose to kill himself." Acaricia remembered what had happened to her in the past when she took her own life. "He will be fine, and if he is lucky, he will start a new life in another sphere."

"Perhaps. But taking one's own life is serious. It is a deep offense. It is a negation of God's will."

Acaricia seemed highly unperturbed, as if another fly had been killed with a swift swatting.

The sage with the dog began to panic. He knew he had more work to do than he had originally anticipated as he saw her continue to caress the warmth of the value ring.

Chapter 17

TRUST ISSUES

I left Eric and walked away feeling a little uneasy and jumped into Kyle's Korvette.

"So?" he asked, rather eager.

"He said he was run off the road but that he was unaware by whom."

"Really? So he didn't see who attacked him?"

I shook my head as if to say no. I was thinking about what Kyle so mysteriously needed to do in the morning when he dropped me off.

"How was your morning?" I asked, going about it in a casual roundabout fashion.

"It was quiet!" he replied.

This was clearly a way to tell me that I don't allow him to think when I invade his thoughts with my blabber; what an open hand to the face.

"They're too many possibilities to what's going on, Kyle. How can I possibly narrow it down?"

"Well, we have to go to the beginning. Who would be after you and Eric and why? If we can answer why, we will have a better idea of who? Did Eric tell you what was in the briefcase?"

"Some current case files and a volume written by one of his ancestors about some myths and prophecies. Eric seems to think it's a strong possibility that it was what they wanted."

"Well, why try to kill him for that if they could have just taken it as they did? If people want you dead, it's either because you know something or they hate you. At least under logical reasons."

"Well, that makes sense. However, what if all they were trying to do was threaten and not kill?"

Kyle and I drove back toward Eric's house in hopes to find some clues. It was the first time I actually took notice that Kyle was wearing different clothes than that morning. I thought this to be an odd detail, since he simply took a few hours. Could he have gone back to his house to have sex with someone and then changed? OK, I know you must think that is ridiculous, but I have an overactive imagination, and yes, my mind does go there.

"So the only person who has keys to the house is the maid who cleans twice a week?" Kyle asked.

"That's what Eric said," I replied.

"And you, of course?"

I nodded.

The house was just as I had left it the night before. Kyle looked at the door to ensure that there were no forced entry marks, as if he doubted my words. We went to the library, and he grabbed the fire poker and checked out the space behind the chimney. He inspected the wood and all the nooks and crannies as if expecting something more than just a secret space to hide.

I felt something different in the house, or rather something that had always been there but up until now had gone unnoticed with all the events that had occurred. Most of the time that I had been in the house, I was there with Eric, and he gave me these feelings—this energy that came along with him—but that feeling, that mysterious energy, was still there even when he wasn't. It was hard to describe the feeling, or rather the energy, but it was definitely there, and it appealed to me especially. This will sound romantic, however; it was like a feeling of bonding or belonging.

"Did you ask Eric why he had this built?"

"He told me simply that he wanted to make it a panic room of sorts."

Kyle kept quiet. He knocked on a couple of spots, poked at others with a pocketknife, and then utterly seemed frustrated not to find anything.

I began to feel uneasy when Kyle wanted to see the rest of the house. In a way it was as though I invited a guest and now that guest was intruding. I hadn't asked for permission to have guests in the house to rummage through Eric's things, even though I clearly had no problem doing that myself. There was a boundary, a thinly veiled line, that Kyle failed to want to see. I helped Kyle go around the house, all the time pretending to be complicit with him but in actuality taking notice of his actions more acutely.

I showed him most of the empty rooms, and by that I mean the rooms in the house that had no one living in them. This brought to light another fact about Eric: all that house for just one person. All that space just served to accentuate the loneliness. Why hadn't he sold the house or rented it out when his wife died? Did he, at one point, have more family? I wondered about it. I wondered even more at the fact that there were no pictures in his house. I had not seen one since I had been there.

Some of the rooms had area rugs, and Kyle looked under each and every one, expecting to find a false wood panel or something.

"You must watch too much TV," I said.

"M, we are all people who show a face to the world. In some rare cases, that face and who somebody really is are one and the same, while in others it is not. Similar to that, there is a negative space to everything and everybody."

"Is this some type of training from your mysterious past?"

"You could say that. It's called life."

When I looked at Kyle's face, he had the look of someone who likes to smile on the inside when no one is looking, as if his nugget of information was somehow precious.

"Listen, I was thinking about Paco and how he would be useful to find info on some of Eric's current case files, and maybe even the McEvoys," I said. "Eric gave me enough money to cover it. You've been more than nice helping me and putting up with me, and I wouldn't want to abuse."

I waited for a response, but there was a ten-second gap in communication, enough to set the tone in the cord of awkwardness.

"We can check that out sure," he responded, with a lacking in surety.

He looked under all the dresser drawers for any papers or items flat enough to be taped under them. Kyle even looked under the couch. I was going to ask why he was looking for clues there or even why he felt the need to go over the house the way he did, but I decided it was best to act stupid, in hopes that he would slip up and reveal more about himself than he did up until this point by me looking smart or attempting it!

I toned it down quite a bit. Eventually we ended up finding some obscure porn magazines and nude pictures of women in very lewd poses. Some were even fingering themselves, but what they all had in common was a happy, open-to-anything look. I forced a smile and shook my head. One shot in particular seemed off key to me, because the woman was wearing red body paint and holding, what appeared to be, a huge penis-like magic wand. I noticed that Kyle took a brief glance and looked away quickly, almost as if taking care to be modest, or perhaps he started to feel too intrusive about Eric's life for once.

When he was satisfied with all the searching, we moved on.

We drove and parked in front of the McEvoys. We waited in the car for an hour, just watching. Alice pulled up in her car, wearing a cream blouse and a light blue pencil skirt. I kept thinking she had a gun under that skirt. Kyle wrote down the address and the license plate numbers; he also wrote down the license plate from another car a couple of houses down and a utility vehicle across the street from it. One of the neighbors, who always ran in the afternoons, gazed by, waving at me. She probably recognized me from the block party. Well, I moved into one place, and not long goes by, before I become a known celebrity, even in a low profile. It figures!

Kyle trained me at his warehouse the rest of the afternoon. We dropped some information over at Paco's for his special type of research.

It had been a lot of hours alone with Kyle, and the awkward silences among us were getting to me. I was waiting for just the right moment to lay some magic on him, but it almost appeared as if he was purposefully being cold toward me. Decoding male behavior was always the worst subject in school for me.

Later on that day, we went to the recovery lot where they towed Eric's Miser-ratti. This was the vehicle I had planned on sailing into the sunset with. It was just pitiful to see it totaled. I said a little prayer and crossed my heart as if I buried the car and that idea altogether.

The sun was setting over the horizon in a very lazy way. The attendant looked greasy. There simply was no other way to describe his shellacked look. His hair had Vaseline and was styled in a fifties sort of way. He wore indigo blue jeans and a striped work shirt with his name on it. "Lou" it read. His collar was pulled up, and his sleeves were rolled up, revealing what once were defined muscles. He looked iconic in a dirty and vulgarly spent sort of way. The rebel without a cause met the trailer trash and carried on with too many beers on a couch; the thought made me smirk.

"Hey," he said, lapping his tongue as if he had terrible cottonmouth. I could only assume he had the bad breath to go with it.

"We are looking for the keys to the Miser-ratti."

"I've been looking for those all my life," he said with a regretful sense of nostalgia and a thick southern drawl. Kyle looked at the ground and started pawing the dirt with his sneaker, looking nervous, but that was an incorrect assumption; this was just his way of making time when he felt impatient.

"My boyfriend had an accident, and his car got totaled. We need the keys. They had his house keys on the ring among other stuff," I said.

My boyfriend…the words echoed in my head, making me feel uneasy. Acknowledging Eric as my boyfriend somehow seemed retarded for a man his age or a woman like me.

"Which one is it?" he asked and then paused in a spaced-out way. "Oh, that's right. There's only one of those cars here. Well, there ain't no keys that came with that car."

"Can we look?" asked Kyle before I could get my words in. I glared, slightly annoyed but exaggerated my expression for a more dramatic effect.

Both sides of the car were deeply dented. I suppose one side from the sideswiping force and the other where the car rolled down and crashed against a tree. If you saw the vehicle from a top position, it would appear as if it had been stuffed in a corset.

"Some accident the old man walked away from," Kyle said with a sort of envious tone. I wasn't quite clear what exactly the envy was for; was it that he was going to be OK, that he escaped death, that he was able to own a nice car, that he had a younger woman? Or perhaps it was all those things that he had despite being an unattractive old man.

We looked all over the car for the keys, particularly the floor. I tried prying open the side door of the car, but under its present condition, it was simply easier to get in through the broken window. There was some minor blood on the car, probably from a nosebleed or scrapes with pieces of glass during the impact. The change that originally was in his cup holder was tossed all over the vehicle.

There were some scattered papers, mostly from his law firm, scattered and crumpled in the vehicle. It was about the people versus Al Denton case (the pedophile).

"It seems like they ran him over to specifically take the keys. I am not sure they wanted to kill him."

"You run over someone with a car like this," I said, pointing toward the car. "To me that looks like attempted murder."

"Why not just shoot him?" he retorted.

"Maybe it wasn't the killer's style?"

Kyle looked at me sideways as if my reasoning was faulty. "Maybe they wanted it to look like a casual accident, one where they expected him to die because of being old and frail."

"Well, until we know who is behind this, we won't know for sure what their motives truly were and why," I continued, but I was beginning to see Kyle was right.

We walked past a few other clunkers in the lot. I took notice of Kyle's mood. Although I did not quite know him very well, I felt he was acting strangely.

"Listen, why don't we question the maid on the keys, for good measure?" I asked.

"No, why would we? They clearly got the keys to the house from the accident."

I nodded in agreement with Kyle and decided this was best to do it on my own later on.

"Kyle," I said, looking him sweetly in the eye, attempting to enchant him once more, "I want to thank you for all your help. I don't know what I would have done without you."

He barely kept his gaze up when I said this, as if he could not hold his eyes to me. *Those who can't look you in the eye are not really worthy of trust*, I thought.

"We should go now," he said, cutting me off. "I am hungry, and I am sure you must be too."

He was only mildly enchanted, as if I wasn't really effective on him. He grabbed my hand and walked me back to his car. This was not in a romantic way; it was in a pushy "Let's get going" sort of way.

"Kyle, can you tell me why you are like this? What happened to you?" I asked, digging into the same subject from times in the past.

"There isn't much to tell. I have always been in situations where I was able to control everything. I like it like that, and most people do too. We should go." He grabbed my waist and pushed me along.

I had a hard time with him always being so controlling of his emotions, his thoughts, and any situations. I suppose me coming along with my problems kind of put a kink in the way he likes his things, but I suppose, then, this is why he was so keen in knowing about me.

Not to be conceited, but I was having a real hard time conceiving why Kyle was immune to me. I felt as though I would need to rape the guy if he was to be subdued by me. Maybe that was what he needed; however, I doubted it really would have worked on him anyway.

That night as we lay on the bed sleeping...I was probably on my fifth dream, one where I was being tongue worshipped by all these handsome men, when a strong grip awoke me. I let out this small yelp, turned to the side where my hand was being gripped, and saw that Kyle was still sleeping and mumbling something unintelligible. He seemed afraid or perhaps full of a large dose of adrenaline.

"Run, get away now!" he yelled, letting go of my arm. He cut so deeply into it, I felt he tore my bicep muscle in half! I sat up and massaged my arm out, trying to heal and ease the pain, when he sat up and, with flailing arms, smacked me full force in the face. I saw darkness for a moment followed by a flash of light as I gasped in pain again. I began to see how easy it was to knock me unconscious; a little more force or a direct hit to a different area of the head would have been enough. Even in his sleeplike state, his auditory senses were quite keen. He started to come at me as if I was an enemy. I wasn't sure if it was wise to wake him, but I tried staying out of his way first, that was until he grasped my neck with such force I could feel no circulation or air going through my esophagus. It was as though my eyes were going to pop out of their sockets.

"Today you are going to die!" he said. I thought that even if I did die, it wouldn't be the end of me; I just needed to start over, but still, survival was important.

I grabbed on to his hands, trying to untangle them from my throat.

I tried shaking and wriggling my way through muffled tones to have him let me go. Finally, I just kicked him in the balls. This was enough for him to cry out in pain and let me go. I fell to the ground, trying to catch my breath.

Kyle keeled over in pain and was finally wide awake. He cursed loudly at me for, like, five minutes while he regained composure.

"Get out!" he shouted in anger.

"I'm sorry, you were choking me."

He seemed completely absorbed and unable to digest reason; he just reacted. He grabbed me from the arm, tugged me harshly out the door, and threw me out like a piece of garbage.

I had to knock on the door to get the rest of my stuff, including my purse and such. That was, of course, if I wanted to pay for a cab or anything like that.

Kyle must have read my mind because he came at the door with whatever little belongings I had and simply threw them out the door instead of handing them to me like a human being.

"Jerk!" I screamed, as I was about to debase myself into a domestic-violence scene. I felt the rage bubble up but managed to control the outburst for that moment.

I sighed. It was past one in the morning. I felt as though I was just in a bad fight with my boyfriend. I tried to laugh it off by thinking this was just how I told Eric that my ex threw me out, except that there was no jealous rage. I walked to the corner, feeling the light breeze of a summer night. I was wearing my nightshirt and walking in my sneakers, holding my purse and some scrambled clothing items in my hand. I felt like a wandering stray cat.

For whatever reason, this got me thinking how I always seemed to lose things in life at an abrupt moment. One moment I am dancing in a contest and the next I am fighting for my life and swimming in rough waters. The next I am in a home, taken care of, and then I am in the midst of some strange, unexplainable mystery that still boggles me too much to move forward with my original plan. Then I seek the only person I know or thought who could help me, only to be kicked out in the middle of the night because he tried to kill me in his sleep. Why do these things keep happening to me? Will all this instability in my life ever end? Is there something that wrong with me that I can never have a sense of security?

I sighed down and out. I needed shelter. I didn't want to risk finding someone in the middle of the night, only to start yet another cycle, one of hope and desperation again.

"I could go for a drink to drown out the anger," I said to myself. That seemed just like an easy fix to kill the midnight hour.

I called a cab with my out-of-date flip phone. In a few minutes, the cab I howled for had pulled over beside me. There was a dark man behind the seat, who looked annoyed, either at having to work his job or to work at that hour. It seemed hard to tell which.

When I entered the cab, I was inundated by an extremely unpleasant smell of spicy armpit! It sounded like an exotic delicacy, but it was more of a horrible commonality. The humidity made the smell ten times more potent. A specialty in its own way for sure! I opened the window and stuck my head out like a dog, minus the tongue.

"Take me to the nearest bar."

The cabbie nodded in silence and drove for what appeared to be five minutes. He stopped at a corner. The bar was a black joint called exactly that: "The Corner Hole."

"Wait for me here. I won't be long. I need to get to a hotel later."

The place looked awfully dark; to say it resembled the asshole of bars was a compliment. Unsavory was not the word that best described the ambience; that simply would have been a very mild adjective.

There were four men inside the joint. One of them was at the bar, completely wasted and practically falling asleep, and the other three were playing pool and smoking cigarettes like seasoned addicts. My assumption was that past a certain hour, nobody cared to follow the restrictions for indoor tobacco use that simply didn't matter anymore. On top of the onerously dim lighting, it had an extra layer of fog caused by the heavy smoking. There was a dirty, large mirror behind the bar, which, in my imagination, had illegal gambling on the other side. Conveniently placed to be on the lookout for cops or trouble.

"You're not from around here?" asked the bartender, in a true cliché style, trying to imply a warning that I leave quickly.

"And this isn't your lucky night!" I said, trying to appear tough in my nightshirt and sneakers.

The bartender turned his back at me and poured a shot. With my luck, it would have had a roofie in it! He tossed it at me with some type of trick while lighting it on fire.

"On the house," he said with a rough voice.

"Thanks. What's the occasion?"

"No occasion. Simply put, when a woman comes in wearing her PJs in the middle of the night into a bar, you know she had it rough."

Well, there goes all pretense. Shit is shit at any hour, but at midnight, shit is worse.

"What is this?" I asked.

"It's called a lightning bolt!"

"What's in it?"

The bartender lowered his head, raised his eyebrows, and popped his eyes as if to say, "Really? You don't need to know."

There was some loud moaning next to me followed by a putrid stomach gurgling; it was the stench from the man in the barstool. Clearly he was resurrected from death, and that is never a good thing. He fell limply toward me and drooled on my shoulder as his hand kneaded my breast in such a vulgar fashion that I nearly threw up!

"Augh!"

"Pretty lady, wanna go home? It's just up the block." I twirled my finger at the bartender and signaled him for two. As quickly as a lightning bolt, two more fire shots were in front of me. I snatched them up, gulping both of them in one swallow.

"I wish my woman would swallow like you," said the drunk, still pawing me.

I raised the man's head and forced him to look me in the eye. I whispered softly in his ear. I spoke to him smoothly, like a song, and surely he submitted to my tune.

He stumbled toward the bathroom, and I knew his future was drowning his half-assed sorry life into the toilet, back to the dead where he truly belonged. The thought eased my anger and made me smile.

I left money on the counter for my drinks and walked out to my cab.

This was definitely the night from hell.

The next day I awoke in my hotel room alone and naked. My neck hurt from the grapple with Kyle. I felt hoarse and weak. I had a few missed calls from Kyle; somehow, to me, it seemed too late for regrets. I am not the type of girl who takes it and then runs back to put the other cheek. I was still angry, and the storm was not done being weathered. Kyle was going to see the end with me in the alley alone one day, I thought.

I needed to get ready and pick up my car. I waited in the lobby for the valet to call me when my cab arrived.

There was a man reading the paper. He seemed to be completely minding his own business; however he appeared familiar to me. I looked at all his common features, the brown eyes, the dark hair with no luster, and the sun-aged skin. His relaxed jean look seemed out of place for a man on a workday. He also seemed out of place for a man on vacation, I suppose, but it was this minor detail that sparked my curiosity. He seemed out of place in such a vague nondescript way, and with that insignificance, I simply brushed it away and thought of it no more. Too much imagination on my part.

I looked at Eric's house. It seemed untouched since I last saw it. I still walked in uneasy but quickly. I took my car and drove out. A few houses down there was that same utility van parked that Kyle and I had seen a few days back by the McEvoys' home.

I remember Kyle taking the plate number down. I drove past it but saw nobody inside. If Kyle were speaking, he would have said that perhaps another neighbor was using their services—nothing suspicious, but then, again, that started to seem odd to me. Why would a man, who clearly had a tortured past with trust issues and para-noia, pretend that everything was perfectly not suspi-cious, when clearly something was going on? Did therapy teach him that trick? He seemed so self-possessed and contained that I couldn't work on him. He was also too damaged to be any good, in my opinion; giving him a chance was clearly a stupid move on my part. I shook my head at this thought and headed out to the hospital before I got angry again.

While I stood at a stop sign, I saw the man from the lobby wearing a different colored shirt in a black sedan two cars behind me.

The light changed, and I continued to drive toward the hospital. Was that my imagination, or did the man from the lobby had one of those looks that he could just have looked like anybody? Maybe the lightning bolts were that strong that I was still suffering from its aftereffects. It was only eleven in the morning, and the day seemed long already.

I walked up to Eric's room and once again passed Emilia's room where she still lay in her coma. I began to think that perhaps death would mean more to her than this form of living. I needed to tie up all these loose ends, and she was one of them.

When I saw Eric, I gave him a long kiss, in an instinc-tive way, without even thinking.

"Do you know that the girl in the room next door has your same name?"

"Good morning to you too! I saw that and thought it was funny, but I also have a very common name," I said, purposely trying to divert attention.

He looked at me with mild suspicion, or maybe it was just my thought. Better stay ahead.

"How do you feel?" I asked.

"Like I took a very long nap. I've been in bed convalescing for a while. I'm ready to get out of this joint and hopefully never revisit it. How were things with your friend?" he asked casually in a roundabout fashion.

"I slept in a hotel room last night like you asked, mister I have trust issues."

"Are you ready to go home tonight?"

"I think we need to change the locks and file a police report for the missing briefcase."

Eric stalled to answer and didn't quite seem so concerned about it. "I'll change the locks, but I don't want to make a big deal getting the police involved," he said finally.

"So you, a lawman, thinks it is OK not to seek the law when you were run off the road on purpose and somebody came to your home and stole what was yours?"

Eric looked at me conspicuously but then gave me his signature grin—the one I had inadvertently grown to love.

"I have a plan, M. I think it is best to keep the cops out of this for now. In my experience, the law doesn't act on 'if' and 'maybe.' They act when the damage is done. So far all I would give them would be an old man's account of a black truck running me over and petty theft. If I go to the law for something, I have to be able to tell them something better and more concrete than mere supposition. I don't want to go into some strange account of my uncle Bernie's diary, because for a man in my profession, it would just discredit me."

"Well, why don't you just leave that out?"

"They won't have the information they need to find the perpetrator. Besides, I think we can do better."

I cackled so loudly it felt like a heckle. "We? I am not so sure 'we' would be a good private-dick team," I said to him skeptically. "I think you know more than you are telling me, because any other person in your position right now, at the very least, would be a little frightened, if not concerned, but you seem as if it was just another day lying in the laurels."

I encountered his quizzical silence. The once transparent man with a good old heart and generous open arms had more tricks and secrets up his sleeve than I had originally anticipated.

Eric was discharged, and we left the hospital. As we pulled up, Alice was at the front door, ringing the bell with a gift basket in her hands.

"Hey," she said, "Ed and I heard you had an accident the other day, and we wanted to stop by and check on you, see if you were doing OK."

"Oh, that's terribly sweet, but how did you find out?" I asked.

"It is a small community. When a neighbor isn't seen for a couple of days, we worry if something bad had happened to them. Of course, we hadn't seen much of M around lately either. I am sure you must have been worried sick." She gave me an odd look, almost as if implying I might have been the culprit behind Eric's transgression or implying I was plotting against Eric's life.

"Yes, I have been awfully worried and spending a lot of time at the hospital with Eric, caring for him," I said, following the falseness of polite conversation. "That is why you hadn't seen me."

I took the basket from Alice's hands.

"Do you want to come in for a cup of coffee or tea?" Eric added. Alice looked at her watch.

"I have an appointment in a few, but I suppose I can stay for just one cup, as long as you are not too tired."

"Please, I've been doing nothing but resting in a hospital bed. I am eager to get back to my usual self. There is nothing worse than being in a hospital."

"I bet it must have been horrible!" Alice exclaimed.

We all walked in, and I made us all some tea. All the while Alice kept looking around the inside of the house as if she was inspecting it and giving it her seal of approval on the decor.

"You know, Eric, I have always wondered about the elaborate mermaid fountain and the centaur image you have on the masonry work outside. I just have to say how exquisite it is."

I couldn't help but wonder if that was a secret code for tacky or if she meant something else.

"Oh, thank you. My family just loves mermaids and centaurs, and I do too."

"That's very interesting," she said with an odd inflection. "I must go now. Otherwise, I won't meet my next appointment. Ed and I will check in with you later this week, if that's OK?"

"Sure, thank you for coming and for the basket as well," said Eric, giving her a very strong boob-crunching hug. Incorrigible man! Even in the face of danger, convalescing, and with a hot, younger woman, the man finds the time to grope a strange woman in a casual semidownplayed way!

The scent of cedarwood started to invade me; only then I vaguely started to notice that in Eric's absence, the scent had left the house. I wondered where this scent came from, because surely at the hospital he didn't have his usual array of toiletries to evoke such an odor, or his odd incense for that matter.

I called a locksmith to come to the house, who gave me an ETA of a couple of hours. Eric shot me a devilish look and asked that I accompany him to a shower. It was my best guess that the hug gave him a jolt of testosterone and that he was feeling quite all right despite his accident.

Old-man lust is more enduring than true love.

Eric grabbed me by the hand as I laid my flip phone down with fifteen missed calls from Kyle. I followed him as if prancing delicately through the woods like a nymph.

"I've missed you," he said.

"So have I," the words escaped me without even realizing. "I thought you had abandoned me when you didn't come back home." I felt as though that came out like a needy young child whose worst affliction was to be left by a parent lonely and vulnerable. I couldn't remember the last time I had felt that way, if ever. For one moment I felt vulnerable and weak and wished to take back my words, but it was just too late. Once you speak something out loud, it has a tonal vibration that resonates, that echoes in the mind even when it is a lie, but when there is truth behind it, it is much more powerful. It is similar to a song that has been so melodious that it gets stuck in the brain even without one's approval.

"I would never leave you like that without a word, and I especially am not leaving my own home," he said sweetly, although part of me expected him to say something more emotive.

"I guess that was a silly thought, now that you put it that way."

Eric kissed me again tenderly and then turned the kiss more passionately and long-staying on my lips. He undressed me, and I undressed him, and we ran the shower. I grabbed the bar of soap and began to lather my lover, pushing him away from the water so that the soap suds would accumulate on his body as the hot water poured over on my skin.

"So nothing happened between you and your friend?"

"No, he is just a friend," I replied.

"Are you sure?" I went to try to kiss him, but he stopped me so that I couldn't, without giving him a straight answer.

"Nothing funny happened, I swear." Typical, you tell the truth, and nobody believes you. I looked into his eyes and hummed a small melody, the same one from the other night. I lulled him with his head in my hands as I gazed into his eyes. I felt him weaken toward me as his trust issues began to dissipate into a dreamy squinty-eyed man possessed by amorous feelings. He pushed me against the tiled wall, and feeling my body against his, he began to ravish me with hungry kisses. I fell into him, reciprocating all his kisses, touch by touch and kiss by kiss. I felt a hunger to be unleashed by him and to love him with the prowess of my body. I heard Eric's heavy breathing and could feel his heartbeat racing and pouring forth the feeling of life and passion; this in itself excited me even more. Soon the soapsuds I had created on his body were transferred onto mine before being lazily washed off by the water. As wet as we were, we began to tremble from the core of our aching loins, giving away to the possibility of standing in the shower while copulating. I opened the bathroom door, and we gently crashed onto the floor like an ocean wave.

Eric beckoned my legs to open with a swift move of his hip and the introduction of one of his legs to part mine. I felt the warmth of his hardened cock ready to seek its satisfaction. I was wet with arousal as his cock glided feverishly into me, producing in me a singular feeling of love, joy, and satisfaction expressed through the movement of our bodies. I was being possessed inch by inch in all parts of my being and surrendering to the freedom of being undone and not caring. For the first time in my life, I wanted to penetrate a man's chest to surpass the laws of physics and go from solid matter to the ectoplasm of a ghost, just so I could invade the space where his body was. I wanted to own him as he had owned me...be a part of him as if I melted away welded into him. The deep ripples of pleasure that passed through my insides as his cock thrust in me pressured me deeper and deeper into a culminating state. He built me up to the pinnacle of pleasure, and as I could no longer hold back, my man released all the juice from his testicles into my body, and together we savored climax in each other's arms. We remained in silence for a few moments, trying to catch our breaths from the vigorous encounters of our naughty body parts. Eric gave me a satisfied smile as he collapsed on top of me.

"I've never felt this way about a woman," he said, still panting as his heart pounded against my chest.

"Oh! And how is that? This is something you probably tell all your women," I said, skeptically guarding my feelings and hoping that my lovemaking didn't expose the truth.

"I have loved another woman in my lifetime. I have lusted after other women quite frequently. But, M, with you I feel both things are one and the same. It's so intense."

The locksmith came and changed the locks on all entries of the house. Even though I was more assured, I was not convinced that continuing to stay in that place was smart or wise. If someone wanted to come into our home and harm us, not much could stop them from doing so. I no longer felt safe.

We could have had an alarm, but that would just be a false sense of security, for by the time the cops would come, the intruders would probably already be inside the house doing damage, and then what? Would you forever live with the thought that your home was the biggest death trap?

Once the locksmith left, Eric put the fire on in the study.

"Isn't it seventy degrees outside?"

I guess he does use the stupid thing after all, I thought.

"Don't you think it's romantic?"

"Yea, very romantic to sweat my butt off!" Eric chuckled and raised the air conditioning to make the temperature more comfortable. This was another super inane thing to do. If you ask me, men are creatures of an incredible complicated stupidity!

"Is that better, your highness?" he asked.

"I suppose, but I still can't believe you actually have and use a fireplace in this weather just to be romantic."

Eric removed a book titled *Endangered Species* and pulled a handle on the bookcase and, with that, revealed a false wall behind the bookcase.

"Wow, you are full of surprises!" I said as he took out some potions and a really small cauldron. "Couldn't you wait until after we got married before pulling the weird shit out?"

"I suppose, but what kind of fun would that be! Besides, if you are to be my woman, there are to be no secrets between us."

"Aren't you supposed to say something like I am not ready for marriage?"

"I'm too old to say that kind of thing. I could die tomorrow, so I need to live today." Eric gave me a genuine smile, one that made me wonder with mistrust.

"I thought that is what we were already doing. What exactly is it that you are doing?" I shifted uneasily. I finally began to see why he felt the need to keep his extracurricular activities out of the side of the law.

"Just watch," he said, and to all this, he still offered no explanation as to what he was about to do or these strange happenings.

For the first time ever, I was beginning to question this inoffensive old man that I had found on the beach with the looks of a clean-cut citizen. Was he truly what he appeared to be?

He put the cauldron on the fire, and an intense smell of cedarwood came about. Was this all some type of special incense? Was that the secret to Eric's special aroma?

"M, is there anything that you feel you need to tell me?"

"Are you going to seriously question me about Kyle again?"

"I am not talking just about Kyle. I am talking about everything." I hated the tone of his open-ended question. I began to feel like a vulnerable rabbit being choked by the neck. Perhaps there was still a saving grace here, if I could just entice him some more with my magic. He gave me this incriminating look, as if he was the law and I was a guilty criminal. Typical!

"Please help me understand what truth it is that you seek from my lips," I said, buying time.

"I want to know the truth about you, the whole truth, the real truth. Not the version of the truth that you claim to have given me as fact. If we are to be together forever, I want us to have no lies. You, my dear M, have been lying to me." Eric had this eerie look; he no longer looked so benevolent as he had in days past.

I felt as though Eric was goading me into revealing things about myself he suspected, but then, how much about me did he really know?

"If I tell you the truth about myself, I fear you will no longer want me."

"I already know the truth about you, and I still want you, but if I don't hear it from you, I cannot trust you, and only then will I not want you anymore."

The cauldron burned deeply, and the smell of cedarwood was getting more intense than ever before as the fire crackled and sparked lively.

I felt the need to risk it all and see what happened. To trust someone for the first time in my life was an awfully hard thing to do, especially someone of whom I was not sure I trusted. I felt as though he was the rock and I was the scissor, and I was not going to cut through this one.

Chapter 18

THE RIGHTEOUS PATH

"I do not care to be good, to be the foot soldier of a God who has done nothing for me—a God who abandoned me, a God who allowed me to suffer pain and hardship, a God who was nowhere to rescue me when I was raped and abused. God does not involve himself in what he feels are petty matters. If you think that by being nice to me you will cause me to change my way, you are wrong."

The sage with the dog did his best to conceal his frustration and continued in his Zen-like form to speak to Acaricia.

"God does not interfere in the life of mortals, unless you will him to come to your aid. God only saves those who seek for him."

"So you say that God stands by the sidelines and watches, while all our souls get condemned and damned.

How is that a God of love?" Acaricia said and paused. Then she continued, saying, "Your God does not hear me quite simply because I don't really matter to him. Quite frankly, there is no God, and your God is a God of fantasy and lies. There is judgment and hardship, and perhaps there is a soul and an afterlife, but there is no God—not the way you claim him to be. That God simply does not exist." Acacia clenched her fist with the conviction of her words.

The sage with the dog looked at the floor, contemplating his pain for such words; he had encountered a macro mission of the thirteenth law, and all his efforts seemed quite futile. The value ring corrupted Acaricia even more by showing her the power of things she could do instead of building the core values of the heart that was needed for enlightenment—the way it was supposed to. Every word he said was quickly rebuffed, and no feeling whatsoever moved or motivated Acaricia in any way toward a righteous path. She was alone, and her heart that was a coal, that could have once burned brightly, was now cooling off as the last bits of light and fumes were leaving with its warmth. What a curse this was for the sage to have this mission, and what a curse it was to have a black heart for Acaricia, yet she chose to wear it with pride.

How does one cure a black heart when the soul is that corrupted? How does one change the course of evil when hope is this forgone?

The sage had resolved to try harder to find Acaricia's weakness, a point of entry to weave in kindness, compassion, generosity, and love. It was the only way he knew he could exercise some control over her, but so far she showed him no vulnerabilities; at every turn she surprised him with a new trick in her echelon of evil ways. He needed more time to get to her, but unfortunately, she was not budging.

"How can you speak of love when you clearly know nothing of it? You have no right to judge God—you who are so forgone from the right path," said the sage.

"I see you with that dog. Do you think that is love? The way he follows you with blind obedience, the way he has no concept of self-love, no selfishness, he degrades himself by simply being your pet," she said with disdain.

"My dog shows me respect, and he does not degrade himself in his obedience to me. He simply obeys me because he loves me and wants my attention and approval. I love him because he gives me company and is a part of me, and we treat each other as being one and the same."

"I keep you company too, but somehow that doesn't make you love me. You just have to do your job and comply with the thirteenth law," she said in a self-righteous tone.

"If you really feel that way, then why stay?"

Acaricia looked up as if the thought of being out in the world would be different without the sage's watchful eye and his recriminations or constant ploys for her self-improvement. She clearly felt he was like stubble on her leg. She gave him a sigh as if his question was a clear nuisance.

"I stay because I am comfortable here," she said matter-of-factly. But could there be more to it than just that?

"And so you are, but you can leave at any time. I have seen your skills. You can easily find comfort elsewhere. You have magic in your voice, a profound magic to overpower the hearts of men. You are also aware of this power, and even more dangerous is the fact that you know how to use it…I fear I gave you that ring to find the more simple meaning to things in your heart, and instead, you found a different type of power. You should not continue to drown the men who fall for you—it is not right."

"Men are not worthy of my love. Why should I stop myself from avenging all the wrong men have done to me?" The scorn in Acacia's low tone was sharp and poisonous.

"Love is a blessed and positive feeling, Acaricia. I have given you sanctuary and am trying to show you the righteous way—not just to save your soul from further damnation or to follow the thirteenth law but also because it is really in my heart to do so. I feel sorry for how you feel about life or the things that have happened to you, but you need to forgive in order to heal."

"That's very easy for you to say when you don't even seem capable of sin, and you have such a status here that no one would ever dare harm you."

The sage paused, paced a few steps, turned around in a thoughtful manner, and continued. "Can I show you something?"

"Sure," said Acaricia, shrugging her shoulders.

"Give me your hands."

The sage took her cold hands, and with a warming sensation emanating from his hand unto hers, he took her into his mental realm so they would no longer speak but, instead, feel.

At first she saw herself with the sage walking side by side. He held her hand softly and caressed her fingertips gently in a very loving sort of way. It was in this way that she understood a sensation of tenderness.

It was rare for Acaricia to ever feel that there was a man in her life who didn't want sex and gave simply for the joy it produced in his heart. The level of serenity that invaded her was more prolific and much more positive than the one she felt when she walked toward the sea on her last breath.

The more they walked, the more she seemed to be in a dreamlike state; it was as though they lived a fantasy. All these new feelings, that perhaps at one point she desired and envisioned but in a way was always robbed from experiencing them, were now embracing her. The sage hugged her, and as he did, Acaricia was overwhelmed with all the emotion and sobbed. She felt a tingle in her heart as though her heart was shaking; it was a rock-solid mass that changed form. It became a liquid, like a watery substance that slowly filled like a balloon, and the bigger it grew, the more it felt the need to burst...Suddenly invaded by the sage's warmth, her heart popped open, and her tears flowed into the sea.

Chapter 19

THE TRUTH ABOUT ME

"Every lie, every fable, every myth has a modicum of truth somewhere behind it."

I sighed deeply like one with nowhere to escape. The path was very narrow, and all roads were closed but one. I nervously rubbed my fingertips together, half expecting some magic to come out and save me; however, that was not how this worked.

"The truth is, Eric, I am not sure who I am. I have been pretending for so long I lost my identity. I have been lying all my life, ever since I learned how to speak. I was born somewhere in Venezuela. I grew up in an orphanage, where some odd occurrences shaped my life."

"What kind of occurrences?" he asked, intrigued.

"I met my first love when I was five, and as unglamorous as this may sound, he was the groundskeeper of my orphanage. They say I was left at his door a few weeks after I was born."

"How can you say you met your first love at five, and he saw you weeks after birth? That makes no sense."

"I guess you believe in love at first sight and not over time," I said half-facetiously. "I first began to love him when I was five, but I knew him as a distant figure who hid in the background where he was unnoticed for the first few years of my life."

"Go on," he said.

"There are things in my life I cannot explain. Some of them happened so long ago that I am not sure they really happened the way I remember them or if they really happened at all. I was a child with a very vivid and dramatic imagination. For example, there was a boy about my age who drowned in a fountain around that time, or so I think. He had called me stupid earlier that day, and he angered me. I imagined he jumped into the fountain and drowned. I willed this so hard that I began to think it had actually happened. I remembered the groundskeeper came running by the rose bushes where I stood and held me. Later on, his death was ruled an accident, and that he had tripped and fallen, as they couldn't possibly conceive how a child that age could commit suicide. The groundskeeper saw what happened, and in some way, he understood what I had done and said nothing, becoming complicit to my evil powers.

"Some time after that, the groundskeeper, who lived across the road from my window at the orphanage, died." I paused solemnly for a moment. This was the first time in my life I was actually telling the truth. I felt my tongue was dry and sore from doing such a thing; it was like speaking a foreign language. The more I spoke, the more the truth choked me up, and my eyes began to well up.

"How did he die?"

I was beginning to feel this was not the truth he was looking for, but all the same, it was buying me some time in this little hiding-the-truth dance, and maybe—just maybe—it would earn me some sympathy.

I continued, saying, "One morning, I woke up extra early to watch him chop the wood. He always chopped wood for the cooking stove and other things here and there. That morning was brutally cold, and although where I was it never snowed, it actually snowed for the first time in history, or so I think I remember. We were too close to the Ecuador, and in a tropical country, snow was an aberration of nature. The woman, who doubled as a mother to me, told me that when the weather does things like that, it's a sign that humankind is not doing well. The man's cabin was in flames that morning. I never forget how beautiful it was in a way—fire and ice met up for redemption and death."

"Redemption?"

"The groundskeeper had a secret that burdened him, and only in death was he free." I gave Eric the dramatic pause and then continued. "That sort of thing happened in my childhood."

"What you are saying is hard to believe," he said, looking at me skeptically. "Do you know the groundskeeper's secret?"

"You once told me that sometimes the truth is hard to believe," I said, averting his other question.

"No, I simply said that sometimes it was just nicer to believe than know the truth," he said.

"Then I suppose it is. Do you think I'm evil for wanting that child to drown?"

"I think you are evil, M," he said and paused for a few seconds. Then he continued, saying, "You are evil, looking to be good."

I tilted my head sideways, and at that instant of bewilderment, I saw in his eyes that he knew most of my story already. It wasn't anything in particular about that moment; it simply was my sixth sense that picked up on his thoughts.

"When I was a teenager, I ran away from the orphanage and tried luck on my own. I did anything—I stressed anything—for food or money. That was when I decided to join a brothel to gain some stability in my life. It was not long before that phase of my life ended that I found myself to be Hugo Chávez's favorite pastime. Hugo was so sweet on me that he would often take me to places, including Cuba. He and Fidel had a small brawl over me, and I ended up in Cuba permanently until I was forced to flee."

"Why were you forced to flee?"

"His wife wanted me dead, and a confrontation with Fidel over his wife's wants would have been no good for me."

"So how did you come here?"

"I swam. How else does one escape from Cuba?"

Eric laughed in disbelief, or perhaps just the comment itself was that ridiculous within its honesty.

"Is there anything else you want to tell me?" he asked.

I looked at him, fearful of confessing more truth than I should, and gave him my pleading eyes as if to allow me to rest with my silence.

"Emilia is not your real name, is it?"

"No."

I wanted to be alone. I wanted to flee in the middle of the night. I looked over at Eric and felt as though he had confirmed his disappointment and could no longer love me. This had such a devastating effect on me that I wanted to cry. It was the first time ever that I felt it actually mattered to me. I wanted to be loved, but how could I be loved if nobody really knew who I was? I was deathly afraid of this newfound vulnerability, and that made me quiver in my panties (I was commando), desperately looking for a place of comfort and finding nothing but the freedom of the air (and no, I was not full of gas).

"M, I am satisfied with what you have had to say so far. I know this must have been really hard for you. I have some things about myself to reveal as well. It is only fair, after all, as I want there to be no secrets or lies between us."

"You are scaring me, Eric. I feel like I don't know what to expect anymore. This baring-the-truth stuff is really beyond what I can handle. It feels like the burden of sacrifice—to say the truth and finally let go."

I was feeling awfully weary and out of control. I wanted to pretend not to be afraid, but somehow pretense seemed to run for the hills, mocking the fact it left me behind to deal with the garbage. The worst part was that I really wanted to run after it and onto those very same hills. Nowhere in the villain's manual is there a clause, a rule, or an escape strategy for being caught in this type of quagmire, but I suppose a real villain loses his or her compassionate heart somewhere before being evil. Why all of a sudden did I decide to have a heart? That was for the weak!

"I thought you said you weren't the type to scare easily?"

"I am not, so I guess you must feel honored then," I said, dismayed. Eric chucked lightly, and I joined him halfheartedly to ease the tension in the room.

"What I have to say is not easy because like your truth, it will not make sense right away. I want to say that I love you," he said and then sighed, as if an elephant walked off his chest.

"I didn't think that was a secret, Eric." We began to laugh at this again obvious confession. "Is there anything else you wish to confess?" I asked with renewed confidence. However, I wondered if his confession was really the remnants of my magic still at work. But then, again, how could it really work when there was no facade?

"I see the tables have turned! I wanted to tell you that I knew you would come," he said as I waited in suspense, hanging on to his every word. "Since I saw you on the beach that day, I thought I knew it was you, but it wasn't until you told me your dream about the mermaid and the archer that I was certain who you were."

"And that is?" I was beside myself with the excessive usage of verbiage in order to get to the point.

"The love of my life, the woman I have been waiting for my entire life!" Eric sounded like a lunatic. This was not the story I thought I would hear from his mouth, not from a mature professional man who, for all purposes intended, seemed to be all there except when it came to me. OK, maybe I want to forget how strange he really was in private. I shamelessly smiled at this thought and gave myself a complimentary and invisible pat on the back! But that was a false sense of reassurance. I couldn't believe this man actually loved me; he didn't even know me, and he was also under my magic, so that wasn't real love. This thought saddened me, but I chose still to live through how bittersweet his words were.

"You believe the story of your uncle Bernie?" I asked even though I already knew the answer. "So you are telling me you are a centaur?" He gave me no response, and more than five seconds of uncomfortable silence went by.

"Are you a mermaid?" Never has truth-telling been so full of fables, but I reciprocated with the same silence.

"It is very rude to answer a question with a question, but perhaps we have spoken too much for one day, and we both need to meditate on this tonight." Eric shifted uncomfortably, and I began to rethink my escape route—the one where I ran off into the sunset with bags full of money and the perfect paradise life, completely unencumbered by all and everything. I wanted to waltz to my happy ending, wearing the last laugh, but somehow that laugh was nothing but a nervous giggle.

At this point things with Eric were still quite vague. I was unaware that his little cauldron had a way to show him if I was telling him the truth so that he had no trouble believing me, even though, by all accounts, my past somehow managed to sound like a little enhanced fib.

That night before bed, I tossed and turned, unable to sleep. Eric lay wide awake and very still as well. I wondered if any of this was due to us or our present circumstances.

"Eric, are you sleeping?"

"No. Are you?" We both giggled; at least we could still carry on even in awkwardness.

"Isn't that obvious? Listen, I am very worried someone is out there trying to get us, and we aren't sure who they are. Do you have a plan?"

"Not quite. Do you?"

"Well, I believe I do. Are you in?"

"Do I have a choice?"

"No. But it's a little risky," I replied.

"Risky is my middle name," said Eric so enthusiastic it made me feel sorry I was luring a lamb to kill and eat it.

"We have to try and find a way to draw the enemy out. I believe what they want, what they are really looking for had something to do with your briefcase, and in some way, they also want you dead. If we can convince them that you died, they may come forward, make a mistake, and do something to reveal themselves," I said, expecting to receive quite a bit of resistance to this plan. Who in their right mind would fake their own death? Besides, it also would give me the opportunity to combine events with my master plan and kill two birds with one shot.

"You know that actually might work. I like the thought that if people think I am dead, I am free to do whatever I want. My enemies will go away, and I can just sail away with my money into the sunset."

"Well, you need money to sail away into the sunset. Your social-security checks and pension will stop," I said.

"Ha! Don't make me laugh! I am not gonna miss my social security. That is not even enough to afford my expensive toilet paper."

I suddenly felt like a deuce on the corner. I thought for a moment that maybe, just maybe, I could use this small faux pas to my advantage. After all, there was a huge power in being underestimated.

"I have actually been planning my grand escape for some time, M," he said, adding to my surprise.

"You told me that you had all your friends and your life here."

"I told you everybody was dying on me. I was alone, and all I have is a job that, although making me feel productive, makes me more enemies and lands me in nothing but predicaments. I am not satisfied and I don't feel fulfilled," he said with a tone that made me feel he was tired of life. "Before you came along, I was almost ready to give up. I was planning some sort of escape where I could just bow out and leave this life."

"Well, what about all your stuff? Were you planning on letting that go too?"

"No, I would liquidate everything and go away forever, sailing into the sunset," he said, hypnotized by the melodious sound of his sails in his ears.

It appeared that his plan and my plan were almost identical. The question still remained: Was I going to sail away with Eric, or would I be sailing solo?

I almost wanted to shake my head that there was something way too easy about this and so many things that could go wrong.

"Well, you can't liquidate everything, fake your death, and then sail away into the sunset. It just doesn't work that way."

"You can if you have some help. I have this beautiful island I bought off the coast of Belize. It is a beautiful five hundred eleven acres of land with a resort built in."

"Nah, you are just being ridiculous." I was beginning to feel conned. This was a story I normally would say to somebody.

"What is the name of the island?"

"Centaurus. I rebaptized the island," he said with his goofy, dreamlike smile.

"This is way too funny," I added. "So we fake your death and move to Belize to run a getaway resort?"

"Yup!"

"I need to hear the logistics on how this is going to work, and I guess I will deal with finding the perpetrator as we go along," I said, convinced there was still something more going on.

"I have a trust set up. All my possessions are supposed to go to my nonprofit called Centaurus, which is a group in charge of ecology and conservation in third-world countries. This trust will fund our venture in Belize. I also have monies reserved in offshore accounts."

"So if you really die, I will be basically screwed to the point of being penniless," I said, disappointed about how faulty this plan was.

"I am not going to die," he said as if he had a solid, well-thought-out plan.

"Well, what is the idea on that front? Are you going to fake a drowning accident or something?"

"I have been planning this for a year or so. I have a friend who used to work for a pharmaceutical company. Since he has been retired, he kind of has had the hobby of developing male-enhancement drugs, mostly using plant and animal extracts," he said matter-of-factly.

"I am beginning to feel that the golden age is something of a rebirth. Who would have known that some choose to make this the most productive years of their lives! That is fearsome," I said, astounded, thinking that old people should really rest, but hey, who am I to stand in the ways of productivity?

"We are a force to be reckoned with." Eric flashed his saber-tooth smile.

"Has he been giving you stuff all this time to try out?" I asked, just realizing his prowess could have been a fake all this time.

"No, no, all this is natural, baby! If I was on male enhancement, you sweet cakes would not leave my bed," he said, with so much bravado that his chin turned upward, winking his wrinkled dimple. I held my hand to my mouth and started giggling but soon elevated to full-blown laughter.

"Well, what happens if you really die?" I insisted, not really liking his plan.

"The drug I will use will simply make me appear dead for a few hours."

"Well, what after that? What if something goes wrong?" I never worry about things like this, but I was worried then. I was so used to pretending that I began to believe my own persona (*no bueno*).

"You have to have faith that things will be all right," he simply said with conviction.

"How is it that a man such as yourself, so self-righteous and morally correct, is so damn crazy in private?"

"I just don't feel like I have anything to lose anymore," he retorted as nonchalant as a pair of clean panties drying on a line.

I blinked my eyes that appeared to be permanently wide in amazement at that point.

"You know, if I brainwashed you myself, you still would not be as crazy as you are," I said.

"I am a clear descendant from my uncle, a clear glutton for punishment. He had a strong reputation for being crazy himself. It's a family trait!" he said proudly and completely unabashed about something that he really shouldn't be proud of.

"Well, if you die, you know I will be completely destitute, and if you get caught faking your death, I believe there is jail time for you, isn't there?"

"Faking your own death is not a crime. It's what you normally would do afterward that is illegal. But I will take care of you. It is part of the plan."

"Eric, I don't really like your plan. There is a lot that can go wrong. I don't like it for you, and I don't like it for myself," I said, not sure if I was being self-preserving or actually caring.

"Well, you don't really have a choice, do you? Besides, this was your plan, not mine, remember?"

"I could just walk away. I could kill you right now and save us both the trouble."

"Or you can do it and live happily ever after, with me off the coast of Belize," he said, convinced that would be the outcome. "Well, I tell you what—why don't we get you tomorrow that new car you wanted? Would that help sweeten the deal?"

I felt hoodwinked at this point and stuck in the labyrinth of my own doing.

Dawn snuck up on us as we spoke and plotted; the sunlight was a cheery omen of things to come, but would things really come?

Chapter 20

SACRIFICE

"I took some of you, and you took some of me, so now we can both walk in the other's shoes for a little bit," said the sage.

"I feel different," said Acaricia.

"So do I," said the sage.

"Do you not have any physical desires other men have?"

"I do, Acaricia, but that doesn't mean I must act upon them. I make sacrifices in order to attain a certain level of enlightenment. I can't be a sage if earthy banal matters control me. I must be above that. Then how do you deal with the need? Do you ask this because you fear I may take advantage of you one day?"

"It is a thought that has crossed my mind."

"Energy is not a force that can be created or destroyed. It simply changes form. Your soul, when you die, simply changes form and moves on. Your feelings are energy. They don't go away but simply change form. In a way that is what makes human relationships so complicated. I can love you one day and hate you the next. Likewise, instead of acting on my physical desires, I simply choose other ways to channel that energy so that I can be this way."

Acaricia looked at the sage, but his words were beyond her comprehension.

"Why did you choose the path of enlightenment?" she asked him.

"I didn't choose it. It was a calling." The sage always had a definitive word.

Acaricia and the sage were getting ready to walk toward the Fire Festival. It was a festival held every year in Atlantis. The sage wore his bright blue robes, and as he placed them over himself, he began to feel the evil he took from Acaricia revolting in his holy body. After a minute or so, he managed to regain composure, but it was not easy. Acaricia wore a fire red toga dress that offset beautifully her platinum yellow hair and her pale skin.

As they walked down the road, more people gathered around them in a procession down to the festival. The other sages came walking toward them, all with their sewn eyes, and the sage with the bird had acquired a new feature. She now had a third eye in the middle of her forehead, whose eyelid was wide open and able to rotate 360 degrees.

"How did you get that?" Acaricia asked, not realizing that she sounded as if she had been hit in the head and lost her ability for censorship. The sage looked over tenderly, and her past rudeness didn't appear to matter.

"The less I see, the more I see, the more I see, the more eyes I have," she said so placidly it sounded like a song. And although her speech was riddled, it was perfectly understood.

"How did you all know to agree to wear the same color robe?" Acaricia began to feel this was a stupid question.

"We wear the same color every year," said the sage with the dog in a loud cackle. "And even if we didn't, we all would still know. I can feel other people's thoughts, wishes, and desires simply by concentrating on them."

"It is a form of telepathy," said the sage with the bird.

"Some people are better at it than others," said the sage with the rabbit, continuing in on some level of unison.

"Our brains produce waves. This energy, when in sync with another, establishes communication, even when the other body isn't quite receptive," said the last sage, completing the thought.

The festival of fire honored the big volcano in the middle of the island, which brought upon them the abundance of vegetation and foods. Ninety percent of all food consumed was in some way produced by the volcano, so every year they honored the volcano with gifts and/or sacrifices that would ensure the well-being of the upcoming year and that all the commerce that occurred on the bay would be for the well-being of the entire island.

The closer they got to the middle of the island, there were performers on open space, dancing in synchrony, wearing little clothing that sparkled like the sun. They danced to the fiery rhythm of drums, resembling a flame in the wind. All movements were forged with much dedication and passion, provoking the roar of the crowd as they cheered the dancers on with gestures, clapping, and chanting.

Acaricia seemed intrigued by these people. They all possessed powers that she knew to be uncommon from her past lifetime. They had a metaphysical type of spirituality, and they all seemed extremely gifted in arts and science. Their God and way of life all seemed very cohesive and aboriginal in a way despite the mechanical advancements she had seen in the dome with the sphere and other structures.

At the very center of the island was an amphitheater, and this one, like the dome, had a floating sphere balanced on top of a crystal cup. The sphere was equidistant on all sides and appeared to be held in place by some sort of electromagnetic force, unseen to the naked eye. It rotated on an axis. Immediately behind the theater was the most impressive of active volcanoes. The force of its tremors kept at bay not only by the gods' will but also by the common goodness that all its citizens seemed to naturally have—all, of course, except Acaricia.

Acaricia remembered the entity she saw before coming to this land and how offended he was that these favorite people of his were losing their way. They worshiped a landmark and not their God.

The ceremony continued with a display of fire arrows lighting the amphitheater. The arrows were shot to animate a firework display that animated the crowd like a domino effect. It displayed first the national bird and then the scenes of the festival, followed by musical instruments, fire flowers, and so on; all this while the musicians played solos in a very melodious, continuous symphony.

Finally the sacrifices had to be made. One by one every person in the population dropped something of value into the mouth of the volcano. Some offered food offerings in gratitude for the past harvest and secretly promised to make a personal sacrifice for an equal return.

"Do you know what you will sacrifice?" asked the sage, looking at Acaricia with his marble eyes.

"I do not know if it is a sacrifice, but to me it is. I promise to try to love. I will try to open my heart to the possibility of love."

"In your case that is a very worthy sacrifice," said the sage. He finally felt contented with his newfound progress.

Chapter 21

CONVERSATIONS AND REVELATIONS

I was at the gym working out, where out of nowhere I see the brooding figure of no other than Kyle, making his way towards me.

"I need your help," said Kyle with some nerve that was beyond my understanding.

"Really? How so?" I said, affronted, waving my hands in the air, trying to disregard him, but all the same very curious as to what he needed.

"I am looking for something, and I need your help to find it. Are you in?" he said, with his usual "on an as need-to-know basis" way.

"Listen, you and I are not on good terms. Even if we were, what makes you think I can help you find what you are looking for or that I would even do such a thing for you?" I asked curtly.

Kyle sat down on a weight lifting bench and closed his eyes; he ran his hand through his hair with anxiety. It was the first time he seemed like he was open to letting me in on something, and I felt like I was at the verge of snatching that right up.

"Well, because I have helped you in the past and right now I am still here to help you, believe it or not."

"How so?"

"Well, I am here to warn you about Eric. He is not what he seems."

"Really? How is it that you know more about Eric than me, the woman who is actually living with him and sleeping with him?" I asked defensively.

"Because he isn't being honest with you."

"Well, how does any of this have anything to do with me helping you find what you are looking for?"

"Because what I am looking for Eric hides in his possession!"

My jaw dropped for a moment in surprise as some pieces were starting to come together.

"What is that?"

Kyle inched in closer to me as if he was about to tell me a secret; he popped his eyes out as if to inspire amazement and said, "It is a huge diamond...Do you remember the McEvoys and how you thought they were strange? You had Paco dig up some dirt on them, and nothing really concrete came up. Paco, on a hunch, used some alternative methods and found out what they were after."

I nodded my head for Kyle to go on.

"Alice, whose real name is Brenda, moved into the neighborhood to watch Eric and to find a very valuable stone called the Koh-I-Noor. Even though nobody has ever seen Eric with this stone, it is believed to be in Eric's possession. The McEvoys are undercover."

"You mean feds? Why do they want this stone?"

Kyle shook his head at me up and down, saying yes to me.

"It is a very special stone, not just due to its size but also because it is believed to have special powers of influence. It was first discovered in India where it was believed to have been manipulated by a survivor of Atlantis, a sage of sorts. This person had an energy deposited into the stone. The energy was supposedly extracted from a damned soul and deposited into the stone in order to help heal that individual as the crystal, over time, could purify that energy. However, this stone has a history of destruction in its path, including the story of the infamous Aladdin. The stone has been stolen numerous times, and those who have had it have been corrupted by the power in the stone and ultimately destroyed or killed by it. Greed and power have motivated all those who have owned it. But because it has been in the wrong hands for centuries, the stone has been unable to purify its energy and, instead, has been collecting more negative energy."

Kyle looked at me, trying to decide whether his words sunk into my brain or not. He was trying to see if I recognized this story, as if there was a reason why I should.

"Why do you want this stone?"

Kyle paused for a moment and reflected and then said, "Because I am the rightful owner. A long time ago, I was a survivor of a great catastrophe." Kyle looked up at me to see my reaction to his words with expectation. The room seemed to be clouded all around as if on the verge of a storm where the clouds appeared heavy and sudden rays of sunlight cleared the path to an epiphany of sorts. He continued.

"One where there was a series of earthquakes that led to a huge volcanic eruption that destroyed the island where I lived. I needed all my positive energy in order to survive, so I grabbed a piece of coal from the volcanic eruption and gave it this negative energy I drew out from this woman. This is the energy it now has. Over time, the coal took its natural course of action and became this grandiose diamond coveted by many. It is surprising to me how much beauty was created out of tragedy. In either case, I was unable to keep the coal by my side during all the havoc and have been looking for it and the survivors of my island ever since then. It has been a long time and a long journey here, where, for one reason or another, I have been always missing out in attaining what belongs to me."

"You have been on this quest for a long time. You've been recruiting people to help you find this stone?"

"Yes, but only people who are survivors of the island," he said.

Kyle spoke with a demeanor that made me realize he was not joking around. As crazy as his story sounded, I instinctively believed it because despite my black heart, the truth is always something that stands on its own two legs, and even if it isn't clear at first, over time, it always comes to the surface. The truth is something that cannot be hidden forever.

"You were trying to recruit me. Do you believe I am a survivor of this island?" I asked, pretending not to know or rather still trying to be convinced some more by him.

"I know you are," he replied with the certainty of a rock being solid.

"How can you tell?" I asked, testing him.

Once more he looked me point blank in the inky darkness of my eyes and said, "We all have the markings that are distinctive to our race. Most survivors of the island do not age. They do not live normal lives for one reason or another, but mostly because they need to conceal their ability to rise from the dead and never quite die—a clear anomaly to regular people. They do possess a keen sixth sense of some sort, either because they are psychic in some way or another or they may also have strong powers of persuasion. You clearly have both. They are normally very tall and, in their own way, very attractive or beautiful, just like you. However, despite all these characteristics, one clear way to know for sure if you are a survivor is to see the watermark. You have the watermark on your right hand. I noticed this immediately that first day on the shooting range—the three raised wavy lines on your hand that tell me how you survived the fire by taking to the water. All survivors of the island have this mark as a symbol of that day's destruction. We had nowhere to go but to the water. We eluded death, and now we cannot evolve or rest to the door of death until we repay God what on that island we were unable to accomplish for him. Our race is looking for redemption." Kyle enunciated his words with such piercing drama in his self-righteous tone that he commanded the respect I had always remembered him to have as a sage, the conviction of an undeniable truth despite how fabulist in nature it sounded.

"You are the sage? You have a watermark?"

Kyle looked at me with his piercing emerald eyes; his stare was so intense it nearly made his eyes turn to the color of ink. I remembered that look from so long ago. So familiar was this feeling. Kyle unbuckled his belt and lowered his pants just enough to reveal on his hipbone the legacy of our watermark. It was identical to mine in shape, size, and texture, and without any more testing or doubting, I knew that in some way he was just like me. We were part of the same group, and it now dawned on me why he was the way he was.

I sighed and nodded for a moment, digesting all this.

"Do you remember me?" he asked as if I was still in denial of things.

"I am not sure I remember. I feel it wants to come back to me. When you live as long as we have lived, it becomes hard to have enough neurons to store all the memories of the past. If I was to be honest, maybe I forgot on purpose. It helps me live a normal life," I said sort of bluffing while I played with my hair and tried not to pull it out.

"When one has as many regrets as you do, it becomes easier to want to forget. You and I have history, M, and if my memory serves me right, I owe you. I cannot rest until I complete what I had set out long ago to accomplish." He paused for a moment as if he had reached a pivotal moment in finding me, in having this revelation.

"Have you been killed?" he asked.

"Quite a few times," I answered with a sigh. "When lust and passion come into play, things get messy, and more often than not, these walk you down the roads of jealousy and rage, and those roads are all literally dead ends."

"Well, then that explains the lack of memories. The first time I was killed, I lost quite a few memories in the process, but I was later able to remember. You can too if you'd like," he said, his eyes still looking intently at mine, and for a moment I remembered…I remembered a feeling that was once there…a purity, a warmth…and then the pain in my heart started twirling around, rejecting that feeling once more.

I wanted to cry, as I was so overwhelmed with everything. The modicum of pure feelings that still laid deep within me were trying to surface, but my black heart tried to push them back and annihilate them for my own protection. Then, again, I always hated looking like a swollen toad that had too much to drink at New Year's.

Crying was for the weak; besides, all this water and being bound by water didn't help not looking puffy now and again.

"I know you need time to process all this, but I really am here to warn you about Eric."

"You said this before, but why should I fear Eric if he loves me?" I said, being and sounding naïve.

"Because Eric is the centaur."

I looked at Kyle bewildered. I had heard this before in some way, and I also almost remembered it, but I still didn't get how this was a threat.

"Is he going to shoot me with a bow and arrow?" I asked facetiously.

"If you were betrayed by the one you loved the most, would you still be good to them?" he asked rhetorically.

I stayed quiet for a moment. I thought of all those times Eric and I were together, where things seemed to be going well. He was under my influence. He loved me. How could he not? I couldn't conceive how the man who loved me would want to hurt me. I shook my head in disbelief.

Kyle placed his hands on my shoulders and looked at me. "Eric and all his family line are cursed because of you. He blames you for all his deep-rooted sorrows. He knows who you are and has always known it. It was you who could not quite remember."

I vaguely recalled what Eric had said to me while we were in bed and I'd had that dream. He was indeed hiding something from me.

Kyle continued. "A long time ago, the Archer, who, by your association, was damned into a centaur status and unable to love again or feel any satisfaction in life, was doomed to death on that very catastrophic day. Eric is not one of us, because he actually died that day. His half-horse state couldn't swim his way out of doom, and his hooves weighed him into the bottom of the sea. You led him there. His soul later reincarnated into a very hard and callous man. It was as if he was angry and just didn't quite know why. With all that rage, it became nearly impossible for him to love, but with wisdom and knowledge, he was able to overcome and gain some insight. He too evolved into a man who used to go by the name of Bernie. On one of Bernie's journeys, he found my diamond. It is unclear to me exactly what happened, but being so close to this diamond made him see and feel the truth of you and, therefore, the truth behind himself. His wife and children suffered some sort of tragic event relating to the family curse. So has Eric, by the way." Kyle spoke suggestively at me, trying to make me feel guilty.

"Through his journals, he managed to explain and reconstruct things about life that should've really remained a secret, including the truth about you, M. The diamond has been passed down through generations in his family. He must have it somewhere. Nobody has seen it since it was exchanged for a fake on Queen Elizabeth's crown jewels."

"Really?"

"Yes. Apparently there has always been drama surrounding this diamond. The last owner to be forced to surrender the diamond was named Ranjit Singh. It became a spoil of war, and on its journey to England in 1850, the son of Ranjit, Dulip Singh, managed to exchange the diamond and hide it in one of the islands where they set port—not without an incredible risk to himself if caught. Sometime later, the diamond was located by a couple of women. One of those women was one of us. Those women were on a quest to find a stone that was believed to bestow the ability to return loved ones together even after the grave."

"Does it?"

"It is within its power, M."

"Then what happened?"

"She and her daughter recovered the diamond temporarily. Again, here the story becomes unclear as to how it ended up in a forest near Bernie's home when it was supposed to be on this island all along. It couldn't possibly be in two places at once. The story is as unclear as any of the Elvis sightings. However, what I suspect is that the diamond, in a way, holds your heart. Your most evil of sentiments lays there, wanting to be pure and good, and in some way it felt the calling of love, the calling into the reincarnated centaur, your one true love. I believe it placed itself in Bernie's way in order to reunite the two of you so that you could solve your unfinished business."

"You make it sound as though the diamond has a life of its own, that it has evolved into other things and that it has become more powerful over time."

"All things change over time, Acaricia," he said, and for that brief moment, I could not sustain his sight. My eyes were welling up again, and in one last effort to retain my emotions, I looked away into the ground, holding my hand on my heart.

"Then why do we stay the same?" I then asked.

"Are we?" he retorted, sounding as a true sage. I puckered my lips in disapproval for not getting a more direct answer. "Are you still the same woman who once took her own life when you now do everything in your power for self-preservation?"

"No," I answered, hating the fact that he had a point.

"Every time we die, we evolve and change. Change is a necessary part of life. If change is called for and we refuse to accept it, inevitably all things crumble down to the floor, destroyed by some form of death, to force change unto those who have refused it. It becomes a painful and traumatic event. Death is a form of change. You, Acaricia, should know this better than anyone. Our island is a clear example of an inevitable change for better or worse."

I hated Kyle right now. I was most certainly not into preacher types. He was so sanctimonious, so self-righteous, and I had no weapons to rebuke the truth of his words. I felt slightly defeated and was sulking and pouting as I pondered in my little corner.

"Well, what do you think I should do now?" I asked him.

Kyle looked surprised at me and then rubbed his chin between his index finger and thumb, almost as if he thought he would never get this far in his plan, or with me for that matter.

Chapter 22

THE WRONG TYPE OF LOVE

One of the archers possessed some of the most grace and charm that Acaricia had ever seen in her very short life. When he smiled, he grazed the heart with his cute dimples. His inky blue eyes and platinum hair were such an Apollonian sight. He was the stark opposite of Acaricia. He had such a jovial touch of righteousness that was exuded in every gestural movement from his body.

"He is the Archer," said the sage with the dog, as if it wasn't obvious that he was.

"Does he have a name, or is he supposed to be just 'the Archer'?"

"His birth name is Verdandious, which means 'presently,'" said the sage, with an overtly solemn tone.

"Presently. That's funny."

"Is it? Why then would somebody have named you Acaricia?"

"Yea, I suppose you're right. It was idiotic to be named caress, as in tender and loving, when that is the least I had been shown in my soul's life," Acaricia said, remembering her ever-present resentment, and the sage quickly understood he had made a mistake in pronouncing such a statement.

Acaricia was left openhearted after the sage had intervened but only just a little, yet she was so full of impetus to explore these feelings that she failed to see she needed more stealth in matters of love. But alas! When the heart is inclined, only the temerity of logic and the almighty fated destiny can stop it.

"I wish to be introduced."

"You don't need me for that, but if I do, promise me you will not drown him," said the sage, raising his eyebrows with concern.

"In life we must all make sacrifices, or so I guess," said Acaricia, rolling her eyes.

And so they walked over to the young man, and the sage introduced Acaricia to him as his prodigy.

"Oh Sage, will you bless me with your wisdom?" said Verdandious.

The sage grabbed the Archer's hand and closed his eyes, as the Archer's were still as open as a night owl. The sage with the dog still had many more tests to surpass in order to earn his full psychic sight, which, of course, meant losing his physical eyesight in the process.

The sage began to feel a surge of lofty warm feelings that waved around in his heart like the softest of velvets but then was surrounded by an intense physical pain in his legs, and it was then that he saw himself sprout horse legs and feel an enormous gauged-out hole of never-ending physical and emotional pain across his chest. The sage knew this was not a good omen for young lovers, and in his greed to succeed with Acaricia, he debated on what to say to Verdandious, for the words of a sage in Atlantis were a sacred decree, and a disappointment in love would lead to nothing but doom from Acaricia, who, the sage knew, had not come about to her fullest potential yet.

The sage opened his eyes, looked at Verdandious, and gave him an encouraging smile and then proceeded to excuse himself without a word, cleverly avoiding a lie. It was then that a young couple offered their firstborn child to the volcano. Acaricia felt a pinch in her chest, a small indescribable feeling for the loss of someone she didn't know. A single tear rolled down her eye. The sage looked at her with a similar sentiment.

"I wish they hadn't done that. I shall see you at home. I must take care of something," said the sage to Acaricia and the Archer, using his telepathy instead of his actual voice.

The two youngsters looked at one another and walked off from the busy roads, the feasting boisterous pedestrians, and the overall holiday fire festivities.

They both walked like this until the silence turned awkward. Neither of them had any idea what to say.

Acaricia looked over at him and giggled nervously. As an impulse of both excitement and fear, she giggled again and ran into the woods, looking at him suggestively. Her instinct drove her to fear men, and naturally, running away from one whom she liked seemed appropriate.

He chased her, playing along with her seduction. He caught on to her by a tree, and with the impetus of the fire in his heart, he stole the most passionate of kisses. Her hair caressed his bare shoulder, and in wavelike movement, Acaricia hypnotized him for a few moments and then playfully eluded his amorous embrace. Acaricia opened the depths of her throat and, as if with the most potent of lights, illuminated the entire forest with her melodic song.

"Physical penetration is not enough for my thirsty feelings to sate,
I feel the clamor for the sweetness within me,
A relish conserved for only a pure self-sacrificing love;
I am bound to you to create
The holy union of wetness to my steed,
A hellish conserve for a purity that effaces evil."

By the end of Acaricia's lovely chant, Verdandious was so afflicted with intense feelings of love and so weakened by such that he crawled to Acaricia, begging for her embrace, and even though she wanted to resist, she too felt the pull between her hips as to compel a union that both satisfied her body as well as her newfound emotions.

Her red dress was both pushed down to her waist to reveal the stout roundness of her bosom and then pushed up to reveal the deliciousness of her sex. Verdandious was not being shy about pressing his enormous penis against her leg, awaiting reception into her little sex oiled with the moisture of lust. Acaricia kissed him in an immortal way, combining her soul unto his and sealing a pact of love that would endure time. The pain from the puncture of penetration brought upon Acaricia a tear, and although this was not the first time Acaricia met a man, it was the first time she willingly acceded to receive one. Verdandious's cock was as hot as the fire on his arrow and as hard as the steel from his bow. All these exciting and new sensations made it hard for Acaricia to control her desires, and the buildup was as inevitable as an eruption to a volcano. Her vagina increased in temperature, pouring out an abundance of liquid. It was like a waterfall drenching his cock and soiling his clothes with the very welcomed climax of pleasure. The feeling encased Verdandious, and with such a snug, wet, hot little space caressing with love his glorious member, he too released his seed unto her soil. He collapsed on top of Acaricia, and both hearts pounded in unison that they were gloating to lovers' glee in hurried wings to the reel of never-ending contentment.

It was then that the creature from the night, the creature from the underworld, dragged Acaricia into the water and forever cursed Verdandious to be a centaur so their souls could not match up for more than a little at a time, with no real satisfaction.

Chapter 23

SURPRISE, SURPRISE!

The Lazarus effect...This was what I thought to be an enormously stupid way to go out blazing in the wrath of fire.

At dawn, after Eric's morning esoteric rituals, that admittedly took some time to get used to, he took me into his library. The smell of woodlands was still very pungent and present. He gave me his saber-tooth grin and handed me a dark, hunter-green book that bore the title, *Necromancy for Beginners*. I did my best to hide my aversion for this. It was almost like having an urgent need to burst out and pee after somebody has had a nefarious case of diarrhea in the only bathroom around. I held back my facial expressions like one holds breath in a stinky situation.

Eric closed his eyes, and for a moment without him looking, I exhaled, searching for relief. He sat cross-legged in front of his fire and stared at it intently, trying to meditate or enter some sort of trance state. He urged me to sit beside him, and with a forced smile, I attempted to copy what he was doing. We sat like this in silence for what seemed a long time.

"Try and concentrate on the fire, and just forget everything else for now," he said.

I played along, the thing I knew how to do best. At a point in our trance, I started to see things in the fire. It was really hard to discern if this was my own psychic abilities or part of what Eric was showing me.

I saw myself speaking to a crowd of people in a light-gray room.

"We all are molded from the ash and clay of the earth. We are figures and characters of a theater, who are always performing until the earth claims us again to close our eyes and rest from the adventure of life," I was saying to them.

I knew I had a vision of Eric's funeral. I also saw Mr. Denton there. Even though I had never met him before, I knew this was Eric's client, the alleged pedophile.

After we were done meditating, Eric got up and smiled at me. He had this eerie smile I had never seen on his face. It was almost demonic.

"This book I gave you, I want only you to use it if I actually die. The instructions to summon me are on page sixty-four. You will turn on the fire and meditate like you did just now. Do you think you can do that?" he asked in a very serious tone.

"I thought you said you weren't going to die."

"If I do, I have things I want to say to you, so you must summon me if I do."

I must have looked visibly upset to him because he grabbed both my hands in his and walked me over to the love seat that was in the room. He had me sit on it, and he kneeled before me, looking at me intently in the eyes.

"You know I love you," he said.

His words sounded so genuine my heart began to shriek in pain as my eyes welled up on the verge of an oncoming tear. My chest was expanding; something inside it was growing, and it was my heart. I sighed deeply to alleviate my emotions and hold them back as best I could. I couldn't speak, so I simply nodded at him to relay my understanding.

"If I die and you don't contact me, my soul will reach out from the afterlife to pull your feet at night so that you can never have a restful sleep again. I will haunt you for the rest of your days and scare the life out of you, I promise."

"OK, but if this is so important to you, why don't you just tell me now instead of waiting until you die?"

"Life follows a sequence and so does death. You can't rush things, M. They just happen when they need to."

There was a long contemplative pause between us and then he continued. "Do you trust me?"

"No," I said without any hesitation in my voice.

Eric stood up and took a step back, appalled by my response.

"My heart be still," he said, holding his hand to his chest in an exaggerated sense of drama and with a touch of corniness that could only come from his generation.

"Don't be so sensitive about it. I just don't think this is going to work. I can't really be expected to trust your judgment when you are so crazy!"

We both laughed heartily.

"What can I do for you to trust me, for me to reassure you?" he asked.

I stood up and, looking visibly upset, turned my back on him and said, It's just that if you die, I will have nothing. I don't know if that matters to you, but if you care about me, you would do something about this. I've grown attached to you, Eric, and considering that you are the first nice man in my life, it is hard for me to let go. It is hard for me to think that I could lose you in this outrageous getaway plan," I said, taking my hands to my face and pinching my nose hair so that I may cry a tear or two. Eric approached me from behind and hugged me, trying to comfort me.

"Listen, why don't we get married?" he asked.

My eyeballs nearly dropped out of their sockets and, with a glazed and nearly speechless low tone of voice, said, "Are you sure?"

"Only if you promise to contact me from the dead if I do die. Besides, if I die, at least I will have a peaceful conscience that I did the right thing here. I am definitely not getting any younger, and I do want to spend the rest of my days with you. I have nothing to lose by marrying you. What do you say?"

"I can't do it."

All along this was my fallback plan, but then why was I betraying it? This was a completely logical solution here, but somehow it just didn't feel right. His words were too perfect. It all just seemed too convenient. I couldn't be completely certain this was my magic working on him or the secret agenda Kyle had suggested Eric had for me.

"Are you going to make me beg?" he asked with his signature saber-tooth smile and a tinge of seduction. He almost looked like a cute little tiger cub. Ugh! I couldn't believe this actually was working a little on me.

"You do have to remember the Island of Centaur awaits us in the end. We can enjoy our money and live easy. This is our happily ever after, M. C'mon, babe, let's do this!"

"Well, I guess we will have to have a quick wedding. Do you think we can do this in a week? Who will we invite as our guests? Oh, there is just so much to do."

"Hold it, bridezilla! I was just suggesting we go down to the courts and have a civil ceremony to make it legal. We have the rest of our lives to celebrate. I'll buy you that car you want, as a wedding present," he said, dangling that carrot in front of me to sweeten the deal up, enough for me to be unable to refuse.

"Well, I feel like I just got a reward for being slapped in the face, but OK," I said, rolling my eyes with resignation.

A few days later…

I was doing laps around the neighborhood, probably looking like a happy ol' dog sticking his tongue out of a car window. I looked into my rearview mirror and saw I had inherited Eric's signature smile. It is amazing how over time couples resemble each other. I was having one of those moments where you feel you accomplished what you wanted and had set out to do. The glee was a feeling that just poured out of every one of the senses I had on my face. It was that uncontrollable, and quite frankly, I didn't want to control anything, anyways.

Some of the neighbors around me, the retired ones who were home, just stared agape as they watered their manicured lawns or crept up the windows to see what the ruckus was about, like cats looking at the birds from the inside of their homes, hopeful to hunt what they desire.

The McEvoys were no exception; they had a mixture of incredulity and envy—Alice (or should I say Brenda) more so than her spouse. I relished in these feelings, and the wings of my heart fluttered as I gloated with shamelessness. I was making my final last dance before the ta-da moment.

After breakfast, I wore an antique cream dress with old-fashioned lace trimming on the edges. It resembled a doily that you would see at your grandmother's house. I must admit it was not the look I was going for, but Eric insisted. I could see this was a presage of the future—his word and my compliance—or perhaps this was all a pretense just to get him hooked. Even I had a hard time seeing how I was going to pull this off. When a plan has these many moving parts, it is best to keep all the possibilities open.

It had taken us a few days to get our marriage license, and Eric, despite his original enthusiasm, did look uneasy about the entire situation. When he presented his deceased wife's death certificate, I noticed how especially uncomfortable he was. He shifted around in his seat as the clerk asked him the standard questions about his name and past marriages. He had the worst case of ants in his pants that the clerk had ever seen. Finally, the clerk asked him if he was mentally competent and if he had come there of his own will without coercion.

"No," he responded as solemn as death.

The clerk blinked her eyes as if this were a first to her, and I just held my breath and opened my mouth, expecting humiliation on the spot.

Then after a few moments, the clerk asked, "Are you sure, Mr. Lieberman?"

Eric composed his jittery body and began to cackle like a true lunatic, causing a huge level of disruption in the office. "I am totally crazy, and this woman caused it," he said, laughing heartily. I sighed and began to laugh with him to relieve my embarrassment.

"Forgive him. He is just incorrigible, and he hasn't had his therapy today," I said in a wry tone.

The clerk pushed her glasses up and laughed while shaking her head to the sides. "Well, it seems like crude humor. Will keep you two going."

She smiled and signed off on the marriage certificate and wished us the best of luck.

Eric held my hand as we walked down the parking lot; he was walking tall like a soldier marching to battle. He had the goofiest smile; it was the smile of a cocktail of mermaid magic and sex! I gloated on the inside about my prowess and clicked my heels along his side.

The ceremony proceeded without any incident, and we had two strangers to be our witnesses. At the end, I walked back into the car wearing, what I would say, a very modest ring. Eric promised to get me a better one later. My black heart was brewing with resentment at this, yet I still smiled and played along.

"I have a surprise for you!" said Eric as he winked his eye at me.

My eyes bugged out, scared. "Oh really! And what might that be? A lovely midnight chant by a fire on the beach? Voodoo lessons? I can't wait!" I must admit I could have done better at concealing my dislike for his hobbies.

He looked over recriminating me but laughed it off.

"You'll see," he said with his signature grin.

When we got to the house, he picked me up in his arms, and as he did, some bone possibly on his back cracked. I smiled as he made a slight grimace.

"Oh my! How chivalrous!"

"Ah, there is more to come of that, Mrs. Lieberman!" The excessive pride in which he said these words made me cackle.

He carried me up one step at a time, using extreme hesitation as if not to fall backward, embarrassing himself. I held my breath, pulling in all my muscles in a very lame attempt to make myself lighter, but of course, that was not possible. I was vulnerable, and I knew it, but I still smiled, hoping for the best.

When we got to his faux animal-print-embellished room, I noticed a few differences. The bed was covered with rose petals, there were red candles lit everywhere that you could possibly set one on, and on the nightstand was a very conspicuous needle and rubber cord, the type you would normally see a drug addict use.

"What is that?" I asked, looking scared.

"That is my surprise."

"Oh."

I felt as though the room was spinning out of control, but it was more like Eric attempting to gently toss me onto the bed.

"I must admit I am surprised! Is this some type of new foreplay?" I asked, sounding naïve.

"You are just too cute," he said, laughing.

He grabbed the rubber cord in his hands and snapped it menacingly. He then made a strange jerky striptease for me that gave my eyes the same intense pain they get when they stare directly into the sun.

"You are by far the most unique man I have ever been married to!" I said, laughing.

"Good times, my love. I am just trying to entertain you!"

"In all my years, I have never seen the likes of this, and I am actually scared," I said, bobbing my head up and down as I gritted my teeth the way one does when tensed at a roller-coaster ride.

Eric then grabbed the cord and wrapped it along the base of his limp penis, choking the thing.

"Does that hurt?" I asked, thinking it must cut off his circulation easily.

"Nah!" he said with mock bravado.

He then grabbed the syringe and stabbed his shaft with it, as you normally see when people get adrenaline shots. To my surprise, Eric didn't even flinch.

"What is that?"

"It's a peptide called Tx2-6."

"Eric, I need a stupefied answer."

"It is venom from a Brazilian wandering spider. It causes paralysis."

"Oh! Sounds wonderful and deathly romantic! Is that safe for my vagina?"

"I hope not!" he said like a child testing out a new toy invention. We laughed together, and then I laughed even harder, rolling around the roses as I saw his cock swell up and stiffen to a ninety-degree angle and point at me as if saying to me, "Hey you! Here I come!"

Eric's penis looked as though it had a mind of its own. He jumped into the bed, eager to test himself out and, with a toothy grin, took me into his arms and kissed me. His bulging erection was creeping between my legs as he kissed me. His cock was instinctual by nature and seeking out the warmth and wetness to cocoon and envelop itself; it was of the most comforting desire, only second to a mother's womb. Despite all the awkwardness of a moment before, I still felt receptive toward him. His steely hardness was calling me, and inch by inch it made its way inside me, causing me to gasp. I could feel him poking all the way to the end of the tunnel; it knocked on the door out of courtesy, but he already had the key to unlock me. Whole was not enough of a word to describe how I felt with his cock inside me, a complete sensation of sun on the skin, an intoxicating wetness that rubbed on the heat of pulsating blood to my sex. I breathed, and he breathed, enamored by the union, the sensation; we held each other together tightly, so snug there was no room between us. My heart started to ache with this feeling, but this time rather than fighting the feeling, I surrendered to it, and for the first time in a very long time, the coldness in my body was gone, and the energy of passion in my red blood suffocated all the bad in my past and filled it with a warmth. I could feel the sun in my heart and the joy rubbed onto my sex, euphoric and delirious, building rapidly and inching in closer with every thrust inside me to a climax that I could almost grasp until the next thrust. Again and again I galloped, pushing into him to reach his orgasms and mine. I panted in his ear, he groaned in mine, and our chests heaved in unison to our final destination, where all our limbs relaxed after the almighty and sought-after release.

Breathe…I lay heavy on the heart and closed my eyes for an instant.

Eric's erection would still not go down, as I could feel it inside me, nor did he really move much for that matter. He still lay on top of me, and I could feel his heart racing and his blood boiling. He began to convulse, and I could feel this intense pain inside me, perhaps a sympathy pain but a strong pain that spread uniformly across the body like the webbing together of the veins. I felt compelled to spasm, and the pain was causing me nausea. Eric heaved and gagged violently on top of me, until this thick, yellowy, stew-like consistency came out of his mouth and onto my hair and shoulder. I felt as though I was swimming in a completely new and appalling wetness. The smell made me gag, and the pain began to drown me. I tried to calm down or even say something, but nothing came out. I was heaving so quickly, avoiding the need to yak, that I couldn't have possibly uttered a word.

Eric's body began to stiffen to the same degree of his penis. There were no limp muscles that I could feel, and his body began to feel heavier by the second, burying me deeper into the mattress, unable to move from the filth and the weight. I was a creature of water, and I was now drowning...

"Help," I said in a bleak voice.

Chapter 24

THE SKY IS ANGRY, AND LIFE IS ON FIRE

After sometime on a given day...

Acaricia looked at the sky and knew it was time to go.

"Acaricia, come to me. Play with my hair like you used to. Play me like the wind in my flute. It is your touch that has a power that no other can produce." His voice begged for what his heart wanted. In sweet tender isolation, two bodies and two souls cried out that they were left outside at the door.

Running, she came with those big chimerical eyes that mirrored the sea in depth and color, not to mention in vastness.

"I could fall into your eyes, Acaricia," said the centaur.

Silence fell to her tongue, but words were not needed, for what her eyes said was far deeper than any sound from her melodious throat.

"Why are you always so silent, Acaricia? I always wonder if you really love me. I always wonder what you think. If you are this silent, are you really there? If you are this silent, can you be anymore? You could be anywhere. Unlike you, I cannot read minds. I was not born with the gift to see beyond my eyes. I am just me and my humble words. Appease me, my love. Let me know you are here. Let me hear your voice that takes over my body and my soul, for my heart and mind are already yours," he said, pleading, almost like a little boy begs his mother for more affection.

And so, Acaricia's sweet melodious voice hummed for her vocal cords to awaken her throat that seemed to be sleeping. Her voice grew louder from the lowest point in her throat, producing a giant sound wave. It stretched itself out like one does in the morning after a long night of sleep with stiff muscles. The look of joy on his face was almost that of orgasm but far deeper in happiness than momentary pleasure.

The sounds from her voice were so piercing and delightful that the vibrations spoke to his bones in volumes but not in words. The air caressed him with those same vibrations like a body massage. As her voice grew louder, it echoed in echelons of tonal keys, like that of a symphony arriving at a climax. She didn't speak to him in words, but he could hear what she was saying. He could hear her so clearly in his thoughts that it was like one and the same.

"Oh my love, let my voice touch you and embrace you like a glove. Allow my presence to touch you as it sings to your frequency. You know my silence speaks volumes, for my voice is your doom. I see the end is coming, and if you look into my eyes, I will take you to see."

The symphony from her throat continued, and Acaricia's face was filled with nothing but destruction; it was so hard to see the danger and so irresistible not to follow.

He grabbed her hands, which were so smooth like alabaster. They guided him like soft waves crashing against the sea. Acaricia moved as graceful as a feather in the wind by the tips of her toes, at the rhythm of her tunes—the same movement the centaur mimicked as they moved together as one.

As they stepped onto the cobblestones outside, her hair flickered in the wind as dark as a starless night. Shining bright as the sun, her hair became a mistress to the air.

"Acaricia, my love, if you are taking me to my doom, are you coming with me? For I will not to be content without you, even if that means my end. You must come with me even to that point after my end."

Acaricia turned to him with her onyx eyes, which were so glassy and empty that they pierced any loving heart with pain. Verdandious followed her with all four hoofs clattering on the floor behind them.

By then Acaricia had mastered the art of telepathy and had acquired some psychic powers of her own.

The value ring she still had on her finger showed her that any desire increased the strength of her enchantment and that real love through physical union intensified her power. Her power had become so strong that she no longer needed words to control her subjects. Like the horsehair worm controls the cricket and forces its host to drown against its natural instinct for survival, so did she overpower her prey.

Acaricia held Verdandious's hand as she led him into the water...

The night smoked. The fire lit up the sky, but the night sat down with the fattest cigar, and from the mouth of the volcano puffed clouds of ash. Its rumble and destruction muffled the screams of all the Atlantyans and scared all into the sea, who were not killed by the volcanic action.

As evolved as they were, their God was happy not to save them of their destruction. All the souls that would be claimed to the underworld were drowning in the sea of bleak hopes. Those who survived had to adapt to the water that damned them. Their hands became webbed, and scales began to grow so they could sway under the vast and dense water. Their fins evaded their fate into the underworld, and the gills on each side of their necks allowed them to breathe under water, until adaptation was fully completed.

The Atlantyans were not a race to be departed from the earth, and although seemingly eradicated, they endured, spreading out to all corners of the world with their knowledge and advancement in their own mysterious ways for centuries to come.

Love binds. It supersedes our bodies. It defies reason, and it is part of our spirits. It crosses over time and doesn't come about in space, for above it all, in happiness and in joy, or sorrow and in torture, it continues to exist even though life itself ends.

Even when words are not much comfort, feelings stand strong, almost unbearable to control.

In the tempest of fire, as all was being erupted through the skies, in destruction too did beauty lay, holding her anger in such a calm dissension of light. The fury overcame them all; even those who survived were forever changed in the fire to take to the water.

Chapter 25

THE SKY FALLS DOWN

I could see the storm clouds forming in the background. They resembled chaotic turbines trying to reach the ground for destruction. It rained heavy for a minute, ceased, and then drizzled; some sunlight came out, and then the dark clouds reached out again, covering any ray of hope.

The ambulance and the police came to the house, and of course, all the neighbors, including the McEvoys, were there too. It was as though we were the hot topic of the town. Somebody called the local news to report on the oddness of the case, or maybe they were there because of Eric's standing in the community, who knows.

By the time I was carried out in a gurney—yes, I was too traumatized to speak from the ordeal and numb from being in the same position over a period of time—hours had passed. I was, however, pretty capable of listening to my surroundings.

"Local man died at home during what appeared to be a sex act with his younger lover. It is currently unknown what caused it," said the newscaster.

I was rolled out covered in barf and with my hair crusted to my face. The camera crew tried to take a close-up of my unattractive state. I simply blinked my eyes and glared as hard as I could and, in my silence, screamed out, "Fuck off," as my upper lip twitched.

The voices in the background all murmured, as if it was too proper to speak out loud what they really thought.

"I saw this coming," said the hushed voice of a man.

"Well, younger woman, older man...there is only one reason for that, and we all know what that is!" said the voice of another woman.

"Wow! I can't believe she killed him. Must've been some sex," said yet another man as if he longed to have "that" type of sex.

"Poor Eric. I can't believe he ended this way, swindled by a younger woman. Men are weak!" said yet another woman in the crowd.

As I listened to this in my catatonic state, I just wanted to get up with a steel bat, crack that video camera that was in my face, and crack the newscaster in the jaw and smash it in pieces until it reached a bloody pulp and go on to all those nosey neighbors one by one and hit them in the knee, the face, but, for the most part, crack their hands for pointing the finger.

After about a day in the hospital, I was more recovered from my original state of mind, at least enough to be discharged. The police came to question me as to what had happened in the bedroom. I could tell they were making their best attempt at being delicate about the situation.

"So Miss Olivares, how is it that you just screw a man to death?" he said in a boxy voice, the type you would hear when in a soundproof small room with no furniture.

"Well, if you ever had sex with me at Eric's age, you would see what happens to you!" I said with a glare while I flicked my nails. "Oh, and it's Misses *Lieberman*!" Of course, my attitude was enunciated here.

"I'm sorry. I just need to get to the facts. When did you and Eric get married?"

"The day he died."

"Can you help me understand a few things?"

"I can try, but as you can see, I am not at my best."

The detective paced a few steps and then asked, "A few weeks ago, Eric had an accident where, if luck was not by his side, he could have perhaps died. Then on his wedding day, he dies during sex. Don't you think that is odd?"

"Well, when death follows somebody, there is no escape, Detective," I said with a smirk.

"Can you tell me step by step what happened the day Eric died?"

I sighed as if weighed by the burden of his words. "Eric wanted to impress me on our wedding day and decided to try out some experimental male-enhancement drug given to him by one of his friends. The man went hard, stayed hard, orgasmed, and then stiffened up even more on top of me until you guys found us."

I could tell the man wanted to laugh, but in a death situation, he felt inappropriate in doing so. He looked away from me and walked toward the window. He cleared his throat. "Do you know who gave him the male-enhancement drug?"

"No, I think Eric was too modest to speak about such things openly with me."

"Hmm…I see." He paused and then continued: "Were you aware that Eric's body was taken from the morgue?"

"Really?" I said.

"Yes, don't you find that odd?"

"Well, of course, the dead don't just get up and walk away now, do they?"

"The medical examiner was getting ready to do an autopsy, and he simply just couldn't find the body. So his death is under investigation, especially due to all the conspicuous events surrounding his life, leading up to his end."

I remained quiet for a few moments.

"Do you know if Eric had a life-insurance policy?"

"No, I don't."

"Do you know if you are the sole heir of his assets?"

"I am not sure, but I am legally his wife."

"Well, if you can think of something that could help us clear up this investigation, just call."

He handed me a business card and walked away, clapping his heels against the linoleum floor. It was as if he said, "Congratulations, now I am going to prove you did this."

Kyle came and got me at the hospital a few hours later. He was very quiet for the most part, in his usual I-don't-talk-much-about-myself way.

In his preferred style of communication—telepathy—he said, "Will you be OK?"

"I don't know yet. I am still not sure of how things are playing out, and I also have no idea about Eric. I am still waiting to see what will happen next. I am not even sure if he is dead right now."

Kyle sighed and, in his silence, was avoiding the dreaded "I warned you."

When we got home, I noticed that things seemed off. The cedarwood scent of Eric was gone. Everything seemed there but out of place; maybe it was because people had been in and out of the house due to Eric's death or maybe because of something else. I couldn't feel the familiarity in the house anymore; I felt more like a stranger with memories of the past.

Kyle, this time, took out a little stone from his pocket that was concealed in a little burlap pouch. It was black and shiny, like a marble. This time he walked around the house with it. His steps were slow, yet assured.

In our usual way, I asked, "What is that?"

"It finds energy in inert objects—like the diamond I am looking for. The stone will grow hotter as it gets closer to an energy source. This time I don't actually have to look around like I did before when Eric was in an accident. The more energy an object has, the hotter the stone will grow."

While Kyle walked through the library, the stone got warmer and warmer and started to look like a small piece of coal that was lit. I followed out of curiosity, because if there was such a diamond that you could hold with two hands, how come I hadn't seen it or even been introduced to it? Diamonds are a girl's best friend!

Kyle got closer to the fireplace, and again it was very noticeable that the energy was coming from that one spot. Again I removed the fire poker from its place to reveal the space behind the fireplace where I once hid from sight. Kyle held the stone close to the ground, but the stone appeared not to have any special reaction to that spot. Then he held it toward the walls of this secret hiding place, and then again toward the fireplace, but only when in the fireplace did any reaction occur on the stone. Kyle walked through the rest of the house, and although the stone got lukewarm in some spots where some talismans were and other artifacts of dubious nature, like a little wooden mallet, or some conspicuous herbs, the energy from these things were not as strong or enough to be the diamond we were looking for.

"Do you really think there is hope for me?" I asked, changing the subject.

"Yes. Change is always a possibility as long as there is life to live and you're willing to take the risk."

I felt cold, the way I always felt despite the weather. Kyle gave me a brotherly hug, the way no other man except him has ever given me. It was the purity within him that feed into me, into my blackened heart, and it warmed me with a longing for all those things that I've missed out on because of my deviant ways. Kyle stayed with me in Eric's house to support me. I felt that since we had found each other, we were now again going to be companions or rather the seeker and the guide like in the very, very old days. This was a very meaningful gesture in this time of need for me.

I went about town later, running my usual errands, checking my account, and going through my PO box. There was a letter in a red envelope that read, "Good-bye."

I got an odd chill going up my spine as if my worst fear had manifested itself. I didn't need to be psychic to know who this was from. I didn't want to believe it. I tucked it into my purse and wanted to head back home to Kyle. It definitely stunk to have feelings. Where art thou, my blackened heart, to rescue me from disappointment?

I was walking slowly, dragging my feer because for the first time in a while (and I had the years behind me to be able to say that!), I was actually ready to admit I had fallen for someone. It didn't matter that I tried to keep these feelings to myself; the result was the same, and the feelings of devastation were the same too.

I felt that for a moment I couldn't perceive reality, but then I looked over at my new car. It seemed like a mirage, or maybe it was the car next to mine. The closer I walked to it, I stared agape in disbelief.

"Is this your car, ma'am?" asked an overweight tow driver with a smart-ass look on his face and sweat on his brow. Yes, the bastard didn't even say he was sorry.

"Yea, what are you doing?"

I was beside myself. My getaway car! I shrieked on the inside.

"Your vehicle is impounded. Good luck," he snarled.

My legs started to give in with weakness as he drove away with my dream of happily ever after, and I simply went down on my knees, raising my hands to the sky in the bleakest, most desperate "Noooooooo, aaaaugh! Grrrrrrrrrrrrrr!"

It took me almost an hour to recover from that loss. It's surprising to see how the older you are, the more sentimental you become, no matter how you try and hide it. In this case, I was doing an awful job of concealing anything at all, and my bag, my knees, my heart, and everything else was on the floor in pieces. I wanted to reach resignation, but I knew I was just not enlightened enough as a person to be there. That road, the emotional high road, was hidden in the outskirts of a town that was just too high for me to reach.

Kyle thought he could recruit me to be part of the people of light. I was not there. I was not that person, and if I didn't know about our past and us, I would have just assumed he was a cult leader recruiting some lackey to manipulate me for his selfish purposes.

All the pieces were just falling into place, the puzzle was coming together, and the picture was becoming clearer and clearer. How could I of all people not see this coming? I was even warned, yet I refused to see what was always right in front of me.

I wanted to shed a tear, and for an instant, my eyes welled up. I fought it for a moment, and then one minute drop, a modicum of pain rolled down to my lips, and I tasted the bitterness and rage inside me. I grabbed that force inside and stood up and screamed out loud in the most scratchy, annoying shriek my normally melodious voice could allow.

The pedestrians who walked along the streets near me were deeply affected by my wrath, and as I walked to the bus stop, because, of course, my antiquated flip phone was at home to call anybody, I could see the effects of my vocals on a couple who immediately started to fight in a heated rage about him leaving the toilet seat up, and then they went on to how much money she spent on junk like her anti-wrinkle cream!

A man stormed into a local store to complain merely for the pleasure of belittling the hardworking lower class, just to give himself a sense of grandeur. A little boy ran to the magazine stand and tore the newspapers apart, probably because he was always alone and misunderstood, and in turn, the man tending to the stand started screaming and yelling as he attempted to slap the boy.

All this energy...the chaos was lifting up from my core, engulfing me. The world was angry with me; I could feel it boiling and rumbling under my feet. Powerful like a sea of fire, it gurgled and belched, stinking like the blackest of waters from the sewer.

My ring was becoming heated from my powers, the ones that laid dormant up until this point in my story. I sat and concentrated until those very dark waters boiled up from the depths and out onto the streets, flooding the road. Finally, I stared at a man with glasses possibly in his forties, and just from my intense look alone, I scared him enough to take a step forward onto the street and trip into the sewer water, where he fell facedown into his final liquid breath. I smiled finally; this was enough for my satisfaction. My black heart was content, and despite its empty color did a backflip in my chest.

Later in the week...

"Only Eric knew life too well. He was a fortunate soul to have labored so arduously and to be able to reap the harvest of his efforts in the most sybaritic of ways. Eric was a loyal friend, a lover of humanity, a good husband, and a model citizen, whose moral character could not be stained. Eric had a happy and fulfilling life with little regrets, but he, like anything living in this earth, was not exempt from the 'last hoorah of life,' the final leap, the last breath of ash that still burns in our mourning hearts." As I said these words, a complete déjà vu moment flashed at me.

I felt as though I were a ghost running through the corridors of the house, lamenting in the corners. I wanted to feel the sunlight, but all the curtains were drawn, and there only lay a sense of darkness.

"May his ashes settle in the peace that he deserves, and our love and kinship for him endure in years to last." I remembered the words of the eulogy I gave at Eric's funeral.

I held the funeral at the house and posted an obituary in the papers for a week to ensure all necessary parties would attend, even those who were not necessary. Kyle helped me tremendously with all the preparations and had been my support all along.

Exactly as in my vision, Mr. Denton appeared and held my hand to console me for my loss.

"Why is the casket closed?" he asked.

"What are you doing here?"

Before he could respond, I placed my hand on his shoulder and looked him intently in the eyes. I spread my mermaid magic on him like warm butter on bread. I inched closer and seductively hummed a tune in his ear that, translated, meant, "Tell me what I really want to know."

He spoke softly near my ear, below everybody else's ear range, and said, "I came to see if my enemy was really dead."

I looked him in the eye and, without words, asked him to tell me more.

"Listen, I am sure you know why Eric was my lawyer?" he asked.

"Enlighten me?"

"Have you ever heard that there are more lawyers than criminals in jail?"

"No," I said, feeling duped.

"Well, Eric almost always got me off or with some reduced sentence. He was known for extorting, bribing, and, in some cases, using witchcraft to convince people to his will."

"Witchcraft? That is outrageous!" I blurted, although once the words came out, it was as though a coin dropped into the empty spots of my brain. I no longer thought or felt the same for Eric; he was an idol that got destroyed with disappointments.

"Listen, if I hadn't seen it, I wouldn't have believed it myself. Eric was a swindler, and he swindled a lot of the wrong people. That was what got his wife killed. I know! I have been his client a long time. I wanted Eric dead, too! That was the only reason I came to his funeral so that I could see that he was really dead."

"Wouldn't you be grateful for all the things he did for you?"

"Would I? Eric was extorting me! He arranged it so that I would appear to be a pedophile. If I didn't consistently pay him dues, he would threaten to have me thrown in jail. I have to say I am not afraid of jail myself, but at least put me in jail for a crime that I did commit, not something that will have my ass raped every day of the week!"

Suddenly a lot of things were spinning and spooling into sense for me. My head didn't want to understand what in my heart I already knew. How did I not see this coming? This was the real reason why he never wanted to go to the cops. He was a crook. He was always planning on disappearing, just not with me. The big question was starting to surface. It was bubbling on its slow way up. Why did he need me?

"Do you know where Eric kept his money?" Mr. Denton asked.

"Do you mean the money he took from you?" I asked.

"He was taking money from everybody, M. Eric accumulated a large bankroll."

"Well, if Eric had money, I would love to know where it is. All he left me was a few dollars in a bank account that I know of. I just found out yesterday that this house is going to be foreclosed on. I don't have anything he promised me when we got married."

"Eric was under federal investigation, M. I know this as a fact. He was hiding his money, evading taxes, not paying his bills. You see those two people there? They are undercovers stalking you and Eric."

"I have always had a funny feeling about the McEvoys. But how is it that you know so much about Eric?"

"I'm sorry all this happened to you, but it is extremely important to know who you get into bed with."

I immediately looked down at the floor. How could this happen to me?

"I would disappear if I were you. Start over with a new identity or something, someplace else." He said to me as if that wasn't what I had been trying to do all along throughout this story. What was this now the fourth time I've been running away? I may not look it, but I am old, and I am tired; can't I just catch a damn break?

My knight in shining armor strolls along, saving me from all my perils, and then what? He makes away like a bandit in the night, leaving me in his shit. I am a suspect in his possible murder, I am in debt, and my image has been shamed for looking like a gold digger, for the way I supposedly killed him and for being his fool. My anger was boiling dangerously at this point. I should have trusted my gut instinct when I heard his ploy. I just wonder how I could have been so blind. *Grrrrr!*

"Listen, the feds are looking for his money. If they believe you are his partner in crime, they might go after you for it. He might have set you up to take the fall. Expensive cars, bank accounts, money. If they seized your car and home, they may seize everything else too."

Great. This was all falling apart just as quickly as I had built it. It was too soon to determine whether or not the feds had caught on to my secret identity. If the cops didn't look into it close enough, I was sure the feds would realize soon enough that the real Emilia Olivares was in a coma in the hospital. I was in so much trouble that I felt like taking a swim back to Cuba and try my luck there again.

"I need a favor," I asked as I looked closely into his eyes. I caressed his shoulder with my hand persuasively.

"Anything, sweetie."

"I need to get a makeover kit and some emergency cash to get me by for a few days."

"I can do better than that."

"Really?"

"Yup, I can get you a legitimate ID too."

"How are you going to do that?"

"Listen, we people conned by Eric have to stick together. I like you, and if you let me, I can be your man." He said in a way that made me feel like he was used to having plenty of women around. "Besides, I know people, beautiful. Stick with me, and your life will change, I promise."

I had heard that more times than there are stars in the sky. Men! They are worse than politicians; they promise and promise and never deliver.

I smiled and looked at him with dreamy eyes, playing along. I would let my magic take its course and let him help me, but I had to be careful with this sleaze bucket. He may not be a pedophile, but that doesn't mean he can't still take a swim with the fishies!

There was a knock on the door. I thought it would be just another person mourning Eric's death.

"May we come in?"

Ed and Alice came to the door to meet the two other men. They were all dressed in suits. Before I could say no, the two men barged in.

"You are under arrest!" said Alice or should I say Brenda.

I took a couple of steps back, not giving her my wrists. "For what?"

"For suspicion of being complicit in embezzlement, money laundering, theft, extortion, and possible murder. The list is long, you gold digger!" she said as if she somehow was right about all that crap.

The pent-up anger grew here. I'd had no chance to properly handle things, and it was just too much at once. I fell to my knees, raised my hands to the sky in wrath, and sang the song of dissonance. It was shrieking loud, collapsing all nearby who attempted to cover their ears. I popped a few eardrums. The sound became supersonic, and I called upon the seas, the waters near in the canals, the dark waters in the sewers, and the mud in the swamps to destroy everything. The bodies closest to me bled through their ears in pain. The vibrations of sound had a mortal effect on those weakest to the noise.

My anger grew a decibel louder, and the sky reacted to the fury of the water. The sky and the water twirled counterclockwise toward one another like a maelstrom wanting to touch each other. The glass all around me started cracking and breaking and going out in waves for miles. The water was coming to take them, the water was coming for us all, but unlike all these people, the water and I were very deep, intimate friends...

Chapter 26

WHAT NOW? THE LAST LAUGH

Months later...

It has been a long swim. The water was warm. I twirled my body in seductive waves, becoming one with the water. In endless circles I moved, looking at my beautiful long and large fin. The scales on my hips were all the perfect size, going all the way down, the color of being iridescent. I let go, suspended in the water, and would start to move again slowly. The eels around me followed me in their own version of synchronized swimming. We danced in this underwater party.

"Come back," I heard in echo. It pulsed. I began to make my way back from the deep sea onto the shore. As I came closer to land, I put my head above water. I began to transition to breathing the air again, slowly draining my lungs from the seawater as my legs found their natural curve, shedding away my fishlike form. My skin absorbed the scales into it, and my legs began to separate little by little the more I breathed. It was time to say good-bye to my friend, the eel. He was so warm inside me, cooing; he insisted on staying, but I told him he couldn't live for long on land. He suggested he could live in the wetness inside me but soon realized I had to indeed go. My favorite eel scurried slowly out from inside my sex and swam off to his school of friends.

I sang to him in my mermaid voice and said, "Tomorrow."

He looked back, smiled, and continued to swim off.

I swam human style back to shore. I must say that being a fish out of water is a huge understatement. Swimming like a human is much more awkward than you can possibly imagine.

I walked up from the shore to our little cottage. It was white in color and made of a very rudimentary material called adobe. It was something that grew on me with a terrible sense of nostalgia for time past long, long ago.

When I walked in, I had a towel waiting for me by the door and a cup of my favorite fire-fruit tea. Then there was the familiar telepathic voice.

"How was your swim?"

"Relaxing."

Kyle had grown out a beard that made him look like a hermit. His selenite eyes always looked serene to me. He was actually watching the news on a TV that he didn't originally want. The newscaster was reporting the following:

"Months after the catastrophic seaquake that over-ran all of southern Florida and left it under water, people are still looking for their loved ones in hopes they may still be alive. Bodies still wash up ashore with salvage. Scientists are still having a hard time configuring the displacement of the Caribbean plate and as to how it managed to shift so quickly and cause this major act of nature..."

Kyle turned the volume lower. He and I were offi-cially, presumably dead. I decided to take one after Eric and recycle his move. As much as I hated him, it was a good one. Normally, being presumably dead after being lost in certain situations takes up to seven years. You can't count on a life-insurance payout at that point. However, when the chances of being alive are slim to none, the declaration of death comes a lot quicker.

"Have you thought about what we will do when we find him?" Kyle asked.

Thoughts about Eric always gave me pause, especially when I thought he was off somewhere, enjoying life after he left me in the gutter.

"What do you believe is the best course of action?" I asked in return.

"Does it matter what I believe, if what is in your heart is something else?"

"Can't you ever just give me a straight answer and not this seeker-and-guide, mentor-and-apprentice crap?" I snapped.

"Can your behavior be less vulgar and more ladylike?"

"I can't change who I am," I said, sounding rigid.

"We are who we are. You and I have established roles. One day, if I am ever successful with you, you will go on to teach those the lessons you have learned so that they too can evolve."

"I am amazed that you have such a deep level of faith in me. All this time…" I trailed off in my thoughts.

Against Kyle's wishes, we got a modest TV set for the receiving area of our humble home. Despite the overall Spartan lifestyle he enjoyed having, he did allow me to add some feminine touches to our new place. I was able to introduce color into his life, and he kept pushing me into the light of a bright white light. From the time I had stayed with Kyle in Miami to that point in time, I was able to expand upon his dishware set and his silverware so that at times we were able to receive guests.

Kyle had become the perfect housemate after I adapted to his nightmares. It was hard for a man of his religious conviction and level of spirituality to actually have endured a few wars without having the scars and trauma to prove it. Over time, I wanted to help him with this, and with healing exercises and meditation, it actually started getting better. Doing something completely selfless for him was good for me. Even I could see that despite time and who I was, he actually was showing me another way. I was not convinced his way was going to work, but his faith in me caused me to want to at least try. I had nothing to lose but time, and that I had plenty.

Kyle had one good thing going for him, and that was, no matter what evil I had done, he was always there to help me recover, instead of preaching and recriminating.

Kyle and I, rather than attempting to locate the very evasive diamond, opted to simply follow the trail of money Eric had left behind. If we knew where his money was, we would inevitably find him.

I had spoken to Kyle about the island where Eric had planned to live his last days and how he spoke to me about the happily ever after that we would have. I thought about that endlessly and overtime. Every time the thought came to me, I would feel angry all over again.

"I just don't understand how my powers of influence just didn't work the way they were supposed to on Eric."

"Because he knew who you were all along, M. He knew he was weak to you, and he also had a very good idea of what would happen if he fell again under your trance. He must have been doing something to counter the effects."

"Do you think he had this all planned beforehand?"

Kyle sighed. I had been going over this with him time and time again, and his patience with the subject was depleting rapidly.

"He definitely was ready for you. He knew his love couldn't and wouldn't change you, so the best course of action was to be at the offensive. He knew that because of the curse, you two could never be together, and because he was cursed, he would never be happy either. Look what happened to his wife. He resolved to concentrate on the only thing he knew how to do best—make money."

"I don't know what happened to his wife. Everybody tiptoed around it as this awful tragedy, and it has been the item nobody wants to talk about."

"Well, Eric got married to his wife out of convenience, or at least that is what it appears to me. He was a good friend with her, and he thought she would be a good wife and homemaker—you know, the practical stuff."

"So he never was in love with her?"

"Hmm…Well, M, it is surprising that love doesn't always happen like a lightning bolt. Sometimes it happens over time and under the right conditions. Love that starts off strong and furious many a times ends just as quickly, but when it's built on more solid foundations, it has the ability to endure the ages, despite love perhaps not being as passionate. I believe Eric had a version of the latter. He loved his wife dearly even if he never was in love with her."

"So what happened to her?"

"Well, because of the unsavory practices Eric had at his job, he and his wife were constantly threatened. Eric and his wife decided it was best to disappear her until Eric was able to neutralize the threat against her. He did, I guess, what any centaur would do and sent her into the woods. She basically went into hiding, out in the middle of nowhere, and practically spent her time in complete isolation. She would get a periodic care package to hold her over, but over time, she began to lose her mind. Eric told everybody that his wife left him to go off and find herself but that he expected they would work things out. One day, Eric's wife actually disappeared, and ten years went by before anybody knew exactly what had happened to her."

"Eric told me he was a widow for five years."

"Well, M, as you know all too well, it takes a long time to be declared dead if you disappear. Eric was under suspicion for his wife's death, so were a few of his clients, and then there was also the possibility that she simply went mad, ran off, or committed suicide. But it's really hard to decide what happened when there was nobody to tell. Who knows?"

"So do we know what really happened to her?"

"Not exactly. Eric, I suppose, spent that decade wondering, longing, lamenting, and mourning his wife with the uncertainty of not knowing what happened to her. There is no closure when an event like that happens. It's not like when somebody dies in an accident or an illness, because you know what happened to them, and in your heart, resignation can eventually come."

"No wonder. Well, tell me what I need to know. You're killing me with suspense here."

"About five years ago, her body was found at the bottom of a cliff. It is unclear if she was pushed or if she jumped or if she lost her balance and fell. Her bones were so deteriorated that it was clear she was down there for some time. However, there was an approximate four-year stretch since she disappeared and the time she was believed to have died."

"How did you find out about this?"

"How else do you think? Paco, of course!"

"Wow, Paco is really good at finding stuff out."

"He is, but only when those things pertain to living objects. Otherwise, I'd know where the diamond is right now."

"How many of us are out there?"

"I am not sure, but what I am sure is that there are hundreds in our group. It's hard to tell how many of us survived, but the only way to distinguish one of us for sure is the watermark. Besides, some of us wish not to be found."

"Why do you think Paco can't find Eric?"

"For the same reason we could never find you."

"And why is that?"

"M, you have been dormant for a long time. Using minimal power, wandering through life, pulling tricks to stay afloat. You haven't tried to use all your power. Look at what you did to our island, and look at what you did to Florida. Don't you think that if you would've been more active, we wouldn't have found you sooner? The truth is, you are used to being alone, and you did not want to be found. Eric does not want to be found."

"I think we should start looking for something else. Eric mentioned an island. Why don't we try looking for small islands that aren't on the map? Maybe we should look at things he absolutely needs. He is a centaur. I would assume wooded areas are important to him. What is absolutely crucial for Eric to have?"

"Hmmm…You have a point. We need to think outside of the box. Paco was able to track the money moving into the Cayman Islands."

"How much of it?"

"Over half a billion."

"Wow, that is a lot! I can't believe Eric lived so modestly for this type of money."

"M, I told you this before. You shouldn't make assumptions about people based on what they show you. Look how modestly I live. Is this really a reflection of what I own financially?"

"I guess you have a point. Why don't you ever spend money?"

"Listen, not everybody can live off their sex appeal and looks forever like you have. I have to make sure that what I have can last me forever. Forever is a long time, don't you think?"

I looked at the ground, slightly ashamed of myself for the first time. I've never done anything that gave me any real value. I never even tried to do anything but take men to their doom.

"I can't believe you are changing me! I hate you!" I said.

"For the very first time ever, you are not using your sex to gain any favor here. I am so proud! Kyle held his hand to his chest as if to say "I am touched."

"You do realize I can always go back to my antics."

"Yes, I know, but we both need to find Eric and our diamond. Besides, I know you secretly enjoy my company. You are evil trying to be good."

Kyle smiled as if he was on the verge of some break-through with me.

"If you find this diamond, what are you going to do?"

Kyle sighed as if he was frustrated with his work or maybe that he had a lot of work to do.

"Without this diamond, I can't complete my thir-teenth law, and I will be stuck in this sphere forever. Like you and all of us. Aren't you tired of this? Don't you want what was promised to you in the afterlife? Don't you want to advance and evolve instead of always chasing your fin in endless circles? You know what was promised to you in the afterlife, right?"

"I was promised to be the favorite and sit by his side. But I still do not see the value in that. Besides, I had to also instill the fear of God in everybody to reform them. I certainly did not do that."

"You destroyed us. You changed our way of life. You were always meant to do that. Do you think that is little? We've all lamented and repented and have had millennia to think about it and make amends, and we are all just waiting on you!"

"What a way to add pressure!"

That night before bed, all I could do was think of Eric's touch. How much, despite everything, I still yearned for him. How much I desired to feel his fleshy cock inside me. The thought kept repeating itself in my brain until with its comfort lulled me to sleep.

That night I dreamt of a very lush forest, where I walked around feeling how humid it was there. There was so much moisture that the leaves were coated with dew.

I was walking, but at a moment later, I felt I was flying at the speed of light through the jungle. I passed a waterfall, mountains, rocks, an anaconda, a leopard tiger, a few monkeys, frogs, and plenty of insects. I smelled something very familiar to me in my dream. It was a scent of cedarwood. There were plenty of those trees near me, and they looked unnatural, as if somebody had placed them there rather than they grew there on their own. As odd as this is going to sound, the tree spoke to me and said, "We protect against evil. We protect him against you."

Once again, I flew through the forest until I reached the sea. It was moving vigorously back and forth the way I recognized the Atlantic to move. How could I not? I come from a place in the Atlantic, which was once called Atlantis.

I felt my soul come back to my body and drop onto my bed. I immediately grabbed on to my mattress. I knew…

The next morning, I woke Kyle.

"I know where to look. We need to take a swim!"

Kyle didn't even fight me. He simply had our luggage shipped over, and we proceeded to take onto the water for our journey.

We were already on the Atlantic coastline. We simply needed to swim further down. The deeper I got into the water, my friends—the eels—came to greet me. They all began to nibble on my legs, and my very special eel slithered inside me, sealing my legs together. What a delicious feeling! Once they nibbled enough of my skin to reveal my scales, I began to fill my lungs with water and breathe. My fingers webbed together, and the openings on the side of my neck began to take the water in, so I didn't have to breathe through my nose anymore. I was ready to relax my way through the water. Kyle swam beside me as he too took a merman form.

The water was warm in the Atlantic, and we glided through in unison.

There was warmth inside me that was new for once. All the time I had been so used to feeling cold, but gradually I was warming up a bit; maybe it was Kyle in my life, or maybe it was knowing I was closer to myself, to the part of me that lay inside the diamond. Who knows? Maybe I just wanted to believe, and this was just the warm weather.

"Are you ready for this?" Kyle asked in our usual way.

"I don't know," I said bleakly.

"Well, there is an honest answer."

The bubbles of a sigh came out of Kyle's mouth and bubbled to the surface. Either that or all the activity was causing him gas!

The swim down to the Amazon took us a couple of days from the coastline of Central America. The closer I got to my destination, the slower I began to go. I was unsure I was going to find the spot I had originally dreamt of. Kyle was close behind me, looking around. He brought his energy pebble with him in order to sense the diamond as backup, even though he did spend months helping me recognize my own value so that if I was close to the diamond, I could feel it calling out to me.

It was an interesting premise if I was to think of it—store my evil in an item of value in hopes that it could transform me into something of value. As with any experiment, of course, the result was yet to be seen. Excitement over the unexpected had me in angst.

I swam close to the coastline, looking for the cedarwood trees.

"I can't believe we're are looking for these cedarwood trees here."

"Why not? It makes perfect sense. Bernie was influenced by Native Americans when he was lost. They have strong beliefs in the cedarwood tree and use it as amulets for healing, rituals and the like. If Eric was hiding anywhere, he would always be close to these trees."

"Here I thought that he always smelled like wood because of the hard-on in his pants!"

Kyle and I giggled for a moment.

"I thought we spoke about your vulgarity."

"I can't help it! You are repressing a good thing here."

"You are incorrigible, M!"

We swam, swam, and swam some more. I was beginning to doubt myself. I couldn't find the place I saw in my dreams. This was beginning to feel just as bad as being lost on a first date.

"So where is this place?" Kyle asked.

I responded with silence.

"Are you sure it's here? Does any of this look familiar to you?"

"Let's circle back, and maybe some landmark will jog my memory," I replied.

"Are you aware this is the Amazon and that we've been swimming for hours?" Kyle said.

"Yes, Mr. Impatience!"

"Listen, let's swim inland. Maybe you'll see something there. But wait, why don't you close your eyes and follow your heart instead?"

We paused, suspended in the water, and I closed my eyes, listening to my heart. At first all I could hear was the trepidation from the act of swimming. I swam a little inland and still nothing. I could see that maybe this wasn't going to work.

"Stop doubting yourself and concentrate!" I heard Kyle say in my mind.

"Fine!"

"Without the attitude! I'm only trying to help."

I tried hard to concentrate, feeling the tender touch of the water waving around me. I breathed in the water and allowed myself to become one with the element. My friend, the eel, poked me to the right. Out of instinct, I followed his lead and swam in that direction, allowing myself to be guided by the water rather than my thoughts. I let go of all the thoughts. I could hear my heart; it beat more slowly, expectantly. *Thump...thump... thump...*it was like the slow motion of a shark stalking its prey just before a climatic attack.

"We're here!"

"I can see that. Good job!"

I opened my eyes and saw a very nicely built cabin. It was my best guess that it was built with cedarwood. There were some baby trees around it.

"What am I supposed to do if he is protected by all this cedar?" I said.

"Why don't you distract him while I get the diamond?"

"It is here. I feel it."

"So do I."

Kyle held out his magic pebble, and it was a reddish orange. "I need to do this alone."

Kyle jumped out of the water and put on a speedo out of modesty, not that he had anything that I hadn't seen before. I said good-bye to my eel friend and got out of the water too.

"I'll be here, lurking in the background," said Kyle, making his best attempt to sound mysterious. Standard Kyle.

I knew he knew what was going to happen; he just didn't want to tell me. He may not even need to be psychic to know. It was obvious.

I stood for several moments and walked around in a circle, not because I was acting crazy but because I needed to regain my balance after being in the water for so long.

My legs and feet felt like lead. I wanted to run and confront him, but at the same time, I was afraid of what may come. I walked over to the porch and opened the door to the cabin.

"Hi there." I heard the all-too-familiar voice of Eric. He spoke to me as if we were old friends.

"I bet you thought you would never see me again," I said with a devilish smile.

"Not at all. I've been expecting you." He repeated my gesture, once again showing me his signature grin.

"Why? Why all this charade?"

"What are you talking about? I've been waiting for you to join me."

"Really? Well, this is not part of the plan we talked about. You left me back in Miami with all those problems."

"Because I knew you'd take care of them. You flooded the entire problem away."

I tilted my head sideways in disbelief. "How could you know? Why did you leave me in the dark, then?"

"I saw in my vision what would happen. Do you remember by the fireplace? I left you in the dark because I wanted you to feel something. I wanted you to be angry. I wanted you to hate me."

"Why would you want that?"

"Because I love you, and you did this to me! You betrayed me. I am cursed because of you. I've been angry with you, I have hated you, and all this time I have had no satisfaction but that of letting you know how I feel by making you feel the same way. Despite all these feelings, I cannot help it—I still love you. But the question is, do you love me? Have you ever loved me?"

"No. Besides, how can you love me? You're just manipulating me. I can't trust you anymore. You are not that good old man you like to portray. You are a lowlife."

Eric looked completely pained. I could have filleted his heart; it would have been less painful.

"I've spent too much time being angry. I am a damned soul. Can you really expect me to love?" I asked. "The possibility of the word 'love' is foreign to my heart."

"Do you hate me?"

"Isn't it obvious?"

Eric didn't seem surprised at all, but his usual light-hearted disposition was gone, and a cloud of disappointment kept him company instead.

"Why are you here then? Are you planning on drowning me again? Do you want my money? Why did you come?" he asked.

"You have something that belongs to me."

"Do I now? What is it that you think that is?"

"You have a piece of my heart," I said, sounding corny as all hell, and Eric looked hopeful for a moment. "You have my diamond."

"What if I told you it isn't yours anymore? You can't have it!"

"I'd say you are behaving like a child and to hand it over."

"You want to redeem yourself and sit by the side of God rather than be your own god?"

"What do you mean?"

"Look at how powerful you are and all the things you can do. Don't you want to answer to nobody and make for yourself the life you want? We still have a chance. We can try."

I paused for a moment. It was tempting to think of myself as my own god. I had all this power inside me that never got used, all the banal things I had spent my entire existence doing. It was definitely time for some change. I thought of Kyle and the rest of our people for a moment.

"We can be together. We can be more powerful than any god," Eric said.

"You are not a god, and you are just telling me what I want to hear again, like you did when you spoke about our getaway to Belize. I'm not going to fall for it."

"Well, M—or whatever your name is—I've seen you manipulate situations to get what you want. What are you going to do right now? If you do kill me, I will just be reunited with my wife—a woman who was truly worthy of love. I will be happy then, at least."

My blood became hotter, and my black heart felt a pang. I needed a moment before speaking, and in my birthday suit, I paced in his small cabin.

"You have a point. I should raise my level of evil then. I am curious why you wanted me to contact you from the dead, if you died."

"I wanted to tell you to be strong and ask you not to hate me for what was to happen. I also wanted you to know where you could find my money and your diamond."

"Repenting in death. Seriously? You don't want to give me your money or my diamond now. Why would I believe that?"

"I guess you won't believe anything I say, so why speak?"

"Well, I wanted to hear what you came up with. It is always amusing to me what someone says or does just before their end."

"The angel of darkness was right. We can never be happy."

There was a pause. His words darkened my black heart.

"With all your money, why did you move here?"

"You like your water; I love my forest."

Eric stood from his rudimentary burlap furniture. The floor too was made of wood. The tapestry on the floor was most definitely a Native American design. This was all too natural.

Once he stood, Eric revealed that he too was stark naked. I gave him a look of surprise.

"Well, I don't get visitors. Besides, it is hot out here. You're one to talk," he said, motioning toward my body.

"You can't use your charm here to persuade me. So what are you going to do?"

"I might have to wait this one out," I replied.

"I might lose my mind by then, like my wife did. Maybe you should do me a favor and just get this on with."

"Stop talking about her!"

I lounged at Eric. I was not better than using physical violence; I was all about it. For an old man, Eric was strong, and we struggled for a bit. Eric attempted to contain me, but I just kept using my Amazonian arms and hands to choke him. I wrapped my legs around his torso and squeezed hard, anaconda style. It is surprising the level of strength it takes to choke somebody with bare hands, especially when those hands are little. I was not going to be able to choke him successfully like this, so I proceeded to bang his head against the floor as hard as I could. He countered my moves by placing resistance with his head and using his neck muscles to absorb the impact. He used his torso and rocked from side to side until he was able to flip our positions, and he was on top now. My leg muscles began to give, and I released his arms from being compressed against his torso. All this training with Kyle, and look at me, overrun by an old man! Ugh!

I was wedged under his stomach, and with a swift upward movement of my hips, I knocked some air out of him, leaving him winded for a moment. It was then that

Kyle snuck up on us and interceded. He grabbed Eric's head, and with his arms and hands, he made Eric unconscious with a sleeper chokehold.

"I had this!"

"Did you, M? You looked overtaken."

I pursed my lips and proceeded to help Kyle.

Kyle looked a little disturbed to see another man naked, and he covered Eric with the tapestry on the floor—after he used some very fancy knots to tie him down like a goat.

We dragged Eric outside of his protective cocoon. I decided it might be nice to tie him to a swamp tree and wait for a hungry, lusty anaconda to attack. The tree was actually a pretty place to die in a creepy sort of way. It looked like a cypress tree and had lots of Spanish moss hanging all around it. The roots of the tree came out above the water, giving it an "I'm going to get you" feeling with its claw-like shape. It was nice.

Kyle and I proceeded to raid the cabin; the diamond was certainly there—I could feel it. Considering how small the cabin was, it shouldn't have been that hard to find it, yet we could not see anything of value despite it having to be in plain sight.

I had to take the time to consider this for a moment: why, with all his money, did he hide here?

"Because, M, he wanted to die just like his wife. Don't you see? He set up the same scenario. Evil lurking to kill him, isolated in the middle of nowhere, losing his mind all alone…he was expecting you to kill him. I hope you're not going to give him the satisfaction."

I growled and pouted and got angry all over again.

"Why are you reading my mind?" I said.

"I only meddle because I care." Kyle smiled at me, expecting me to have fortitude of some sort.

"I am going to wake Eric. I need to know where this stuff is."

I went outside and walked over to his tree. I slapped him around in the face. I must admit it was quite refreshing.

He began to come to. I forced him to look me in the eyes, and I sung to him in my mermaid voice so that he could tell me what I needed to know.

I looked into his face, and even though I knew it wasn't real love, I wished it were. He looked completely subdued toward me.

"The diamond is buried under the cabin with all that you need to get to my money."

I looked him in the eyes once more, yearning for that love that never was but could have once been.

"My love…" he said as I was about to walk away. "You are always so silent that I wonder if you are even there. Do you remember when you used to sing to me? Can you sing to me before you leave? Can you kiss me good-bye and tell me you love me?"

As a parting request, I sung to him. I hummed the most nostalgic of tunes from the depths of my precious throat, in my own way, letting him know how I truly felt. I gave him a long, emotive kiss.

"Until we meet again—but for now, I will let you go."

I untied him from the cypress tree, where he convulsed for a moment; he sprouted out two of the hairiest legs from his pelvis and bucked up and placed them on the ground under the water by the tree. His legs elongated enough to form a horse's back, and finally his hind legs sprouted out an equal amount of hair as his front ones.

He galloped over to me and held out his arms as if to receive some sort of anointing. I went to give him one last embrace.

He galloped slowly away into the horizon, and I walked over to Kyle, who was watching everything from the doorstep of the cabin.

"So you decided to let him go," he said proudly in his usual way.

"For today. That doesn't mean tomorrow I won't get angry again and finally get him. Besides, don't you think his chances of survival are the same as his wife's out here?"

The centaur wandered off into his freedom, and the mermaid went into the water to cool off. Maybe they would meet again in another lifetime...

Alternate Book Cover.

For upcoming news and books visit the authors website
and Facebook page at:

Http://www.lonnylee.com
Http:// www.facebook.com/lonnyleebooks